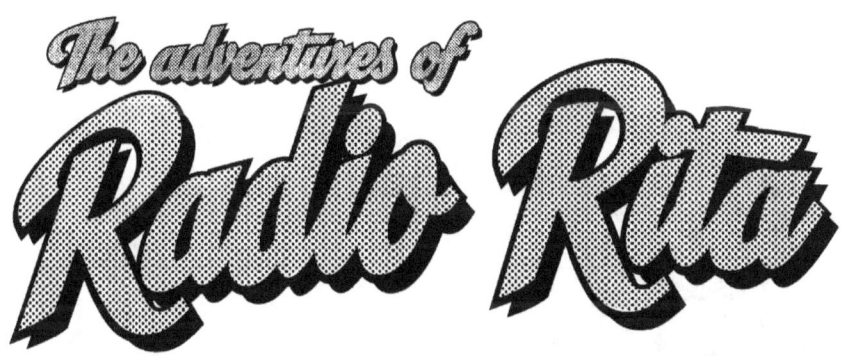

The adventures of Radio Rata

Airship 27 Productions

The Adventures of Ratio Rita

"Radio Rita and the Pearl of Shanghai" ©2022 Teel James Glenn
"Radio Rita and the Genesis Machine" ©2022 Samantha Lienhard
"Frequency" ©2022 Gene Moyers
"Operation Rocket Man" ©2022 Mel Odom
Introduction ©2022 Ron Fortier

An Airship 27 Production
www.airship27.com
www.airship27hangar.com

Cover illustration ©2022 Ted Hammond
Interior illustrations ©2022 Rob Davis

Editor: Ron Fortier
Associate Editor and Production Designer: Rob Davis
Marketing and promotion: Michael Vance

ISBN: 978-1-953589-43-9

Printed in the United States of America

10 9 8 7 6 5 4 3 2 1

Contents

Introduction...5

Radio Rita and the Pearl of Shanghai....9

Radio Rita and the Genesis Machine.....48

Frequency...97

Operation Rocket Man.....................143

Introduction

You hold in your hands a book that came about, as lots of books do, by a strange series of events. Years ago my publishing partner, Rob Davis, and I launched a monthly podcast called "The Airship 27 Podcast." The plan was to do a monthly show in which we would talk about current activities with the company; what books had recently been released, which were in production and other assorted topics all having to deal with what has become known in the publishing industry as New Pulp. That's what we publish and hope to continue doing for a long while.

Once the show was established and we'd taped several episodes, we began letting people know about them by announcing each new episode on our Facebook platform; each of us having several pages there. It worked out smoothly and our colleagues began to follow the show. One particular month, prior to letting folks know we had a new show on the way, I started thinking about how it might be fun to spice up the announcement with a picture of a beautiful woman.

In many of our videos, we often mentioned we were broadcasting from Hangar 27 as if it were an actual locale that housed our flying airship, our logo icon. So what if Hangar 27 actually had a working staff that kept the operation going? And what if the person in charge of the hangar was this good looking dame. Hmm, that could be fun. Next step, I begin net surfing, my parameter query, "Pictures of girls operating Ham Radios." If you've ever done this kind of searching, you are already well aware of the millions of pieces of art out there. Soon enough I was being flooded with all kinds of images of girls using a portable radio.

Among these I found a 1940s style pin-up. It was of a beautiful, long-legged redhead, using a sophisticated transmitter, while stretching out in her chair with a slit in her short dress providing us a nice glimpse of a truly shapely limb. It was exactly what I was looking for and I saved it to my files. Later in the day I posted it to my FB page ready to let our pals know a new show was coming soon and I began the post in words similar to these. "I just got a call from Radio Rita down at Hangar 27 reminding me we have a new podcast episode to record this week."

Alliteration is always a sure fire way to get folks to remember a name and

Radio Rita just sprung to mind from that pin-up picture which was posted with the ad. I would keep using that same picture every time I'd make another announcement and in very little time started getting feedback from people wanting to know more about our gal. In fact after months using that single pin-up piece, I found another image on line of what looks to be a very young Renee Russo, the actress known for starring with Mel Gibson and Danny Glover in the "Lethal Weapons" film series. It's a torso shot and could easily be the pin-up model brought to life. Of course I instantly began trading them back and forth each month and by then our pals loved it. They were getting hooked on Radio Rita.

Invariably one of them sent us a question to answer at the end of episode.

"Are we ever going to see stories starring Radio Rita?"

Here we go, Rob and I, looking at each other via Skype and Rob pretty much hands the ball to me, as I was her initial creator. We were joking, as we do most of the time on the show and as we do so, a truly bizarre thought began to formulate in my mind. I proceeded to vocalize it.

"What if I wrote up the barest of bibles concerning who she is, then we had four different writers each do a story having only that little data to work from?"

Rob immediately pointed out we'd most likely get four totally different Radio Rita characters. "Exactly" I replied laughing merrily. I then looked at the camera and put the challenge out there. If there were four brave pulp writers willing to participate in this madcap project, they were to e-mail me. If we could get four then "The Adventures of Radio Rita" would happen. Thus the segment ended and we went on to other topics in the agenda.

The day after the video went live, I received an e-mail from Pulp Factory Award winning writer Teel James Glenn saying he wanted in on the Radio Rita project and asked me to send along the miniscule fact sheet. I was both stunned and delighted and hurriedly told Rob about it. That very afternoon, Gene Moyers, one of our most popular writers here at Airship 27 wrote in saying he wanted in on the Radio Rita anthology. Within a 24 period, we had half the volume filled.

I got busy writing the few but pertinent facts on the character. Obviously the smallest such I've ever done, and sent that off to Teel and Gene.

Four days later, Oklahoma based scribe, Mel Odom, wrote asking to be a part of the book. Wow! That was three. All we needed was just one more writer. Which was when I began thinking that if we were going to debut an amazing new pulp female hero, shouldn't we have at least one lady writer on board? It only seemed the right thing to do and I knew who I had to reach out to.

Samantha Lienhard came to Airship 27 shortly after graduating from college. She attended a lecture given by veteran writer, and good friend, Fred Adams Jr. wherein he talked about the emergence of this New Pulp thing. After his talk, Samantha asked him to suggest a publisher she might submit such thrilling stories and Fred told her about Airship 27. In the past few years she's written several stories for us in various genres and they are all fantastic. Her talent to spin a yarn is remarkable. Thus I wrote Samantha and asked if she would like to fill the fourth and empty slot.

She agreed and the book was officially in production. Below is the exact data sheet I sent Teel, Gene, Mel and Samantha. It is the only information they have about our girl. Nothing else. Nada!

RADIO RITA
Starring in – "The Adventures of Radio Rita."
Known facts –
Female – 5'8" tall. Statuesque with long, shapely legs.
Weight – 125 lbs.
Hair – Fiery red…shoulder length.
Eyes – Emerald green.
Skills – Pilot

"And that is all you get. The rest is up to you. What's her full name? In what age does she live? What other skills does she possess? Does she have a family? All of this is for you, THE WRITER, to fill in.

"All we ask is that the stories are fast paced action yarns and Radio Rita IS THE HERO! Not ever the villain. She is the hero of your story and everything revolves around her. Now you go and create her world and give us a rollicking old fashion pulp adventure."

That was it. And playing fair, the stories appear in the book as they arrived on my desk. None of the writers ever read what the other three had invented. Due to the uniqueness of this book, I requested that all four writers, upon completion of their tales, also write a post-essay detailing their own experiences in creating their own Radio Rita and how that came about. Something we often hear at Airship27, letting you, the readers get a peek into the creative process.

Now that the four stories have been written, read and edited, Art Director Rob Davis set about doing twelve black and white interior illustrations, three for each story. Plus bonus illustrations for each tale. Something we rarely ever do. Then Canadian artist Ted Hammond delivered the absolutely stunning cover that graces this volume. I so love his take our Rita.

And there you have it, dear reader. You are about to meet Radio Rita. Four of them. I honestly think you are in for one hell of a ride. Enjoy the surprises!!

Ron Fortier
Managing Editor

Radio Rita and the Pearl of Shanghai

by
Teel James Glenn

August 12, 1937:

"**Z**ee Chinese race are mere children," the German businessman said with a smile as he adjusted his monocle. He held out his empty martini glass and waited for the stoic Chinese waiter to step in and take and replace it with a new one in a smooth, practiced action. "That ist why we have to guide zhem with a strong hand, an iron hand; and if we can make a profit from it, so much zee better."

Two of the other four seated in the lounge area off the lobby of the Cathay Hotel in Shanghai both nodded their heads to agree with the German. The hotel was the most glamorous one in the city, which itself was a roaring port of frantic energy and opportunity in high style.

The international nature of the city was mirrored in the four seated in the lounge; the German, an American businessman named Harcourt and Baron Akio Takoda, a shaven-headed Japanese in traditional kimono and wire-rimmed glasses.

The last of the group, who'd disagreed with the German said, "After all it is their country, *Herr* Von Totten; we are here by their forbearance and the European strength of arms. I truly doubt humanitarian concerns are upmost on your mind when you are selling small arms to warlords."

The speaker stood out in more ways than one from the others. She was a stunningly beautiful woman with pale skin and emerald-green eyes that bespoke a powerful inner fire. Her long red hair was held back with a single blue ribbon, and she was dressed in a stylish green pants suit with bolero jacket. She nursed a whisky and soda as she spoke.

"Surely, Miss O'Riordan," the Japanese said in a cultured voice with an English accent, "*Herr* Von Totten's point is that the Han are a chaotic race and have always needed a strong hand to guide them."

"Like in Manchuria?" She asked with a slight uptick in her sensuous lips to hint at a smile.

The Japanese made a show of adjusting his glasses and replied in a soft voice, "Indeed our aid has helped the poor of Manchuko. But also that we are in this international zone is proof of the Herr Von Totten's point, is it not?"

"Y'all here to profit from the populace just same as us, little lady," the American said with a deep Texas drawl. "Seems to me you're on a pretty high horse to be spoutin'."

The German stifled a laugh with a cough, but the redhead seemed un-ruffled. "Pilots fly well over horses, Mister Harcourt so I'm used to looking down on things. And I didn't come here to run anyone's lives or live off them. I simply offer service for pay."

"You seem a bit too moral for a businesswoman, Miss O'Riordan," the Japanese said. "To profit, is that not the very essence of business ethics? Herr Von Totten and Mister Harcourt merely see opportunities and take advantage of them with their shipping and import businesses."

"I didn't think morals and business ethics were mutually exclusive, Ta-koda-san," she responded. "Oh, I have a skill to sell to be sure, one I learned from my Da in Montana—he'd shot down more than a few German pilots in the Big War—no offense—" she nodded her head to Von Totten who nodded back and sipped his drink. "But he taught me and my brothers that making a dollar was only incidental to being useful to the world—he saw too much waste in the trenches. So, yes, I have a skill with a plane, but I sell only that skill, not my soul with it."

The German was about to speak again when a uniformed Chinese bell-hop stepped up to the young woman and held out a silver plate with a red envelope on it.

"Miss Radio?" the Chinese asked.

"Whatcha' say, Fu Manchu?" Harcourt said to the bellhop. He pushed his Panama hat back with a thumb so that a shock of straw-colored hair escaped as he fixed the servant with a cold look.

The redhead's laugh was a bird song. "That's what they call me when they can't pronounce my name." She took up the envelope that had "*Radio Rita,*" written on it.

When she looked curiously at the bellhop, he nodded across the cavernous lobby to a Chinese in traditional coolie garb, with pigtail, standing at attention.

"Excuse me, gentlemen," she said and opened the envelope to peer into it.

"Something urgent, Miss?" Baron Takoda asked.

In the envelope was one half of a torn British hundred-pound note. She smiled at the Japanese after she tucked the envelope in her clutch, "Oddly timely considering our conversation, but I don't know how urgent yet." She set her drink down on a table by her chair, picked up her clutch and stood.

When the others moved to stand, she added, "Please, don't rise, gentlemen. I thank you for a stimulating talk and apologize for my leaving before we have solved all the problems of the world with our discussion."

"We shall speak again," Baron Takoda said with a slight bow.

"I'm sure," she threw over her shoulder. "Shanghai is too small for any of us to avoid each other for long."

The eyes of the three men, indeed those of most men in the lobby, followed the lithe woman as she moved gracefully to the bearer of the message, the soles of her mules making hollow sounds on the marble floor.

The Chinese messenger was elderly with a hang-dog expression, a white beard, eyebrows and scholar's mustache and had the look of a man who had labored with his hands. He also had the hunched-shoulder stance and attitude of one used to servitude. He kept his eyes averted when she stepped before him.

"Who sent this?" She showed the envelope. "And why?"

The man shook his head as if he did not understand her but pointed to the envelope in the clutch. "More, you come now." When she looked skeptical, he continued, "Much more, just to come."

"Okay, I'm game, Macduff," she said, "I wasn't up for Peking Opera tonight anyway. Lead on." She followed the messenger out the wide front door of the elegant hotel.

Outside the August air was humid and heavy with the promise of rain later that night and the street was, as usual a sea of people all, seeming in a hurry to be somewhere else. The smell of the city—the exotic scent of spices, cooking smoke, and too much humanity jammed into too small a space, was a heady mix to Rita.

So different from the ranch, so much promise of excitement and danger, she thought.

She waved to the liveried doorman. "Hi, Ling."

"Afternoon, Miss Radio," the doorman said.

"You seen Frenchie?"

The doorman looked past the redhead to the messenger who stood at hand but said nothing. Instead, he nodded toward a cluster of the rickshaw drivers off to one side of the hotel crouched in a circle playing dice.

The building stood at the corner of Bund and Nanjing Road, beside the Huangpu River and in the late afternoon was a nexus of humanity, with rickshaws and a few private touring cars—including Rita's—parked nearby

Of course, I should have figured, she thought, then turned to the messenger and said, "I'll be with you in a minute."

The redhead moved to the gamblers and tapped one on the shoulder.

"Hey, I'm on a roll—Oh Hi boss," the man she tapped said. He was Caucasian, with dark curly hair and a face that showed the memory of some time in the squared circle. When he stood to face her, he came barely to her shoulder at five foot four. "What's up?"

"I won't need you to drive me to the opera house later, Frenchie, you can put the car away," she said in a clear, loud voice so the messenger could hear her. She slipped the envelope out her clutch enough for him to see. "You can take the rest of the night off for further…uh…cultural pursuits."

"You got it, Boss lady," he said with a distinct Brooklyn accent to his voice. He held up a wad of cash and smiled, speaking as loud as she had, "I've been pursuit-ing pretty good so far." He looked past her to the messenger and nodded. "Have a nice night."

"You too," she said as she turned to rejoin the messenger who was now standing beside a rickshaw. "Okay, buddy, where to from here?"

The Chinese man indicated she should enter the rickshaw as he moved to grab the tongues to pull the two-wheeled cart. She climbed in the padded seat of the vehicle, feeling, as she always did, a little uncomfortable to be hauled around by the running man ahead of it like a harness animal.

She generally preferred to walk or drive in her touring car, but for an occidental a rickshaw was the fastest way to get through the crowded street of the city and, being a female with her flaming hair, she took one when she wanted to move with relative anonymity.

She always thought it funny that the *jinricksha* was a Japanese invention, now in every major city in the Far East in light of the fact that the Japanese said their culture would conquer the world. *I guess this is a start on it.*

She did not dwell on the existential however, her mind alert to danger as the messenger pulled the cart through the early evening crowds. Rita kept pressed to the back of the rickshaw, staying in the shadow of the canopy alert for attack, especially when it was forced to stop at congested thoroughfares along the way.

In the three years she had been flying for various companies and individuals in China she had made her share of enemies and had a reputation for a woman who would take a dare. The half hundred-pound note would be a great way to lure her into trap. Even without a specific enemy she knew she would still be a catch for a kidnaper, and kidnapping was a cottage industry up in Japanese occupied Manchuria, especially in Harbin City.

It made Rita glad she still had her .32 caliber pistol hidden in a calf holster.

Shanghai was where West met East, with narrow claustrophobic streets that disgorged onto wide boulevards in its famous Riverside Bund, "the Wall Street of the East." The Bund had been built by the British in the International Settlement, after the Opium Wars, when the European nations imposed their will on the Imperial government and established footholds in China. It was two imposing kilometers of dignified marble, granite, and concrete buildings, built in a world of architectural styles.

The rickshaw skirted the International Settlement to go along the Huangpu River turning off Yunnan Road toward the Night Market District. It turned into the warehouse district that was more sparely populated and turned into an alley that came to a dead end where it stopped.

"Here," the messenger said. He pointed to a door all but hidden in the gloom at the back of the alley. "Go!"

She gave him a mock salute. "I'll miss the conversation, but thanks for the trip."

The messenger bowed and stepped back up the alley, disappearing around the corner and leaving the redhead alone. Even though the alley was in the midst of the bustling city she felt very much alone—but felt comforted that she now had hidden her pistol behind her clutch as she opened the door.

There was a long dark, twisting corridor behind the portal that ended in a second door that was slightly ajar. Light shown from beyond. She slowly moved toward it, alert for trip wires or trap doors.

This is looking more and more like a set up.

She paused just before the inner door and was about to open the door when a deep voice from inside stopped her.

"There is no reason for Radio Rita to fear, Miss O'Riordan," the voice said. "All subterfuge is done; please enter."

In for a penny, Rita thought as she took a deep breath and pushed the door inward.

The room that Rita entered was startling only because it was as elegant a windowless study as one might find in any European Manor house. There were oak bookshelves floor to ceiling on two walls, a large map of Asia on one wall. There was a daybed, a couch, an overstuffed chair and central to the circular room, was a marble topped desk.

Behind that desk, facing the entrance door, was a middle-aged Chinese man dressed in a scarlet Mandarin robe. He was just pouring a cup of steaming tea from a silver teapot. He looked up at the redhead and gave a genial smile. "Please take a seat, Miss O'Riordan. Would you like some tea?"

The woman scanned the room noting that no other doors obvious, which meant there could be many hidden. When she stepped in and closed the door behind her she noted it all but disappeared into a wall panel that showed a silk painting of a mountain.

Her thoughts went back to the secret doors behind bookcases in so many films, but she squared her shoulders and walked with confidence to the high-backed chair facing the desk.

"Yes," she said, "I think that would be delightful. No milk, but some lemon if you please."

The robed man poured and then slid her a china cup across the top of the desk. She leaned in and noticed that his hands were rough, like someone who did manual work. She sipped the tea in mirror of him while the two of them regarded each other like two circling cats.

Finally, she asked, "Why the masquerade? Practice, or is good help that hard to find?"

The man behind the desk looked at her with piercing, dark eyes then he laughed, a deep, genuine laugh. "You deserve your reputation, Miss O'Riordan. What gave me away?"

"The makeup and posture were good, I admit," she said. "And if I were not a devotee of Peking Opera, I would not have realized it was a typical scholar look, but while you were able to take it off quickly—kudos on that, by the way—you can't change your hands."

He held up his rough, blocky fingers and wiggled them. "Ah yes, my youth at hard labor resurfaces. As Kong Qiu—who you call Confucius said, *Everything has beauty, but not everyone sees it."*

"Now that the pleasantries are done," she said, "who are you and what is this all about?" She held up the torn note. "And why the play acting?"

"Ah yes," her host said. He slid the other half of the note across the desk to her. "This was a rather vaudevillian way to entice you here, I admit."

"But it worked," she smiled and took the half-note. "So?"

He stood and gone was his subservient manner. Now the individual behind the desk had broad shoulders and an almost military posture. He folded his hands behind his back and smiled down at her. "First, I have reports from several sources that Radio Rita's word is to be trusted and so I place myself at your mercy: I must ask that this meeting, and all we discuss remain between us. That is upmost important. That is the reason for my elaborate impersonation, so that no one would suspect I contacted you. Should we not come to an understanding that note will be compensation for ruining your evening at the opera. Agreed?"

"Agreed," she said. She tilted her head and licked her lips, obviously intrigued by his offer. "It was a show I'd seen already anyway."

"Good." He walked to the map of China on the wall and stood before it, back to her as if he were Alexander surveying his domain. "As I have heard of you, perhaps you have heard of me. I am Ying Xue Po."

Despite her attempt of calm Rita stiffened. "The Blood-hawk!"

"See, you have heard of me."

"What I heard of was the one with that name was a warlord more vicious than any other in the western provinces."

"Really?" He said turning to look at her. "Such a tone of judgment? Did you not fly for Ho Chien in Hunan?"

"I flew medical supplies and mail for him," she said quietly. "He did not burn villages that opposed him." She rose and kept a tight grip on her pistol behind her clutch.

"I brought order!" He snarled, turning to face her now all sharp angles with fire in his eyes. "I began schools; I brought in better farming methods. My rule was benevolent."

"And you killed anyone who opposed you," she said, her voice steady and calm. "That doesn't sound so benevolent to me."

He started to take a step forward, his shoulder tensed, his expression furious but stopped himself suddenly. Rita stood her ground though her hand tightened on the handle of her pistol.

"You have steel," he whispered, his expression relaxing. He even smiled, "Your reputation is not exaggerated."

"If there is nothing else, then," she said, "I will take my leave." She set the teacup down and turned to move for the panel she had entered through.

"You do not want to hear my proposal?"

She turned back to give him a cold smile. "I hear a dozen proposals a day, Po, I'm sure yours will not be any more attractive to me."

"Please—" he said, forcing the word out as if he seldom ever used it. "I beg you to listen; five minutes of your time."

His tone caused her to stop, and she looked directly into the eyes of the man. "Okay, the magic word was please. I'll give you those five minutes."

"Thank you. Please sit." He walked behind his desk obviously working to compose himself as he sat.

"You have heard about the incident with Oyama at Hongqiao Airport three days ago?"

"The Japanese officer who tried to force his way into the airport against the accords and got himself shot?"

"Yes.

"Well, because of that the level of tension with the Japanese, representatives from United Kingdom, France, United States and Italy along with Japan and China are in conference here in Shanghai to try and keep a cease-fire."

"Like the Japanese will be appeased," she said. "They have a hunger for land and resources that Manchuria and Mengjiang will not satisfy."

"That is what Chiang Kai-shek and the Communists believe. The Emperor's army is too weak to do much to stop them so they hope to gobble up all of China."

"How does that have to do with you getting me hear with our play acting?"

"You have said yourself I have troops at my command, and armaments," he said, his voice taking on an edge. "And the death they could bring is at a premium."

"Not something to be proud of."

"You are harsh Miss O'Riordan, but Confucius says, *'In a country well governed, poverty is something to be ashamed of.'* China is poor for the looting of it."

"You forgot the rest of that quote," she said. *'In a country badly governed wealth is something to be ashamed of.'* You don't look very poor to me." She waved a hand at the furnishings of the room.

He slapped a hand on the desk, anger flaring in his eyes. "I have worked hard for what I have—" When he saw the cold green fire in her eyes he sat back. "But yes—I agree. Still, the Japanese have made alliances with some warlords to allow them to absorb more land. And now they have approached me."

"And?"

"You may think me nothing more than a bandit, but I love my country. I have kept the Japanese at arms length while I talk with Major Yu Hung

Chun about how my forces can best serve the Imperial Army to hold off the invaders."

"Why have you asked me here then? It seems you have decided to come down on the side of the angels." This brought a tight-lipped grin from the warlord.

"So much is never easy in the world." He had a great sadness in his voice now and his posture more resembled the old character he had portrayed. "I have had love once in my life—I know you look askance at me, but even one such as I can have deep feelings. I kept our relationship secret to protect her so that few knew of it."

He walked to the map again and ran a finger along it, tracing a path to northeast of Nanking. "Alas she was called home to tend a sick parent and with her went our daughter, my only child. My wife died a month ago, I received word only today."

"I am sorry for that," Rita said sincerely.

"Thank you. But my sadness is compounded for the Japanese intercepted the message and now know of my child. They would use her against me to force my hand in their favor." He turned to look at her and she saw pain in his eyes. "I must give my answer to the Japanese by tomorrow night. I cannot lose my daughter, nor can I betray my country to invaders."

"And you want—?"

"Bring my daughter back to me. Fortunately, they do not know exactly where she is. Once I know she is safe I can act."

The room was heavy with silence after he finished speaking, his breathing a bit labored. After a time, he added, "All I have I can give you I will, name your price. And as a father I will owe you more than any gold could ever pay."

She moved to the door she had come in.

"We'll discuss numbers when I get back with your daughter. By the way, what is her name?" As she said it she saw the darkness leave him.

"Pearl."

"I've always liked pearls better than diamonds," she said with a bright grin. "Another quote from Confucius fits here." She continued, "'*Faced with what is right, to leave it undone shows a lack of courage.*'"

"You do not lack that," he said with some hope in his tone. "Of that I am certain."

"You may think me nothing more than a bandit, but I love my country."

Rita opted to make her own way back to the Hotel Cathay after the warlord had explained, "I should call you a taxi, it would not do to tempt fate by us being seen together if I should take you back."

The warlord escorted her through a series of corridors to another exit. "My Pearl is in the village of Changshou, northeast of Nanking in the Japanese occupied area," he said. "Please bring her back to me, Miss O'Riordan." He'd told her where the girl's relatives were.

He slipped a Hawk head ring off his finger and handed it to her with a piece of paper. "I will monitor frequency to know of your success. This ring will identify you to the family she is staying with, that of old Wo Fung."

"I'll do my best, Po," she said as she slipped the ring on her left index finger, "Not for you, but for her and China."

"For whatever reason, I will be grateful."

It was dark as Rita found herself on the street in a different alley than she had entered Ying Xue Po's lair.

Okay, redhead, she thought. *You may have bitten off more than you could chew this time.*

She knew that the village was only a couple of hours flying time, but it was in an area that the Japanese patrols and her plane swooping in would certainly draw their attention. It would not be a cakewalk.

Rita moved down the empty alley to a busy street feeling safer in the crowd. She had no fear of Shanghai's streets, rather she embraced and was fascinated by the city. In her time in China the energy of the place excited her. She was not naïve, however, and always was aware of how she stood out.

From her time hunting on the Ranch with her brothers in Montana she had a hunter's instincts. She seemed to sense when she was being watched. She had that feeling now as she wove through the early Friday evening crowd.

She started to linger in front of store windows and randomly cross the street but could not be sure if she was indeed being stalked.

She had made it back to the Bund where the number of those strolling about was nearly at daytime levels as people went to shows or restaurants. She decided that she would hail a rickshaw and head back to the Hotel to get some rest and get ready for her morning flight.

She flagged one down but as she stepped into it two men suddenly appeared out of the crowd on both sides of the cart and sprang almost magically into the seat on either side of her.

"Hey," she yelled but before she could react or even bring her pistol to bear, she felt two knife blades pressed into her sides and hands clamped on each of her arms holding her tight.

"Just street thugs or are you specifically hunting redheads, boys?"

"Make no noise, Miss Radio," One of the men said as he took the clutch from her. "And keep your eyes fixed ahead."

The rickshaw driver seemed to be in on the kidnapping and knew just were to go, racing off through the streets while the two men kept their blades pressed hard into the woman's sides. The ride was a tense with neither man saying anything else. Rita did her best to not lose hope and kept up a calm exterior.

"Mind if I have a last cigarette, boys?"

The kidnapper to her right poked her harder with his knife.

"Health nuts, huh?' she hissed, then remained quiet for the rest of the ride, playing with the ring on her finger and grinning.

After a long time, the rickshaw pulled into a private courtyard of a townhouse on a quiet side street. There was an armed Japanese man waiting for them who opened the wrought iron gate.

"You will come this way," the tall Japanese said. His hair was cut short, he sported a pencil thin mustache, and was pointing a pistol at her. He was in civilian clothes, but his manner was pure military.

Rita looked back to see the now closed gate.

"Gee, guys, you act like I'd want to leave such pleasant company."

The gunman grunted and waved with the pistol. "Move."

With a knifeman on each side and the Japanese behind the redhead walked through a doorway into a well-lit room off the courtyard, which was decorated in minimalist Japanese fashion with tatami mats and *shoji* screens. In a formal area of raised tatami mats knelt the Baron Akio Takoda.

"Please remove your shoes, Miss O'Riordan," the nobleman said. "Then join me so that we may talk in relaxed fashion."

"I didn't realize you were so anxious to finish our conversation, Baron," she said as she sat, shoeless, on pillows opposite him. "I would have come by sooner had I known and brought cookies."

"Tea?" the nobleman asked with a quiet voice. He waved to a geisha in full regalia who was kneeling nearby with a full tea service.

The Japanese woman looked like a living porcelain doll, almost not human for the rounded perfection of her white and drawn on features. Her kimono was the full formal *de* that exposed her long, elegant, whitened neck. It was impossible for Rita to tell the girl's age, but the redhead suspected she was on the younger side, possibly a Maiko or apprentice Geisha.

Rita's two rickshaw companions stood just outside the doorway while the gunman slipped off his shoes and entered the room behind Rita. She noticed the guard kept himself positioned to have a clear field of fire so as not to endanger his leader.

"No thanks, Baron," she said. "I've had my fill of tea for the evening."

"Perhaps something stronger?" He gestured to a liquor cabinet. "There is *sake*, of course, but I must confess—if one could not judge me as disloyal to my blessed homeland—I have come to prefer your Kentucky Bourbon."

"Now, you're talking. I'll take a couple of fingers."

The Japanese waved for the geisha to pour a drink for Rita and one for himself.

When both had full glasses, the nobleman removed his spectacles and handed them to the geisha who diligently cleaned them and returned them while he waited. After he re-donned them, he gave a salute with his drink and he and the redhead tipped them back.

"Ah! Truly something the west has to offer us; perhaps the only good thing from such a vulgar culture." he said with a smile. "Now, please tell me what transpired when you met with Ying Xue Po."

She smiled noncommittally.

"Please, Miss Radio," he continued "or I will have Captain Yamaguchi here cause you great distress."

She glanced over at the civilian garbed Captain who smiled at her with anticipatory joy.

"Po?" she said with a laugh. "That warlord character? I would never talk to someone like that." She did her best to project innocent confusion, but the Baron's expression darkened.

"Do not insult me, *baka gaijin* trash." He waved at her and Yamaguchi flashed forward and suddenly slapped Rita before she could even get a hand up to defend herself.

The blow knocked her to the floor.

"Now," the Baron continued. "We had no idea what you received this afternoon, but fortunately we did have people outside Po's home as we have been keeping him under observation. You were seen to exit his lair, so you see, denials mean nothing."

Rita sat up, a trickle of blood from a split lip, gave a cold smile and looked daggers at Yamaguchi. "Where I come from, we always pay debts, Smiley; that is one I owe you."

Yamaguchi stepped in again and slapped the redhead before she could block it once more, this time with a little laugh.

"You're running up quite a tab, mister," she whispered.

"Bravado will do you no good," the Baron said. "Your stubbornness will not be allowed to stop the progress of the sons of heaven." He rose smoothly with the grace of a much younger man and spoke a few sharp words to his subordinate in his native tongue.

Afterward the geisha helped the Baron change from his leisure robe to a dress kimono. "I have an appointment, Miss O'Riordan," he said. "When I return, I trust you will have told the captain all that we wish to know. If you do, I will allow you to die quickly; if not I can assure you that you will pray to die for a very long time."

As the Japanese nobleman swept out of the room, sliding the door closed behind him, Yamaguchi swooped in and threw Rita on her face, handling her with the skill of a jujitsu man. He bound her hands behind her and then, using her hair as a handle pulled her painfully to a sitting position.

"You tell me what Takoda-sama want to know," he said. He removed his suit jacket and loosened his tie, a broad grin on his face. He called to the geisha and had her bring him a cup of *sake* that he downed with delight then continued, "But not soon. We play first."

He stepped forward and without ceremony to grab Rita's jacket by its lapels to bodily lift her off the floor. He started to shake her like a rag doll, not bothering to ask her anything.

She had to work hard to keep her teeth clenched as her head was tossed around like she was in a car crash. She got dizzy and saw red spots before her eyes.

Yamaguchi kept up the shaking for almost a minute, drawing involuntary grunts from her until both of them were coated with sweat. When he stopped, he held her limp form at arms length. Her feet barely supported her, and her head lolled to the side so that she seemed barely conscious.

"That all you got, Goliath?" Rita managed in a hoarse whisper. "Not even a good rumba."

He stared into her eyes, his pupils contracting to black dots as his rage grew. "*Baishunpu,*" he cursed. He shook her violently once more but when she only laughed, he roared with annoyance.

That was when Rita drove her right knee up into the groin of the interrogator, striking hard and fast. It connected on target enough for him to grunt and let go of her so she dropped to the floor. He staggered away, stomping his stocking feet hard to 'shake it off.'

The woman hit the floor hard but had expected it so took advantage of the moment to roll on her back. She was limber enough to wiggle herself to get her legs through the bound wrists and got her hands in front of her. They were still bound but there was about three inches of play between her balled fists.

Just as she struggled up on all fours the Japanese had recovered enough to grab her again, spinning her around to grab her jacket lapels once more, but this time instead of shaking her he drove the knuckles of his thumbs into her neck at her ceratoid arteries in a naked choke.

Rita felt the raw strength of the man's jujitsu hold. As much by instinct as by memories of wrestling with her brothers she realized she would black out in seconds. She drove her fists up hard and fast so that the taut rope slammed into Yamaguchi's Adam's apple like a garrote.

Yamaguchi gagged and coughed, his hands releasing the redhead to claw at his neck.

Rita pressed her momentary advantage, whirling to snatch up a bottle from the liquor cabinet and swung it hard into Yamaguchi's face. There was a 'chunk' sound. Contrary to the movies it is not that easy to break a bottle, especially one full of hundred-year-old Bourbon. A deep gash opened on the Japanese's forehead that fountained blood.

Rita swung a second time hitting a glancing blow that nonetheless broke Yamaguchi's nose. Before she could swing a third time, he got his hands up to intercept the bottle and got a hold of it.

She let the bottle go and kicked out hard with the instep of her right foot to collapse inside of the man's right knee. He went down.

Yamaguchi was blind now from the blood from his forehead and so did not see her when she leapt onto his back, slipping her bound hands over his head and pulling back with the rope he had tied on her, to crush his windpipe.

He tried to rise but she clamped her legs hard around his waist. All her weight was too much for his torn knee tendons and he fell over with her leached on to him. He clawed at her and flopped like a fish out of water as he tried to throw her off, tried to gasp for some air but she hung on with all she had.

Eventually his movements grew spasmodic and his fingers clawing at her, that scratched her forearms, became weak and vague and then stopped moving altogether.

Rita hung on for a full minute longer till there was no chance there was any life left in the officer.

When she rolled away from him, she was out of breath and her arms ached. She pushed herself to her knees and then noticed that the geisha was standing in the corner of the room, making herself small, her eyes wide with terror.

Rita rose slowly, her breath ragged. She rubbed the ring that Po had given her. "He's paid in full, honey," she said, "I don't owe you anything, its okay."

The geisha seemed to relax and slowly moved forward. She came right up to the taller Rita and now, not in 'professional mode' the youth of the girl was clear under the make up.

The geisha suddenly pulled a small knife from her Obi sash and before Rita could react cut the redhead's bonds. Then she bowed.

The girl looked down at the distorted face of Yamaguchi and suddenly lashed out and kicked the body.

"Well," Rita said. "I guess he ran up a lot of debts. Thanks."

Rita knelt and removed the pistol from Yamaguchi's holster.

The geisha bowed and then left the room via an inner door.

That left Rita alone with the dead interrogator and the two guards outside in the courtyard.

Rita hefted the pistol and racked a bullet. *Okay, here goes nothing,* she thought as she slid the door open and stepped out—prepared for anything but what she saw.

In the center of the courtyard there were three figures engaged in violent, physical combat. Two of the figures were Rita's companions on the rickshaw ride but the third was a hundred and twenty pounds of human fury.

Antonio Giovani Moran had been a boxer in the 'States but after a 'misunderstanding' in a bar fight that led to the death of a man he fled to the far east and joined the French Foreign Legion. It was there he acquired his nickname 'Frenchie' and where he studied *Savate des Rues,* the deadly street fighting version of the combat art, birthed in Marseilles.

Now Frenchie Moran was using all that skill as he whirled and kicked the two knife-wielding thugs. The two Chinese kidnappers were clearly skilled with the broad bladed weapons they brandished, but if the little American boxer was afraid, he did not show it.

As the taller Chinese slashed at him the American threw a *coup de pied bas*, a low kick into the man's shin. It stopped the attacker cold, but before Frenchie could follow up the second man lunged in at his back.

The boxer ducked under the attack and lashed back with a chasse lateral—kicking into the man's breadbasket to bend him over. That was when Frenchie moved in to uppercut the man, rocking him on his heels.

The first opponent had recovered and attacked again but the scrappy little American delivered a devastating *fouette* whip-kick to the man's left temple and it felled him as if poleaxed.

Frenchie whirled apparently anticipating further violence then saw Rita.

"Hey, boss," he saw the gun in her hand and smiled. "I should have guessed you wouldn't need me."

"It's the thought that counts, Frenchie," she said. "I was afraid you hadn't gotten my signal back at the hotel or had trouble trailing us."

"When you came out of that place by a different door, I almost lost you," he said. "I had to play catch up and circled the block then I spotted one of these goons following you."

"All good now," she joined him heading out of the courtyard. "But we'd better head back to the hotel right away; we have a trip to prepare for."

"Oh really, anywhere scenic?"

"Beauty is the eye of the beholder, my friend, so ask me that when we land tomorrow."

Frenchie slept that night in the sitting room of Rita's suite on a daybed, the shotgun she kept in the place beside him, and a chair propped under the outer door handle. Rita slept in her own room a pistol under her pillow. Still, both slept soundly and were up at first light, eating a hearty breakfast.

"So, you plan to just swoop into Japanese held territory, land and fly out just like that, boss?" The boxer asked as he finished his second cup of coffee. "They tend to be touchy about that sort of thing."

"That is exactly what Radio Rita is gonna do, Frenchie." she was attired in jodhpurs, boots, a sturdy shirt and had a shoulder holster with a .38 caliber pistol already strapped on. It was an Army Colt single action six-shooter that had been her grandfather's and was never far from her reach. She also wore a smile and had a joyous light in her green eyes.

She took a last piece of toast from the serving tray and bit it. "This was just a job, albeit a profitable one till Takoda stuck his nose in it; now it is a dare."

"I should have guessed you wouldn't need me."

"And you can't turn down a dare," Frenchie said. He was still dressed in the chauffer's uniform he'd slept in.

"Some people say so," she threw over her shoulder as she went into her room to grab her leather flight jacket. "But like my Da used to say, 'I didn't come to play—I came to win.'"

"Your old man didn't mess around, boss."

When she came back into the room, she was zipping the jacket up and carrying her cap and goggles. "Nope," she said, with a wistful smile. "All the way to the end, he stood up for what was right. He was flying mail in a storm one winter when his plane went down."

"Sort of died with his boots on, eh?"

"Yup," she said. "He'd have had it no other way." She led her friend out into the hall of the hotel.

"Well, Rita," he said as he followed behind, making sure to pick up the bag with sandwiches they'd had sent up from the hotel kitchen, "Let's hope all the other lessons he taught took more than that one, I'm not looking to go down in flames today."

The drive across the city was a strange one. It was a cloudy day, so the morning sunlight had an odd, muted quality. There was tension on the faces of the people bordering on fear. The populace as well as Rita and Frenchie were aware that things were changing.

"Word on the street yesterday was that the Japanese were not gonna take the Oyama thing lying down," he said as he negotiated the already crowded streets at eight AM. "They've been looking for an excuse to do down here what they did in Manchuria."

"I know," she said. "From what I heard the Japanese guy tried to force his way onto the airport."

"I talked to another driver who had been out here at the airport that day," Frenchie said, "Lieutenant Isao Oyama of the Japanese Special Naval Landing Forces came speeding up to the gate and when the guard stopped him Oyama shot and killed the guy. Other Chinese guards plugged Oyama."

"What the hell was he trying to prove?" she said. Their car came to the gate and the very nervous guard who, fortunately recognized Rita and Frenchie from their frequent visits. Construction on Hongqiao airport was started in 1921 as purely civilian, but now was mixed use with the Chinese

Airforce based there so security tightened of late.

"Hi Chong," she gave the guard her best smile. "What's the news for to-day?"

"Miss Radio," the guard gave a tense smile back, "bad day today."

"How so?"

"Much Japanese noise," he shrugged. "Everyone armed and ready."

"Well," she said, "stay safe."

When the touring car drove through the checkpoint they saw other Chinese soldiers, all armed and kitted for war. And all looking tense.

"It's all about to hit the fan, Boss." Frenchie pulled the car next to the hangar they rented for Rita's plane. They decamped and she unlocked the side door then he drove the car inside.

"It sure seems it, Frenchie," she said. In the hangar was their pride and joy, Rita's "Radio Flyer" a modified Curtiss Hawk, bi-wing and a small office. "So, let's get in the air as soon as we can."

"She's mostly fueled," he said as he threw his jacket on a coat tree. "I'll top it off though."

"No," she said, hanging her own jacket up. "You shower and change while I top off the belly tank and check the sparks." Then as an afterthought added, "And let's leave the shotgun here. Grab a rifle and bandolier of ammo."

They proceeded about their tasks and by the time both where finished it was just nine o'clock.

"You look almost human again," she joked to him as he exited the office. He had his own flying clothes on—he kept a spare set in the locker in the office—and a Winchester carbine with a belt of ammunition for it.

"I ain't qualified for that description since Jack Sharkey took me apart years ago in an exhibition bout."

The Radio Flyer was a naval model 64 Goshawk that she and Frenchie had modified to enlarge the cockpit by enough to allow for a passenger and installed the best radio set they could get. A cartoon of Rita with her flying cap on—some of Frenchie's artwork—decorated the fuselage. There was no mistaking it for anyone else's plane than hers.

"Store the popgun and our lunch," he called up as she climbed into the cockpit, "I'll get the door and kick it."

He slid the door back then stepped up to spin the propeller. "Contact!" he called

"Contact," she called back as the powerful R-1820-80 engine coughed into life. She taxied the plane out of the hangar, he slid closed and locked the door behind and then moved up beside the wing.

"Okay, you monkey," she called over the roar of the engine, "climb aboard."

He did, nimbly scaling the craft. She had to fold forward for him to get into the enlarged cockpit. It was really not a 'full space' for a second seat; the backward facing seat was minimal, but Moran was not a big man, so it was enough.

Once he was buckled in and had donned his leather flying cap, he was able to plug into the intercom.

"Everything's kosher, boss," he said.

"Let's take a little ride then," she said. "Radio Rita to tower, Radio Rita to tower, request permission to take off."

"Radio Rita," an accented voice came through the radio. "You are clear for take off on runway number three. Good luck, Miss Radio."

"Roger that, thanks." She checked the windsock then aimed the plane into the wind, gunned the engine and they were off!

"Get the wheels, Frenchie." She circled the airport while he used the crank to raise the hand-operated retractable landing gear.

"Up and locked," he called. There were some storage spaces in his back area and he checked them to make sure nothing had shifted with lift off. There were their lunch, some water, and coffee in one, a medical kit and a pistol in another. A larger one had some spare parts and tools. He hung the rifle with the ammo on some straps added for that purpose.

"I'm gonna head over the city and then take the coast up," she said, "To avoid any chance of ground fire."

She gained some height then headed over the northern fringe of the city. When she did a wingover they both noticed something strange.

"Was that gunfire?" She called back.

"Looked like it."

She looped back, passing over the Wusong, and Jiangwan districts and swooped lower.

"There," she yelled, "At four o'clock."

He craned his neck around and partially rose to see where she was indicating.

"Oh my gosh," he said. "Those are Japanese troops and the Chinese army."

Below them in was a pitched battle in the streets between uniformed troops using small arms. The sound of machinegun fire and even the yells of men in agony were audible above the roar of the plane's engine.

"It's come to open warfare now," Rita said. "Its even money there is even a city to come back to; but now we know why the Japanese were pressuring

Po—they must have been planning this."

"What do you want to do, boss?" Frenchie asked.

"What we set out to do," she said, "Get Pearl; then we'll figure out what to do when we know she's safe."

Rita O'Riordan's love of flying was born early in her life. As long as she could remember the freedom and joy of the sky had touched her soul and made any troubles she might have had on the ground disappear.

When she was four her Da had come back from the war troubled by the shadows of what he had seen but found his escape from those dark visions in his delight at flying. It was truly the times he was happiest and even as a child she saw that.

When he took little Rita with him on her first flight, she felt his joy as well and it was in the air where the two of them bonded. From that first flight her love for the air grew. She would beg him to take her with him on his barnstorming trips to air shows across the whole of the Midwest. By the time she was fifteen she was flying solo and putting on exhibitions at small town air shows and the smile her father gave her and the 'thumbs up' after an aerial maneuver were the best moments of her life.

Rita's brothers were more interesting in running the ranch, never really interested in flying so when their father died in that crash it was up to her to carry on the O'Riordan flying tradition. And the desire to see the world over the horizon was the logical choice to pursue her flying dreams. For the last three years those dreams had been in the skies of Indochina.

Now the turmoil of the war had come to her in a very real way, was it the hope of adventure or danger that drew her?

It's still about the sky, she thought. *Just let me fly.*

"According to the map we should be almost there, boss," Frenchie said from the "rumble" seat. "Maybe ten minutes."

"Gotcha," Rita said, pulled back from her woolgathering. She had been flying as high as she could out over the ocean for as long as she could in hopes of avoiding any unwanted attention but was forced to turn landward as their destination neared. She now kept her plane low, almost skimming the treetops. "If we are lucky, we get in and out before nightfall; I don't want to have to spend a night on the ground."

"Bound to have noisy neighbors," Frenchie said, "with guns."

The village of Changshou was in the midst of plowed fields and Rita skirted it with an eye to seeing if any of the Japanese forces where in the area. They saw a column of Japanese troops on horseback moving along a road heading toward the village.

"Gonna be tight, boss," Frenchie said. "They are moving pretty leisurely but if they speed up…"

"I know," she said, "But this is our best chance. If we can get in and out before that column get there—if they are heading for the village—we can avoid trouble. I saw a field over that hill about two miles back, I'm gonna see about setting us down."

She skimmed the treetops and did a flyby of the field with Frenchie scanning the ground carefully. She banked up and swung back.

"Looks good, Boss, no obvious roots or boulders, but it's gonna be tight."

"Wind is stiff enough," she said, "I think we can do it." She headed into the wind and cut back on power till she dropped to treetop level then killed the engine altogether and brought the Radio Flyer down deadstick.

The wheels hit dirt with a delicate touch; the plane bounced once then skidded across the rolling field with deft skill.

"Not gonna make it," Frenchie said. He was craned around to look ahead of the plane as it bumped along the field heading toward the far line of trees.

"We'll make it," she laughed, "or die trying!"

"That's what I'm afraid of."

Just before the plane would have made the tree line Rita worked the rudder pedals and swung the craft in a sharp left. The Radio Flyer skidded along and the one of the wheels caught in a clump of earth then the plane stuttered and fishtailed.

It spun around almost one hundred and eighty degrees and then came to a jarring stop.

"Damn!" Frenchie cursed.

"Oh, don't be an old lady," she called back. She jumped from the cockpit to the ground barely before the plane had stopped moving.

"'Damn' is right," she cursed as she landed in a crouch. "We messed up a wheel."

He was out with her in a moment and crawled under the craft. "It's twisted, Boss, but it's not a total loss."

"You can fix it?"

He nodded. "I'm pretty sure. The issue is that this clearing may not be enough to get out of with the two of us in the plane."

"The three of us," she pointed out.

"Hope she is a little girl," he said. "And if we can clear the field of any other rocks."

"Can you do it without me and get the plane turned around?"

"I think so, but why—"

"I'm gonna get to the village and find that girl."

There was a new growth of woods between the field they landed in and the plowed fields of that surrounded the village and the going was slow for Rita. It took her over an hour to reach the outskirts of the cultivated fields where some villagers were working.

It was past noon and the peasant women she encountered were startled and a little fearful to see the leather cap wearing stranger. The children, most barely older than toddlers, were not the least bit shy, however, racing up to stare with delight when she removed her flying cap to become a redheaded apparition.

"Hi," she said with as warm a smile. "*Jau, Jau!*" she called, 'Friend' in Cantonese. In her time in China, she had learned enough Cantonese to get by so it only took her a few minutes to find someone to direct her to the hut of Wo Fung.

The hut as a simple one with a pen out front with two goats and a pig wallowing in a mud puddle in the corner. Chickens in a coop squawked behind the hut.

Strange, she thought, *no one in the village at all.*

She stepped to the front of the door and knocked, the very normalcy of the action feeling strange in the oddly quiet town.

After a long time, an ancient voice called out in Cantonese. Rita answered, "I have come from Ying Xue Po to bring his daughter to him." In both Cantonese (as best she could) and English.

There was another long pause then the door swung inward, and an old woman stepped into the space. She leaned heavily on a cane and regarded Rita with hawk eyes. "Proof?" She said in English.

Rita held out the ring. The old woman looked hard at it, taking Rita's hand to pull the ring closer to her face. Then she looked up and nodded. She called back into the hut in Chinese and a figure stepped out of the shadows.

The girl that stepped into the light was dressed in simple black pajama-like peasants' clothes and had short cut hair so that she almost looked like a boy. She was four feet tall and around nine years old, thin but healthy. "I am Ying Zhenzhu," she said with a pronounced English accent. "How is papa?"

Rita could not help but smile at the poise of the young girl as she could see echoes of her father's features in hers. "He's fine, Pearl. I saw him last night and he asked me to come for you because he misses you."

The girl looked to the old Chinese woman who gave a weak smile. "She has the ring."

The girl smiled then. "Okie, dokie, let me get my stuff."

"Pack light," Rita said. "We're flying out of here."

"Flying?" the girl's face lit up. "A plane? From here?"

Rita laughed. "Only way to fly!"

The girl raced off into the hut and followed by the sound of her gathering her belongings. The old woman looked at Rita and said in halting English. "She is a good girl of a bad father; but family is family."

"Are you not?" Rita asked.

"Her mother was my husband's child by his first wife." She spoke with pain in her tone. "Yet she is a good girl; it has been good to have her underfoot"—that brought a smile—"but exhausting."

Pearl was back now, a small cloth satchel slung over her shoulder. "Is this okay?"

"That should be fine," Rita said. "But we have to go, we—"

Just then another child ran up from the center of the village jabbering in Chinese. Both the young girl and old woman evidenced shock.

"The Japanese, they come," the old woman said.

"Dang," Rita said, "They must have speeded up the column." She turned to the boy. "How far?"

The boy pointed at the other end of the village and spoke in Cantonese.

"He says just at the edge of the North field," Pearl said. "Perhaps a half hour away."

"We have to go fast then," Rita said.

The girl moved to the old woman and embraced her, speaking softly in Chinese. Both looked like they were on the verge of tears but controlled themselves.

"I'm ready," Pearl said. "Where do we go?"

"Will you be all right?" Rita asked the old woman.

"No one here knows who Zhenzhu is but me," the woman said. "And I am old. I have no fear of the invaders."

The girl moved to the old woman and embraced her.

"Okay," Rita said. "This way, pumpkin, we better double time it."

The two ran back out of the village toward the field that Rita had crossed before. The word about the coming invaders had already reached the farm workers and they were coming in from the fields.

Pearl embraced several of them, but Rita had to press her. "We have to move, honey. We have a ways to go."

The two of them headed into the woods at a fast walk. "It is going to be a bit rough," Rita said, "The plane is in a clearing on the other side of this wooded patch."

"Oh, I know that place," Pearl said. "There is a path that is easier than this."

"You lead on then," the redhead said. The girl did, striking off on a tangent from the way Rita was going, and for a time the woods were just as dense then, suddenly they broke out onto a rough path.

"This goes up and around to the clearing," Pearl said, not the least bit out of breath from the rough terrain. "In the spring there are lots of pretty flowers there, but the ground it too goopy for crops."

They moved along the path at a good pace in silence for a time, but finally when they stopped for a moments rest Pearl asked. "Are the Japanese coming for me because of my father?"

This took Rita by surprise and took her a moment to answer. "I think so, but they don't know you were in this village exactly. At least I'm not sure."

"Will they hurt the people in Changshou because of me?" The girl's soft face took on an angular quality and she looked suddenly much older.

"No," Rita said truthfully. "The Imperial Army is rough, I've seen what they've done in Manchuria, but there is no reason for them to be especially rough in the village. No more than they would have been anyway."

"But they are after me?" The young girl was clearly wrestling with a hard reality.

"Maybe not this group, but yes, the Japanese want to capture you to put pressure on your father." When Rita saw how this weighed heavy on the child she added, "But because of that they won't hurt you if they do."

Rita had misunderstood, however for the girl straightened up and put on a brave face. "They won't use me to hurt father. I won't let them. Let's get going—" Then the girl smiled. "I do not know your name."

Rita laughed and stuck out her hand. "Rita O'Riordan."

The girl shook it. "Wait," Pearl said, "I know you, Radio Rita?"

"Uh, yes, people call me that."

"My father called you that," the girl said with her cheeks coloring, "But he usually prefaced it with 'that bloody damn.'"

Rita laughed and it encouraged the girl to continue. "He said you had taken this or that shipment out of his hands. He was angry you worked for Ho Chien."

"Well," Rita said, "I guess it's nice to be known; and frankly, I've been called worse." This made the girl giggle and the two rose and headed off with much less effort along the worn path.

In a short time, Rita became aware of sharp cries in Japanese that told them there were others in the woods not far behind them.

"They haven't discovered the path," Rita whispered. The two of them moved more quickly now, not quite running, but moving as fast as the uneven ground allowed. The sounds of the troops behind grew steadily louder.

"Don't worry," Rita whispered when she saw the fear on the girl's face. "We'll be soaring soon and away from them." She did her best to sound positive but was beginning to doubt her own words when they broke through the screen of underbrush into the clearing.

They were halfway down the clearing from the Radio Flyer. Frenchie had succeeded in turning the plane back into the clearing and was tinkering with the motor when Rita waved to him.

"Hey, Boss I—" He started to call but she waved him to silence and the two women ran faster. He realized something was wrong and quickly closed the engine housing.

Rita gestured to wind the prop and he got the message and scrambled up into the cockpit to pick up his Winchester. The two racing women picked up speed and were in the middle of the clearing when the first of the Japanese troops emerged from the tree line.

The soldiers were at the far end of the clearing and began to shout when they saw the plane.

"Knock on it," Frenchie yelled. He was back on the ground now and cocked his rifle just as the Japanese soldiers began firing at the two runners. The range was too long for an accurate shot, but the bullets kicked up dirt around the two.

Frenchie started to fire back, knowing his chances of hitting them wasn't any better, but in hopes of halting the Japanese attack. It worked.

The shots broke the charge as the troops threw themselves to the ground to find cover.

"Move it," Frenchie yelled. He kept firing from the side of the plane but after the troops realized only one person was shooting, they started to rise again.

"Up you go!" Rita called. As she bodily hoisted Pearl up to the wing, she swung off her leather jacket. "You'll need this. Get in the back seat."

"I cleared the path," Frenchie said as he fired several more shots, "but I didn't expect to have to roll over the laughing boys out there."

"We'll make it," she said as she slipped into the cockpit. "Contact!"

He spun the propeller and then scurried up on the wing, crowding into the jump seat with Pearl.

"Hi, Kiddo," he said. "I'm Frenchie."

"I am Pearl," she said calmly. "I'm not afraid."

"That's okay, honey," he said as he strapped her into the seat and jammed himself into the floor section. "I'll be afraid for both of us."

Rita gunned the engine, revving it to full power before she released the break and the plane surged forward.

"Hold on to your hats," she yelled. "This will be close!"

The Japanese soldiers started to fire at the plane, but Rita's plane still had some of the original features from when she bought it as a warplane, including two fixed synchronized .30 in M1919 Browning machine guns in the fuselage. She depressed the trigger and opened fire, shooting above their heads.

The charging Japanese once again dropped face down to the ground and the plane roared at them, just inches above the ground.

"We're heavy," she called back, "Drop the belly tank."

Frenchie reached forward to the release handle by her left side and pulled. There was a hard click sound. The plane shot forward and up as the gas tank below the ship dropped clear. The 'Flyer rose immediately, and Rita yanked back on the stick hard.

The boxer then grabbed the landing gear crank and worked hard to retract them.

He was just in time as the belly of the plane barely cleared the line of trees. As soon as she was sure they were clear Rita veered off to the right out of the clearing, out of small arms range of the troops.

"You okay back there?" Rita called.

"That was fun!" Pearl giggled. "Like a ride."

"Yeah," Frenchie said, "just like Coney Island, complete with a shooting gallery. I think I left my stomach back there."

"Let's see if we can find it," Rita said. She made a wide loop with the plane to fly back over the clearing again. The confused Japanese soldiers had all gotten to their feet and were being berated by an officer, all standing around the off-loaded belly tank.

"What are you doing, boss?"

"Can't leave Coney Island without fireworks, Frenchie." Just as the soldiers realized she was bearing down on them again they opened up with their guns with some of the less rattled of the troopers sending shots into the wings. "Hand me the Very pistol."

The boxer handed the single shot breech-loading, snub-nosed flare gun forward. Rita leaned over the side of the plane as they passed over the belly tank. She took a quick aim and pulled the trigger.

Suddenly the tank erupted into a massive explosion of flame, throwing up a huge blast that seemed to chase the plane as she gave it full power. The fire and debris were carried by a blast wave that threw the soldiers across the field.

The Radio Flyer was buffeted by the concussion, and they all felt the heat.

Rita kept control as the plane was rocked by the explosion.

"Why'd you do that, boss?" Frenchie asked. "I mean, except general orneriness?"

"This way they can't give the village people any trouble," she said. "Not enough of them left to do any damage."

"What's next?" Frenchie asked. "Gonna be a squeaker with the belly tank gone."

"I used the belly as primary on the way down," she said, "just thinking ahead, not knowing how big Pearl was. I think we can make it back if I nurse the Flyer and take a more direct route."

"Are we going to papa?" Pearl asked, plugging into the intercom. The leather flying cap was as large on her as Rita's jacket, so she looked like she had melted.

"That is the idea, pumpkin," Rita said. "I have a radio frequency to call him on, but we're too far out to get him yet."

"Can I talk to him?" Her voice had a plaintive tone, and it was clear she missed him.

"If he comes on, we can try," Rita said, "but I can't pass the mic back there very far."

"Okay."

"You'll see him soon, kiddo," Frenchie said. "You're on the Rita Express, so not to worry."

Rita turned the plane south and headed back toward Shanghai hoping he had not lied to the girl.

The afternoon skies clouded and soon the Radio Flyer was fighting its way through a summer downpour. The cockpit was only semi-cowled, so Frenchie was ducked down and Pearl huddled in her borrowed jacket. Rita pulled her goggles down and wished she had a second jacket.

At least the rain is keeping any prospective potshot takers indoors, Rita thought.

There was not much wind so even with the rain the plane made good time. And they were soon in broadcast range so she warmed up the radio and called.

"Radio Rita to the Hawk," she repeated several times until a staticky voice replied.

"I am here, Miss O'Riordan. Did you succeed?"

"Pearl is with me, Po," she said, "but we're not set up for her to talk to you."

"Where are you?"

"Probably about fifteen minutes out of Hongqiao Airport."

"You must be very careful, Miss," his voice crackled from the radio. "Things are very bad in the city, open warfare has broken out in the Zhabei, Wusong, and Jiangwan districts. The Japanese crossed the Bazi Bridge. Navel ships have begun bombardment."

"Oh, June and junipers!" Rita exclaimed.

"I have moved to a safer area then you visited," he said. "I am in contact with Chiang Kai-shek and can commit my forces to him, but I need to know my Zhenzhu is safe."

"We're on the way to you, Po, just tell me where."

"Ask my Pearl," he said. "The monkey place. She will know where that is."

The signal cut out then and after a few tries with the dial Rita gave up. "I heard from your Da," She called back to the girl on the intercom. "He said to go to the monkey place, do you know what that means?"

"Yes, Miss Radio," the girl said with excitement. "A compound near the Jade Buddha Temple on Jiangning Lu Way."

"Good," Rita said, "We can get there pretty quick from the airport, faster than his place near the Bund."

"What's the news, Boss?" Frenchie asked.

"Later, pal," Rita said, her tone conveying her dark meaning. "After we get dried off."

As they neared the airport night was on them. In the darkness the flashes of navel guns and even small arms fire could be seen ahead of them. Rita made a wide Eastern circle toward the airport and made radio contact to announce herself.

The tower cleared her for landing when they recognized her, and it was just in time as were almost flying on fumes. She made the landing with no incident, taxing directly to their hanger. Frenchie climbed over Pearl and opened the hangar's wide door to allow her to taxi the plane in.

"I have to change my shirt," Rita said when they were all on the ground. She was soaked.

"Is there any food?" Pearl asked.

"I think there are some candy bars in the office, pumpkin."

"I'll get the top up on the car while you change, boss."

Rita did find some candy bars in an office drawer for Pearl and a dry shirt for herself in the closet. She brushed out her hair, only slightly damp from beneath her leather flying cap. She removed her shoulder holster and strapped on a hip belt with a holster, then donned a duster from her closet against the rain.

"You look like a cowboy," Pearl said, happily munching on a Baby Ruth bar and sipping from a Coke.

"I should," Rita said, drawing, twirling and re-holstering the single action gun. "My grandda was a lawman in Montana and used this gun and rig."

"Like Tom Mix!" Pearl exclaimed.

"Just like," Rita agreed. "Now, come on let's go see your Da."

The rain was not heavy, but the normally busy streets were all but deserted. The distant sounds of gunfire and explosions mixed with far off thunder gave the whole trip from the airport a nightmarish tinge.

"You sure this is the right thing, boss?" Frenchie mouthed to Rita as they drove toward the Jade Buddha Temple. Pearl was dozing between them on the front seat, her enthusiasm at seeing her father tempered by the long flight.

"The only thing, Frenchie. A girl should be with her da. Might make sense for us to think about a change of scenery though after we deliver her. Fancy Saigon for a bit?"

"I got some friends that way from my legion days," he laughed. "Some enemies too."

Ying Xue Po's compound consisted of two buildings with a wide court-yard between them protected by a high iron fence. As the two guards opened the gate for the car Rita could see why it was called "the Monkey Place" as there was an intricate sculpture of Hanuman, the Monkey King, scribed on the gate.

"This is a happy place," Pearl gushed as they parked the car in the center of the courtyard. "My papa's office is there." She pointed to a lighted room and bounced out of the car to race ahead.

"I gotta say, I'm glad we did this," Frenchie said. "But I'll be just as glad to be done and out of here."

"Yes," Rita said, "I always liked the French food in Saigon; be a nice change from Chinese food."

The two of them entered another book-lined study, much like the one where Rita had first met the Blood-Hawk. Pearl was hugging her father but his face evidenced anything but joy.

In a moment, the two friends saw why; Baron Takoda stepped from behind a curtained arch, pistol in hand pointing at Pearl.

"Thank you for bringing our little guest to us," the Japanese said waving his pistol like a wand. He was in full military uniform now, sword at his hip.

"I am sorry, Miss O'Riordan," Ying Xue Po said. "After we spoke this—man and his soldiers descended upon us."

Two guards stepped into the doorway behind Rita and Frenchie. They had bayonets on their rifles and grins on their faces as they took up relaxed positions in the door jam.

"Sorry to say I'm not surprised, Po," Rita said. "Snakes gotta way of slith-ering out of the shadows."

"The Sons of the Rising Sun will always prevail," Takoda said, indicating his guards with his gun. "We had kept observers on Mister Ying and monitored all his communications. So we were prepared to take advantage. We will take this city in three days and then the rest of China."

"Never," the warlord said. "The Chinese will never bow to invaders." This made Takoda laugh.

"We will see if your attitude improves," the Japanese said. "Now that your little daughter is in our hands."

"No, papa!" Pearl said, clinging to her father's waist.

"You're pretty low, Takoda," Rita said with a hiss. "Snake is the right term for you."

"You will pay for what you did to Yamaguchi as a comfort woman for the Emperor's forces." Takoda said making a wide gesture with his pistol. "You will learn your place, soon, American,"

"In a pig's eye, you sidewinder!" Rita spat. "Frenchie—left!"

As soon as Takoda's gun barrel was pointed away from Pearl with his gesture Rita moved like lighting, slapping leather, drawing and firing her six-gun. The move was so quick that she put a bullet through the Baron's forehead before anyone realized what had happened.

Frenchie snapped a kick to the left guard's jaw and Rita spun and fanned her gun to finish the other with a bullet through the heart.

In two eye blinks there were no Japanese alive in the room.

"Get their guns," she called to Frenchie as she raced into the courtyard. Two more uniformed soldiers appeared out of the shadows, but Rita fired twice, each shot a fatal one.

By then Ying Xue Po and Frenchie both were out the door with the soldier's rifles and soon discovered the other three Japanese soldiers that were guarding the household staff.

It was a short firefight with the surprised soldiers gunned down before they could get off a single shot.

The house staff were freed and set to guarding the compound while the warlord, his daughter and the two Americans moved to the sitting room. Servants brought in tea for the four of them, though the adults spiked theirs. Other servants cleared the dead away.

"They will dispose of the bodies where no suspicion will come upon us," Ying Xue Po said. "And as soon as possible I will take my Pearl away from this city." His voice was choked with emotion.

"I can not thank you enough, Miss O'Riordan," Ying said hugging his daughter. "Name whatever you wish—"

"I think that hundred pounds to cover gas will do it," Rita said. "And there is an orphanage in Hunan that could use a new well and some medical supplies." He looked at her, stunned, but when he realized she was serious he nodded.

Pearl stepped forward to offer her the flight jacket. "Thank you," the girl said. "I will always be in your debt."

"The jacket is yours, pumpkin," Rita said. "Keep it as a souvenir so you won't forget my name."

The girl started to cry then and threw herself around Rita in a hug that took her breath away. "I'll never, ever forget you, Radio Rita."

"Don't you mean bloody damn Radio Rita?" Rita said with a smile, looking at Ying Xue Po.

"Perhaps before," the warlord said, returning her smile, "But now it will be bloody damn amazing Radio Rita."

"I'll drink to that," Frenchie said. He did, and the others joined him.

THE END

Who is Radio Rita?

Radio Rita –at least my version of her—jumped into my head as quick as a six-gun draw. It happened like this—

I work late at night spinning my tales, often writing through the night. One of those nights I saw the Airship27 podcast where the Captain and the Chief Engineer (Ron and Rob) were joking about Radio Rita and how that little cartoon lady/mascot was getting to be so popular that people were asking "when will you do stories with her?" and they said "Okay, we will!" and put out the call.

I literally wrote them right then and there and said, "I want in!"

Why?

Well, Rita O'Riordan told me to.

Yup—in that moment I had clear picture of the redheaded aviatrix and knew I had to tell her tale. She was as clear as any character I'd ever written and sort of jumped into my brain fully formed.

But let me backtrack a bit.

To me the most interesting period of the twentieth century were the years between 1936-1940. This prewar period was when all the forces of the old world that had been disrupted by the destruction of WWI were beginning to find a new way to move forward. Old institutions still cast a shadow on the world, but new institutions and attitudes were taking hold.

The great depression was in the rear-view mirror for much of the world and it seemed like a new age of science was coming with inventions like television, nylon, and plastics that promised a better world.

And at the same time, new powers were rising—dark powers—and not only in Germany, Italy, and Japan, but also in South America.

On the newsstands pulps like Argosy, Adventure, Blue book, and Flying Aces, and radio shows like Ripley's Believe it or Not brought the world into the living rooms of America. There was a public that was beginning to have a world view that was focused over the horizon.

In the movies adventure films let us see that world beyond (even if India looked like California and all European villages looked pretty much the same, 'cause there were only three European sets).

Even though the American public pretty much wanted to ignore the atrocities in Ethiopia, Manchuria and the rumors of what was happening in Germany, films where beginning to hint at it and help raise consciousness.

Films like *Secret Agent of Japan, The Mortal Storm,* and *Escape,* as well as comedies by The Three Stooges and Charlie Chaplin were all sounding the alarm of what was to come.

"Frenchie"

The yellow menace trope was still part of the culture and many radio show villains had suspiciously Germanic names or accents, though no one wanted to specifically name their country of origin before America was in an official war. Captain America, however, was not shy at all in his comic book premier about who to punch.

At the same time the place of women in the world was being redefined with Eleanor Roosevelt, Amelia Earhart, and Catherine Hepburn leading the way to establish them as self-determinant and powerful.

It was that sense of "I can do it!" that I saw as a key factor in my version of this heroine. It is why she had to come from the ranch culture with a pioneer background to connect her to the strong women of the past that had crossed the plains and made the west.

And I gave her the Irish background because of that questing Celtic sort has always appealed to me, and well, we were told she had to be a redhead so that was not a stretch.

All these things collided in that moment when Radio Rita crossed my 'radar' and I knew I had to write a tale about her.

And it had to be a straight up adventure, not a weird tale, nor mystery such as might have appeared in Adventure or Argosy Magazines on the newsstands back in the day.

But why Shanghai and why on that day?

Well, if you look at the pivot points of history one of them was August 9th 1937. On that day a Japanese officer tried to force his way onto a military airport and was shot in an exchange of gunplay.

It was the final straw in the delicate balance that the international city had managed to keep while the Japanese were pressing territorial claims to the north since they had invaded and annexed Manchuria in 1931.

The Saturday that followed, August 13, at 9 am the Battle of Shanghai began, and started a bloody conflict that lasted for over three months with a Japanese victory and over 180,000 Chinese dead.

Many historians consider this is the first battle of World War II.

That is why I wanted my Radio Rita to be there, at the critical moment in history and, while honing as close to real facts as possible, give her a vital role.

I tried to make as many facts accurate as possible so that this is not an alternate world take, but could indeed have happened.

I hope you have enjoyed the tale and if you did, let us know and maybe we can see what the future brings for the redhead from Montana who loves to fly!

Teel James Glenn 8/24/21

TEEL JAMES GLENN has stories have been printed in magazines from *Weird Tales, Spinetingler, SciFan, Mad, Black Belt, Fantasy Tales, Pulp Empire, Sherlock Holmes Mystery, SciFan, Sixgun Western, Crimson Streets, Silver Blade Quarterly, Tales of Old, Blazing Adventures* and scores of other publications and dozens of books and anthologies in many genres. His short story "The Clockwork Nutcracker" won best steampunk story for 2013 from Preditor and Editors poll.

His novel Cowboy in Carpathia won the 2021 Pulp Factory Award as best novel and he is also the winner of the 2012 Pulp Ark Award for Best Author, his website is: http://theurbanswashbuckler.com

Radio Rita and the Genesis Machine

by
Samantha Lienhard

Jazz music played over the radio as Rita waited behind the desk in the radio station studio. A large window overlooked the coastal town below, and sunlight filtered in to illuminate her posters featuring Louis Armstrong, Frank Sinatra, and Bill Haley, displayed in between the record-laden shelves. On the opposite wall, a second window gave a dazzling view of the North Atlantic waves crashing against the rocky cliff upon which the radio station perched. Stacks of popular albums sat on her desk alongside a microphone, and in the middle of it all, a record player spun out the final notes of the latest jazz hit taking the country by storm. A crisp scent like that of fresh pine filled the air. Rita relaxed back in her office chair, headphones partly buried in her fiery red hair, until the song concluded.

As she switched to the next record, a rock single that had been gaining traction, the phone to her left rang. She spun in her chair to face that side of the desk and grabbed it.

"This is Radio Rita, coming to you live from Maine to play the songs you love the most. How can I help you?"

"Hi, Rita." The familiar voice on the other end had a trace of a Russian accent, and her heart skipped a beat. "This is your number one fan, calling in from a snowy getaway. Even though I'm on vacation, I miss you terribly. I'm glad your station can always bring me the welcome sounds of home no matter where I am. Could you play 'The Fire Burns at Midnight'?"

Rita kept her voice composed despite the racing of her heart. "Absolutely. It's always good to hear from you."

She hung up the phone and rose from her chair to find the song in question, an obscure single from a little-known band that never did anything else after that. The record sat at the top of the stack just alongside her desk, and she set it up to switch to it next.

When the current song ended, she turned on the microphone. "Folks, we've got a request for 'The Fire Burns at Midnight.' Let's get that song on the air, and don't forget that you can call in at any time to request your favorite songs!"

The brassy chords began, and she settled back in her chair to think. If anyone looked in at her, she would appear relaxed, but her mind raced.

Vacation. Misha had traveled somewhere.

He missed her terribly. This required someone else to be sent out there.

Welcome sounds of home. HQ would have the details.

"The Fire Burns at Midnight." This mission was time-critical.

She'd play a few more songs before turning over the studio to a colleague for the day, and then the real work would begin.

In an office building on the corner of the city's busiest street, the same in appearance as all the others around it, mail was delivered to Reports & Accounting in a brown bundle. Mail left the office in a similar format, and was sent to DC to be filed away.

Rita entered the building in which Reports & Accounting had its offices. She passed rows of bored workers busy in their cubicles, entered a hallway at the back, turned right into an unlabeled room, and gave her credentials to the man waiting inside. He opened the door to a hallway that most people didn't know existed, although it was from where the Reports & Accounting mail usually came.

At the end of that hallway, Rita entered the elevator. Most attempts to use it would result in a message saying the elevator was out of order, but she didn't select just a single floor. Instead, she pressed the buttons for floors 5, 3, 2, 6, and 1, in sequence. The buttons remained lit for only a second, then darkened, but the door slid shut and the elevator descended to the deepest level.

The quiet hum of activity surrounded her the moment she stepped out into the hallway. Deep underground though it was, it had more life than the fake office above. Warm lights on the ceiling lit up the hall and the numerous doors that led to various offices, labs, and meeting rooms, and the smell of coffee filled the air along with a pine-like scent. It was abustle with activity, as people went about their business from one room to the next.

Two colleagues in black suits passed Rita on their way from the break room and nodded to her in greeting. An elderly man raced past with a stack of papers hugged tight to his chest, and she almost called out to him—but old Dr. Stevens looked like he was on the verge of a breakthrough; when he got like that, he probably wouldn't hear her anyway. Another agent marched past her with only a stiff nod, clearly focused on his next assignment. Hushed whispering drew her attention to a group of clustered recruits who ducked their heads when they realized they'd been noticed.

At last, she reached Simmons's outer office, where his secretary tapped busily at her typewriter. She glanced up. "You can go right in. He's expecting you."

"Thanks." Rita walked past her to the next door and opened it.

Her boss sat behind his desk looking over reports with a pained expression, dressed in his usual crisp black suit. The thick mahogany desk was covered in stacks of paperwork, and the rest of the room was richly furnished with paintings, statues, and even an experimental video screen intended to simulate an outdoor view despite how deep underground they were.

Simmons looked up when she entered, and a smile crossed his aging features. "I'm glad you came quickly."

"You know me," she said, "I never can resist an invitation to a party."

She first met Simmons during the war. Rita was a pilot, and although most women didn't participate in combat missions, one day he introduced himself to her and said her piloting skills impressed him. He saw potential in her and wanted her to fly some covert missions that the public would never know about. Rita didn't care about recognition or glory, so she accepted.

The missions were a success, and their partnership grew from there. She went behind enemy lines to gather intel and took on increasingly dangerous assignments.

When the war ended, Rita found herself part of his network.

Simmons headed the government agency officially documented as Reports & Accounting, unofficially known as the Hand of the Law. At 5'8", with fiery red hair and bright green eyes, Rita was a bit too distinctive for a lot of the Hand's undercover work, but she made up for it as a pilot. At her boss's behest, she had then studied the material from the Moore School Lectures and every subsequent paper on computing, later getting permission to experiment with one of the government's UNIVAC I machines on her own.

She eventually found a permanent post at the radio station to accept and pass on intelligence from their contacts throughout the world under the guise of song requests.

"So," she said, "what's the situation?"

Simmons let out a long sigh and rubbed his forehead. "A group of unknown persons is constructing a device of unknown purpose—possibly a weapon."

She raised her eyebrows. "Unknown persons constructing an unknown device? Is there anything we *do* know?"

"Whatever they're doing, it appears to involve nuclear power."

She sat down in front of his desk and frowned. After so long with the organization, this office felt homey and comfortable. Yet tension hung in the air between them today. Aside from the obvious, she also had a strange sense of uneasiness she couldn't shake no matter how much she tried to settle back in the cushioned chair.

Oblivious to her discomfort, Simmons launched into his explanation. "A few weeks ago, our agents picked up reports of shipments being delivered to an isolated area far to the north and high in the mountains. These shipments often took circuitous routes as though trying to go undetected. Looking into it further, one of our agents traced them back and determined that several of the ordered items are materials you'd needed if you were constructing a nuclear weapon."

"You said it's in the mountains?" she asked.

He nodded. "It's within the bounds of the United States, but a highly isolated area in the north. It is home to Whitehollow, a small mountain village that has seen an unusual amount of activity as of late."

"An organized group, then?"

"Most likely."

Always a danger. "So you sent Misha in to investigate?"

"That's right. He was able to determine that a man named Carter Hawke is involved." Simmons passed a folder across the desk toward her. "Hawke was an American businessman of some renown, but he vanished a few years ago."

Rita opened the folder and looked at the photo of a bald man in a suit giving a press conference. "So he reappeared in the mountains constructing a weapon?"

"According to Misha's report, yes."

She scanned the portfolio on Hawke. He was the head of an oil company until his disappearance. He had no close relatives, and his colleagues never heard from him. Attempts to locate him ceased after a year, and he was presumed dead. Now he'd suddenly reappeared.

"Unfortunately, we've lost contact with Misha. His call to you earlier today was his final communication out of the village. All attempts to get in touch with him have failed."

"It's only been a few hours," she said. "Are you sure it's cause for concern?"

"I'd rather not take any chances after the message he gave you." Simmons furrowed his brow. "He was supposed to send a full report today and keep a radio nearby at all times. For him to contact you instead and then fall silent makes me fear the worst."

Rita grinned. "Sending me out to rescue him? He won't like that."

Simmons ignored her comment and continued his explanation. "The region in question is surrounded by mountains, and we have reason to suspect anyone who enters is being monitored. Therefore, I want you to fly in."

He passed a map of the mountainous region across the desk to her. The small village was marked on it, and another location in the mountains was circled.

"This clearing in the mountains should have enough space for you to land, although it will be tricky."

"I live for tricky landings," she said, "but won't the villagers wonder where I came from? Small place like this, I expect strangers to stand out right away."

Simmons nodded, his expression pained. "That's definitely true, and you can't avoid the village and hope to learn anything useful. However, our attempts to monitor the area suggest the organization is minimizing its involvement with the village. Therefore, while information will eventually reach them regardless, entering this way should buy you some time."

"I see," she said.

"Can you do it?"

She folded her arms. "Getting in is no problem. As for the rest, I'll figure something out."

"Please go in with a plan more concrete than 'figure something out.'"

"Always." She winked.

He shook his head. "Head to the lab to requisition anything you'll need before you leave. If you have any other requests, please let me know."

"I do have one," she said.

"What's that?"

"Would you assign someone to watch the radio station in my absence?"

He laughed. "I wouldn't dream of leaving it empty."

"Good."

Everything was settled, then. She would get some gear from the lab and head on out. Planning could be done on the way; Rita had confidence in her skills and those of Misha once she tracked him down. Even against a secretive organization with unknown resources, she liked their odds.

Yet something tugged at the back of her mind with an ominous whisper that something about this wasn't right. A cold chill in the air made her uneasy, and that sharp scent of pine increased her growing headache. The situation sounded like it was under control, but Rita's gut said otherwise.

Better to be safe than sorry. Rita snapped her gaze back to Simmons. "One more thing. If Misha really has vanished, things might be worse than we think. I could be in grave danger out there."

Grave danger.

"I'll check in once every 24 hours," she said. "If I miss a check-in, you'll know something went wrong. That's when we should turn to Plan B."

"The usual Plan B?" he asked. "The emergency dispatch?"

"Exactly."

"Very well. If you miss your check-in, an elite squad will be sent in after you and Misha. There will be no attempt at subtlety; they'll storm the place with the assumption that the worst has happened."

"If neither of us can check in," she said, "it probably has."

In all the times she had worked with the Hand, an elite squad only had to be sent in once. She and Misha had been on the Monaco job together, but they weren't prepared for the enemy's resources. Captured, interrogated, and about to be executed, they only survived because no one expected the rescue team until it was too late. It left the intended mission in shambles, but they got out with their lives and damaged the enemy's operations.

If the worst came to pass, she wouldn't be out of hope.

Her next step was to take a short trip down the hall from Simmons's office to meet with the head scientist. He greeted her with a smile, although once she told him she suspected she would be in grave danger on this assignment, he sobered. This was no time for pleasantries, after all. She was only there to get her requisitioned gear.

Insulated clothing, boots built for the snow with blades concealed in the heels, a small radio hidden beneath the false bottom of her purse, a gun disguised as an ornate bracelet, and a small vial of acid contained within an ink pen—these tools would help her complete her mission without needing to resort to calling in backup.

Equipped for the mission, but otherwise dressed like a civilian in a blue blouse and a black skirt, Rita checked on her replacement at the radio station and then headed down into the underground hangar beneath it. The radio station itself was under the Hand's management, with the resources to ensure she could get the job done right. A switch on the wall opened the large hangar doors. Light filtered in from above and danced across the gray body of the plane. It had a basic design to avoid drawing attention, but it was a modified F-94 Starfire equipped with the latest technological advances. Seeing her plane in the light always made Rita's heart skip a beat.

It had been a long time since she sat in a cockpit and pulled on her helmet and goggles, but the familiar routine brought back memories of when she flew in the war, first on exercises and training missions, and then on secret missions for Simmons. Her head still pounded, but sitting in her plane restored a sense of calm.

The job had its perks. Flying her fighter plane was definitely one of them.

She guided the plane onto the runway, picking up speed. As she cleared the rocky outcropping that concealed it from above, she let out a long breath. Things would intensify when she reached the mountain region, but for the moment, she could relax.

Misha's silence concerned her. His radio message might mean he had no safe way of getting in touch, but it was still worrying.

Still, if she had to rescue him, that would certainly give her an edge in their arguments. Then again, if she rushed out there all worried about him and he was fine, he'd never let her hear the end of it. Maybe he could be in a slight amount of danger. Just enough to need a rescue. Probably the best outcome.

Rita settled back for the journey.

Partway through the flight, the clouds outside grew dark and heavy with snow, and she pulled on a thick fur coat. Soon the snow-covered mountains came into view. She flew carefully, alert for any sign of her destination. If she was on track, she wouldn't see the village yet; her flight path circled around to bring her in from the north to avoid flying directly overhead and being spotted.

She located the clearing picked out by Simmons and brought her plane down into a graceful landing.

Then she removed her goggles and cap to replace them with a fashionable fur hat that matched her coat. She checked through her purse to make sure she had everything she needed and then climbed out of the plane.

The frozen ground crunched beneath the heels of her black boots as she tugged down the tarp she'd brought. Hiding an entire plane was impossible, but concealing it would buy some time by making it difficult to identify from the air. It was cumbersome to cover the plane without any help, but at least her boots gave her solid footing. This would be a cinch if Misha were there to help, but if he were there, she wouldn't be.

At last, she finished hiding the plane and hunched over to catch her breath.

Once she had recovered, she began her cautious journey over the rocks to circle around, intersect with the mountain path, and reach Whitehollow.

Few people were outside when Rita stepped into town, yet the handful who were looked at her with curiosity. It might have been safer to devise some means of transportation when arriving at the villager proper, but that was the sort of thing that could draw their enemies' attention. Instead, she kept herself composed and hid her exhaustion, to look less like she just hiked over the mountains in the cold and more like she took a ride partway and simply left to enjoy the scenery on the way into town.

The mountain path shortly changed into a brick road leading to a central plaza with a cluster of small evergreens at the center. Smaller paths branched out to reach various parts of the village, and the brick buildings around the plaza provided a cozy feel. Snowflakes drifted down from the sky to cover the streets, but paths had been cleared earlier and kept the snow low.

A small sign above the door of the building at the north of the plaza marked it as a bed and breakfast. Rita breathed a sigh of relief. With how isolated this place was, she worried there might be no formal lodgings. The other buildings adjacent to the plaza appeared to be a town hall, a bank, a post office, and a grocery store. People gave her curious looks but seemed utterly disinterested in engaging with her in any way.

She walked up to the bed and breakfast and opened the door.

Inside, the small lobby had the look of a converted parlor, with chairs along the walls for guests and a single large counter to check in at. A fireplace filled the room with warmth, a welcome relief after the frigid air outside. Rita crossed the white carpeting to reach the counter, suitcase in hand.

The bored-looking clerk looked up from the book he was flipping through, and his eyes widened.

"How may I help you?" he asked.

If seeing a guest caused that much surprise, it was a miracle this bed and breakfast stayed in business. Maybe it was a family-run business on the side, with other work for their primary income.

Then again, his startled look could be due to her specifically. Dressed as an affluent woman, along with her flaming red hair, she stood out compared to the people she saw outside.

"I'd like a room for the week," she said.

His brow furrowed, but he opened a thin registry. "Name?"

"Dolores Smith."

He marked down the fake name she'd use for this mission. "What brings you here?"

"Vacation." She smiled. "I need to get away from the bustle of the city, and a snowy mountain village like this is just so charming!"

"I should warn you that there isn't much in the way of things to do around here."

"That's exactly what I need."

He looked dubious, but gave her the price along with a few details about their service—breakfast in the lobby at eight, housekeeping in the afternoons, very little else in the way of amenities—and handed her a thick iron key. "Don't lose it. There's no spare, only the master key used by the staff."

She closed her fingers around the key. "I'll be careful."

Her room was on the second floor, just a few feet away from the stairs. It was hard to tell if the other rooms of the quiet building were occupied, but there was a good chance other guests might be her enemies.

But while Rita had to be cautious, an innocent tourist like Dolores Smith had no reason to think anything was wrong. She unlocked her door and stepped into the small room.

It was richly furnished, with a thick bed, a large dresser, and numerous paintings on the walls, in addition to a cushioned armchair in the corner alongside a small desk. She set down her suitcase and sat on the edge of the bed. If only she really was here to relax, it might not be a bad place for a snowy getaway.

However, Dolores Smith might disagree. A city woman used to mingling in high society would struggle to grasp the idea of there being *nothing* to do, just as the clerk seemed concerned about. She'd spend a few days showing mild curiosity about the village, after which her cover story persona would conceivably get bored and start digging for more information.

And she wouldn't stop until she learned the truth.

A noise startled Rita awake during the night. Tense, she looked around the darkened room for any sign of what disturbed her.

It happened again, a low scratching sound from the hall.

She lifted herself as quietly as possible, gaze fixed on the door. The knob moved the tiniest bit. A shadow visible through the crack in the door indicated someone standing on the other side.

Great. She didn't even get to ask any questions yet. So much for going undetected.

She grabbed her gun from the bedside table and slipped out of bed. The cool air made her shiver under the thin chiffon of her nightgown. She crept to the wall alongside the door and waited.

A moment later, they got past the lock. The door slowly swung open.

Two men stepped inside. Both wore black suits. They wouldn't look at all out of place in the city. One was short and fairly nondescript, while the other was taller and had a thin mustache just visible from her angle.

"She's not here," the shorter one said in a frustrated whisper. "You sure you got the right room?"

"Positive. I checked the records at the front desk myself."

The two men moved toward the bed. The mustached man's gaze landed on her suitcase, and he reached for it.

"Wrong room?" Rita asked.

They spun around to face her.

She kept the gun concealed behind her. "As you can see, this room is occupied."

"Perfect," said the man with the mustache. "We've been looking for you."

Rita placed her free hand over her heart and took a step toward the open door. "I'm flattered, but personally I've always preferred chats over lunch to these midnight meetings."

"We have a few questions for you."

"How about breakfast, then?" Another step carried her a little closer to the door. "You're lucky; I usually don't suggest breakfast together until at least the third date."

"Enough jokes. You're coming with us." Mustache reached into his jacket.

The door slowly swung open.

Rita sprang back toward the doorway. Footsteps alerted her a second before a third man tried to grab her from behind. She ducked to avoid him and spun around as he lunged forward. She dashed past him into the hall.

Gunfire rang out, and she dove for the floor. The rough impact jarred her, but she twisted to face the room and fired back.

"She's got a gun!"

"That proves it; it's her."

Well, it wasn't as if she'd held out much hope that they were merely well-dressed criminals unrelated to her mission. She flattened herself against the wall alongside the room. The bed and breakfast was silent aside from the sounds of their scuffle, with no sign of any guests or staff who might intervene. At least she wouldn't have to worry about innocents getting hurt, especially if most of the guest rooms were unoccupied as well.

A gun-wielding hand poked out of the room, and she fired a second before he could. Her shot missed, but the man snatched his hand back inside.

She held her breath. They appeared to be at a stalemate. On one hand, they were cornered while she had the freedom to move. On the other hand, they were now holed up in her room, and being outnumbered meant she couldn't hope to face them directly.

Most of her gear was in that room, with only a handful of things still on her person. A nightgown wasn't exactly the best choice of clothes for infiltrating an enemy base, either. Maybe Misha had the right idea; he swore he always slept in full dress when away from home. Then again, he was missing and possibly captured.

This all suggested their intelligence completely misread the situation. The mysterious organization didn't have limited contact with the village, but possibly full control. That would explain how her arrival already drew their attention. Either that or she had the worst luck in the world. She'd have a talk with the intel department when she got back.

As quietly as possible, she crept down the hall toward the staircase.

The covert approach was already out, so she'd need to start searching for the enemy base immediately. With any luck, those men would eventually leave her room to search for her, and she could circle back to slip inside and grab her gear.

Downstairs, the lobby was silent and empty. Rita snuck down the next hall in search of a place to hide—when a sudden crashing sound from the lobby made her double back. Harsh voices rang out, and she peered around the corner. Armed men poured into the bed and breakfast. They all wore some sort of uniforms, tan jackets marked with an insignia she couldn't quite make out.

Great. This situation was *much* worse than what they expected.

"Split up," one man said. "She can't hide forever."

It was going to be a very long talk with the intel department.

So much for getting her gear out of her room. She wouldn't be leaving through the entrance, either. At least she still had her gun. Rita raced back down the hall, where a beautiful glass window provided a view of the snowbanks outside.

Sometimes she wondered why she even bothered making plans.

She smashed the glass with her gun and leaped through the window.

Shouts rang out behind her, and she hissed in pain as one shard of glass scraped her shoulder. More snagged her nightgown, so she pulled free to land in the snow. An icy chill pierced through her, but she rolled and clambered to her feet. Bare feet. In the snow. It seemed like the best option at the time.

The thick drifts made it difficult to run, but she struggled forward with the shadows of the bed and breakfast as her cover. Around the back, the white-covered ground gave way to a garden of evergreens, with red berries the only different color amidst a blanket of green. A stone path wound through the garden, and she stumbled over to it to cover her tracks. She made it behind a large pine tree just as guards rushed past the building in response to the shouts.

As one passed alone, she stepped out and pressed the barrel of her gun into his back. "Don't say a word. Turn around slowly."

The man froze, then turned to face her. He was younger than she expected, barely a kid. Like the others, he wore a tan jacket. His was paired with a thick black hat, probably to guard against the cold. Thin strands of blond hair stuck out from under it, and he stared at her with wide eyes.

"What's a nice girl like you doing in a place like this?" he asked.

Of all the things to say while being held at gunpoint, he picked *that*? "That's my line," Rita said. "What's a kid like you doing here?"

He drew himself up as much as he could. "I'm asking the questions!"

"Fine," she said. "Ask away."

He blinked and furrowed his brow. "Um, what are you doing here?"

"Customer service isn't what it used to be. I ran into a little trouble checking out."

"You'll never get away with this," he said.

"Stop taking my lines." She shook her head. "Exactly what do you think you're doing out here?"

He frowned. "What?"

This kid seemed harmless enough, not to mention rather clueless. Did he not know his organization was up to no good? Well, there was no time to worry about it. For all she knew, he was stalling her to wait for reinforcements.

"Forget it," she said, "just take off your jacket."

"But it's cold!" He sounded more indignant about that than about being held at gunpoint, which didn't bode well for his life expectancy.

"Funny, I noticed that too. At least you've got buddies to borrow a jacket from. In fact, they could probably give you *mine*, since they've taken over my room. So, the jacket?"

With a sigh, he took off his jacket and shivered.

"Drop it on the ground. The hat too, while you're at it."

He dropped both in front of him.

"And the shoes."

"You want my *shoes*?" he asked.

"Right now, it's better than nothing," she said. "Borrow some shoes from a friend."

He scowled, but took off his shoes and kicked them toward the pile.

"Now, take three steps back, but don't move any further."

He obeyed.

After that, it was a simple matter of grabbing his clothes and pulling them on—she wouldn't fool anyone who got a good look at her, especially with her nightgown's skirt fluttering below the edge of the jacket, but at least she was warm. She kept one eye on him while she did it, but he didn't try to run or shout for help. Good.

The insignia she'd noticed on the jackets appeared to be a small ship. Strange.

But there was no time to relax. Shouts still came from the bed and breakfast, and it was only a matter of time before someone came back to the garden. Sheltered under the trees, the scent of pine heavy in the air, she almost could be fooled into thinking she was safe. But reprieve or not, she was still in grave danger.

"Grave danger," she whispered.

The young man frowned. "What?"

"Never you mind that," she said. "You're going to do something for me."

"Haven't I done enough?" He looked miserable, shivering in the snow.

Unfortunately, there was no other way. "You're going to get me inside your base," she said. She lifted the gun tellingly. "And if you don't, it'll be too bad for you."

His face stiffened, but he forced a nod.

She didn't have time to return to her plane and hope it had gone undetected. Certainly not enough time to contact Simmons. The most she could hope for was to get this kid another jacket so he could be her ticket into the enemy base.

With her gun concealed beneath her stolen jacket and pressed against her captive's back, the two of them left the garden.

"What a pity."

Rita blinked slowly against the harsh light above her. She was manacled to a small metal chair, in a tiny room with a single metal door and no window. A man stood nearby, a bald man dressed in black, with a cold smile on his face as he regarded her.

"By now you've missed your 24-hour check-in," he said. "I suppose you think that elite squad is going to rescue you."

Her head throbbed. After the kid got her into the base, they started through the underground tunnels together, into the halls of a building that was alarmingly well-constructed for being a secret base underground. Her borrowed jacket meant they avoided notice from a distance, and a stolen security card gave them access to an elevator. Two floors down, they made it to just outside what appeared to be a lab, with a huge array of equipment visible through a thick glass window, before the guards ambushed them. An alarm went out, and too many men rushed them for Rita to fight her way out.

Then she had the unfortunate displeasure of meeting this man, whose associates called him Noah despite his appearance matching that of the missing Carter Hawke. When his initial attempts to interrogate her failed, he merely smiled and produced a hypodermic needle. It contained a serum, with a strong scent oddly similar to pine, which he said would put the subject in a hypnotic trance and cause them to recount any relevant memories with the proper urging.

She vaguely recalled boasting that hypnosis never worked on her seconds before everything faded. She gritted her teeth and strained again at her bonds. He knew about headquarters, as well as their use of radio requests for communication.

"Your rescue team is about to meet quite the welcoming committee," he said. "I daresay they'll be surprised."

"You don't know what you're up against," she said.

He smiled. "Oh, I think I do."

She scowled and looked away.

"Clever of you to conceal that pen on your person," he said. "I never would have thought to confiscate an ink pen. Since you were separated from the majority of your gear, I suppose you were relying on it to get you out of this."

She refused to meet his gaze. At least they'd let her keep the jacket for modesty. Sitting here in just a nightgown would make this even worse.

"No longer in a mood to chat?" Hawke asked. "Pity. I like you better when you're talking." He shrugged and turned away. "Perhaps poor Will has something to say. After you forced him to bring you in here, he's probably eager for revenge. I'll tell you one thing I've learned, nothing motivates a man more than the desire for revenge."

"What's your aim here, Hawke? What are you planning?"

"Hawke…" He shook his head. "It's been a long time since I've been called by that name. I'm Noah now, prepared to guide the chosen into a new future."

Great, and she'd *really* hoped that name didn't indicate delusions of grandeur.

He walked to the cell door. "Don't go anywhere, Miss Rita—I have a feeling you might be quite useful to our mission if you decide to ally yourself with us. Think about it, while I visit your reluctant friend."

Hawke and the two guards with him who oversaw the interrogation left the cell, and the heavy door swung shut with a *clang*. Rita was alone.

She drew a deep breath and let it out slowly. He made no mention at all of Misha. That was concerning. She certainly must have rambled about her missing partner during the trance, and a man like Hawke would normally use that against her. Maybe he assumed she would prioritize the mission over Misha's safety. Best-case scenario.

Worst-case scenario, he was already dead. But she tried to be an optimist.

At least there were no guards in the cell with her. Hopefully, Hawke's conversation with Will would keep him occupied and give her the time she needed.

Rita looked down at her hands. Her fingernails were coated with a translucent solution undetectable to the naked eye. She spat on them, and the chemical she'd chewed ahead of the mission fizzed as it interacted with the solution. Thank goodness they didn't bind her hands behind her.

She twisted her hand in the manacle and winced as the metal cut into her skin. It gave her just enough leeway to bend her fingers and press her nails against the metal. The acid was fast-acting, so she should be able to break through the lock before Hawke returned.

As the metal weakened, she closed her eyes. Everything had been taken from her when they were captured, not to mention the unfortunate incident at the bed and breakfast. The base was crawling with Hawke's men, and Will's knowledge of their security only extended so far since he wasn't that deeply involved.

Still, she should have the advantage of surprise now, ironically enough.

The acid finished working through the lock, and a sharp tug of her arm snapped the manacle. With one hand free, she was able to repeat the process more naturally on the other side and free herself from the chair.

She rubbed her wrists with a grateful sigh. No acid burns, either, which proved this method *worked*. She'd point that out to Misha after all of his nay-saying.

Assuming he was alive.

Rita hurried to the door. It wasn't locked, so she pushed it open. A single guard stood outside the door, and he turned toward her with a startled gasp, mouth open to raise the alarm. She grabbed him and slammed him back into the wall, knocking the air out of him. His grip on his gun loosened, and she snatched it, then clubbed him on the back of his head. He slumped to the ground.

Footsteps hurried down the hall toward her, and she whirled around with the gun raised.

Will, the man whose uniform she'd taken, stopped and stared at her with wide eyes. "You work fast."

"Nice to see you too," she said.

"Noah barely questioned my claim that you forced me to bring you here and that I wanted revenge," he said. "I didn't expect that." He hefted a gun. "Let me go after just a bit of questioning and told me to follow my own judgment."

Rita grinned. "I have my ways." She folded her arms. "So let's get out of here before he comes to see how things are going."

"What's the plan?" he asked. "Escape?"

"Nope. We find out way back to that laboratory and get inside."

His eyes widened further. "How?"

"Trust me," she said. "I've been right so far, haven't I?"

"Then you have a plan?" he asked.

Rita looked down the hall to make sure no one else was coming yet. "Not exactly."

"What does that mean?"

"It means I'm making it up as I go."

"*What?*"

"Don't worry, we've got this." The coast was clear, so she started down the hall.

Will caught up with her and grabbed her shoulder. "Did you forget how heavy the security is around here?"

"I'm not too worried." She grinned. "After all, Hawke is rallying the troops to fight an elite squad that doesn't exist."

Simmons was big on mental training.

They couldn't always rely on physical strength or weapons, he warned. Mental defenses were essential. Torture was always a danger in their line of work, and even the strongest will could be cracked under the right circumstances.

Therefore, they all went through a specific sort of mental conditioning that let them temporarily tamper with their memories by raising false ones through the use of specific keywords.

In Rita's case, she had set her false memories to be triggered by the phrase *grave danger*.

Revealing some of the truth was unavoidable. It wasn't possible to create a new set of unique memories to fit every situation. But whenever her subconscious mind recognized that something was wrong, such as Hawke's pine-scented serum creeping into memory, her mental conditioning kicked in and caused her to fabricate a response about being in grave danger, which triggered the false memories to rise to the forefront of her mind and overlay the actual events.

Her false memories contained three key elements that could be adapted to merge with most situations.

First, they included a discussion with Simmons about a false contingency plan to send an elite team on a rescue mission. Hawke would devote considerable resources and manpower to countering this expected strike.

Second, they included a list of gear and equipment she took from the lab. Some were legitimate, or else they'd notice the deception right away, but other parts were completely false—she almost wished she could watch Hawke's scientists attempt to find the acid in her ink pen—and didn't cover everything, hence them not knowing about the nail polish solution.

Finally, and most importantly, her false memories included a portrayal of herself as colder and more ruthless than she actually was. That one tended to seep through the recounted memories more insidiously than the others, and she'd suspected False Rita would threaten Will. As a result, she'd instructed him that if they were captured, he should claim she forced him to bring her into the base.

In truth, after she took his jacket, she warned him to get out while he could since his bosses were up to something bad. Then she had let him go since she intended to be long gone before he could tell anyone where he'd seen her.

She went back to the clearing and found that her plane hadn't been discovered yet, and took the opportunity to grab some rations and medical supplies. She spent the next few hours climbing through the mountains to find a high vantage point. It was rough enough for her to make a mental note to do more physical training once she was back home.

The high peak she finally found let her overlook the village and the organized activity of Hawke's men. Enough movement toward the north convinced her she would find the base there.

Staying high in the mountains for cover, she followed the trail parallel until she neared a hidden entrance built into the side of the mountain. She spent some time there observing the security procedures—unfortunately high, with checks done of every single person who showed up—and was just debating ways to take out the guards without being noticed when someone else acted on the same idea.

The young man from earlier, fully equipped once again, jumped the guards after they checked his ID. Rita sprang into motion to take advantage of the opportunity, and between them, they subdued the two guards.

Then she turned her attention to her unexpected ally.

"Well," he said with a smile, "I figured you'd join me eventually, but I didn't realize you were quite *this* close."

"What are you doing?" she asked.

He folded his arms. "After what you said to me, I got to thinking. I don't like the way things are handled around here, and you don't seem so bad. If there's a chance that you're right, I want to find out what's going on."

"You'd be better off getting out of here," she said.

"What about you?"

"I have a job to do."

"Then I want to find out the truth too."

She sighed. "Thanks for the help."

"No problem."

"But if you didn't know I was there, what exactly was your plan?"

"I was going to steal their ID for the security clearance."

Rita raised her eyebrows. "*That* was your plan?"

He let out an annoyed huff of breath. "I suppose your plan was just to sit behind a rock and hope for something to happen."

"Hey," she said with a wink, "it worked."

With an alliance formed, they exchanged names and entered the base together.

The gray hallway felt as cold and unwelcoming as it had when they first entered. The steel doors and wide corridors so deep underground felt completely out of place compared to the rural village above. The base appeared to be massive. For such an undertaking, Hawke must have started work on it around the time of his disappearance three years ago.

According to Will, the official explanation was that they were conducting classified government research. That justified the secrecy for the rank-and-file members.

But what were they *really* doing? Building a weapon felt too small in scope when she looked around at this facility.

"Remember," Rita said, "if we run into anyone, pretend I'm your prisoner."

The tables had turned. Unlike when they initially entered, they would be safest now if anyone who saw them assumed she remained in the hands of her enemies.

Will frowned. "Will that work?"

"If you're a good enough actor."

"I don't know," he said. "I'm not good at acting aggressive."

"I'll cower a lot."

However, the corridors were nearly empty thanks to the rush to face the fake elite squad. As they walked, Rita realized they were on the second basement level. They had stopped there briefly before and found an elevator, which led them down to the floor that contained the lab. She took the lead, and they reached the elevator without much trouble. One guard stood alongside the elevator doors.

Will froze for a second, but Rita slumped and tried to look like a subdued, threatened prisoner. He took the hint and pressed his gun against her back, marching her forward to the elevator. "I need to get through. Noah ordered me to take her down to the lab."

"Another one already?" the guard asked.

Unease prickled Rita. *Another one?* Will's excuse was smart enough, but that suggested prisoners being taken to the lab was a common occurrence.

"I don't question his orders," Will said.

"Fine, just let me see your ID."

Will handed over his ID, and Rita bolted. A good phony escape attempt was always nice to maintain a cover as a prisoner. She made it three feet before Will caught up with her and hauled her back to the elevator.

The guard handed back his ID. "You're good to go."

"Much obliged."

They entered the elevator, and the door slid shut.

As they began the descent, Will shook his head and let out a long breath. "You didn't tell me you were going to do that."

"You needed to be surprised," she said. "He'd have noticed if it was too staged."

"I guess so."

"Now we're on our way to the lab and no one's the wiser."

"Unless he reports to Noah about me bringing you down here." Will shook his head. "Maybe I shouldn't have used his name."

"It got us in," Rita said. "If you just strolled up and said you'd like to visit the lab with a prisoner, we'd probably still be up there."

"Good point. I expected to be stopped, but no one questions Noah's orders."

"Why do you call him Noah?" she asked. "His name is Hawke, Carter Hawke."

Will blinked. "Everyone calls him Noah."

Interesting. Her gaze drifted to the sleeve of her borrowed jacket, and the ship-like insignia emblazoned there. "Your organization's insignia. It's an ark, isn't it?"

"That's what we're called," he said. "The Ark."

"Noah's organization is called the Ark?"

"I don't question his orders"

"Yes."

She winced and closed her eyes. "It just had to be delusions of grandeur."

The elevator came to a halt, and the doors slid open. They stepped out together, Rita assuming a prisoner's posture once again. There was more activity on this level, with scientists hard at work. Men and women in white coats hurried back on forth, with barely a glance to spare for the two of them.

At the heart of it all, the glass-windowed chamber housed mysterious, humming machinery.

Few guards patrolled, although two stood stationed outside the chamber's door. None entered the room. An occasional scientist went in and out, sometimes with papers, other times emptyhanded. It was impossible to judge what they were doing from the outside.

The machine itself didn't look like a weapon. It was a massive box or tower that encompassed the whole of the wall, like some of the computers back at HQ.

One of the passing scientists looked up at them and paused. His gaze went from Will to Rita. "Prisoner?"

"That's right," Will said. "I was told to bring her down here."

He nodded, his expression grim. "Do you know which one it is?"

"Uh." A note of panic flashed through Will's eyes, and he glanced at Rita. She had no advice to offer, even if she could speak freely.

The scientist sighed. "They didn't tell you?"

"No," Will said.

"Fine, follow me." He strode toward the chamber.

Will looked at Rita again, and she offered a slight nod. They followed the scientist up to the door, where the guards barely glanced at him before stepping aside. All three of them walked into the chamber.

It *was* a computer, although one unlike anything even the government had. The towers along the walls hummed and blinked, and out of view of the door was a massive screen that the scientist walked up to. Unlike the printouts produced at HQ, this machine's information appeared straight on the screen. Strings of numbers filled it, some sort of data output from the looks of it. Energy readings? Rita's fingers itched to take over the controls. She'd never seen a computer like this before, and she wanted to know what she was looking at. How they had something so advanced compared to the government's machines was another concern.

The scientist typed *root* with the attached keyboard, a form of computer input she'd heard early discussions about but didn't expect to see at this level yet. The numbers vanished, and then he typed *status*. A diagram popped up. Rita furrowed her brow. It showed a central node with three other nodes connected to it. Each of those had a status indicator, two green with the word "Stable" printed, and one red with the word "Unstable" flashing instead.

He entered something else, and more numbers appeared. These looked like vital signs. "Hmm…"

"Something wrong?" Will asked.

"I just wouldn't think it's time yet. What exactly were your orders?"

"Uh. Take the prisoner down to the lab."

"That's it?"

"That's it."

The scientist frowned. "I can't imagine he thinks we're out of time with the locals, although he did have some concerns about the Russian."

Rita's blood went cold.

He turned back to the screen and tapped the screen itself, his fingers on one of the two nodes marked "Stable." One series of vital signs expanded, and a video feed popped up. It showed a small room and a strange machine, and an unconscious man hooked up to it.

And although his head was bowed, she recognized him even on the grainy footage.

"Misha," she whispered.

He was alive. Captured and in a dire situation, but alive. And stable, according to the machine, even if this was something that could apparently change often enough for them to need replacement prisoners.

She grabbed the startled scientist before he could react and twisted his arm around behind his back. "Change of plans."

"Do something!" he shouted at Will.

Will blinked and pointed the gun at him.

"What are you doing?"

"Change of plans?" he said, a note of uncertainty in his voice.

Rita released the scientist since the gun trained on him should do the trick. "Mind if I borrow your lab coat? It'll be a better disguise for me."

"Yes, I most certainly do mind," he said with a splutter of indignation despite the panic in his eyes.

"Better do what she says anyway," Will said.

The scientist scowled, but only hesitated a moment before pulling off his long white coat and handing it over. Rita took off her jacket and donned the lab coat in its place. It was a little small, but a decent enough fit. While there weren't a lot of women down here, she'd at least seen some, unlike among their guards.

She held up the jacket she'd taken from Will. "Do you want this back?"

He shook his head. "No need. I don't plan to stick around after this."

"Smart." She set the jacket down and pushed past the scientist to stand at the computer. "Keep an eye on him while I check things out."

Will nodded and stepped back a few feet with the grumbling scientist still at gunpoint.

Rita watched the video feed on the screen for a moment. Then she touched the screen like she saw the scientist do. Nothing happened. She tapped around for a bit until she got the video feed to disappear. Not what she was aiming for, but it was progress.

"Do you, uh, know what you're doing?" Will asked.

"More or less."

"*More or less?*"

Despite his skepticism, she learned technology best by using it. No amount of explanations from the scientist would compare to experimenting herself to see what happened. She didn't have the luxury of time to play around with it as much as she'd like, though, so she needed to focus on the most important parts.

She found the diagram again that showed the three nodes, then tapped the one to bring up Misha's video feed. She returned to the diagram and scanned the screen. There was nothing obvious to tap to get what she wanted, but the scientist typed things to get here from the start.

"Is there a way to bring up a map?" she asked.

He didn't answer.

Will lifted his gun. "You'd better tell her."

"I'd rather die," the scientist said.

"You're that invested in all of this?" Rita asked.

"Noah is going to lead us into a brighter future. His plan will set the course for humanity! How could I ever stand in the way of that just because some small-minded fools such as the two of you don't see the bigger picture?"

"Funny thing about that," Rita said, "when you've got my buddy locked up and unconscious, the bigger picture stops meaning a whole lot to me."

"Does it really? Look at what we're capable of!"

"Explain," she said.

"I don't have to when the proof is right in front of you."

She frowned and looked at the computer. "You're saying this fancy computer is part of that brighter future Hawke is looking for?"

"No country in the world has technology like this."

It sounded like the truth. This certainly went far beyond the computers even Simmons had access to, and the Hand was generally given priority when it came to high-tech advances. "Still not interested if it involves whatever you did to Misha."

"Why *do* you have that man imprisoned like that?" Will asked.

The scientist sniffed and turned away.

"Forget him." Rita typed *map* into the computer, then *blueprints,* and then *where-am-I,* none of which got a result. "I'll figure it out."

He'd typed *root* before anything else. Mimicking that made everything vanish from the screen—probably a good sign—and then she repeated her attempts. This time, *blueprints* brought up a map of the facility.

"Nailed it!"

The facility was less complicated than it first seemed. There were four floors in total, and the bottommost level, marked B4 on the map, had three distinct areas set off from the hallway. When she compared it to the diagram, those lined up with the three smaller nodes, while the central node appeared to be outside the facility proper. Curiously, while the arrangement meant the three nodes weren't symmetrical, the blueprint was; a fourth small room alongside Misha's cell was labeled "Emergency." It looked like there was elevator access nearby, too, and it lined up with the one there in the lab. A stairwell was also marked, but only on the opposite end of the hall. If they took the elevator down, they'd only need to head right to reach Misha's cell.

Uneasiness filled her as she brought up the video feed again. That machine connected to him might be a problem. What *was* it? What were they doing down here?

She experimented with more typed commands, and *output* brought back the screen first visible when they entered. Numbers, equations, formulas... She frowned and tried to make sense of what she was seeing. Half of them seemed unrelated to one another. She scowled at the screen, but as the incomprehensible array of data continued, she returned to the root to try again.

Notes. Nothing.

Log. That brought up a long list of system logs for the computer, not what she needed at the moment despite her curiosity. She'd need to try something else.

Records. Success!

A string of documents appeared on the screen, and she tapped the first one. It brought up a written record.

The visitor was the one to show me the way. When I was lost in the darkness, the visitor brought me into the light. Together, we are capable of great feats. I've gathered those I trust and many more besides, the chosen who can help us embark upon this journey. This is the dawning of a new era. As such, I will discard the name men once knew me by. The age of Carter Hawke is at an end; he will fade into obscurity alongside the dregs of humanity that cling to the past. Now I will be Noah, building an Ark to pull us all out of the darkness.

A chill ran through Rita. This was about Hawke's disappearance from public life and his decision to change his name and start of this organization. "Will, do you know anything about this visitor Hawke mentions here?"

Will shook his head. "It's the first I'm hearing about it."

"Hmm." She glanced at the scientist, but he remained obstinately silent.

She closed the record and brought up another.

We have come so far thanks to the information provided by the visitor. Computers! Aircraft! Weaponry! All of these areas will see great advancements in the near future, advancements overseen by my Ark. First and foremost, however, we must establish a more efficient way to process the visitor's knowledge.

The image of the data output on the screen flashed through Rita's mind. Was that what it was? Information obtained from Hawke's visitor in such great amounts that it needed to be fed through this advanced computer in order to make sense of it? She brought up the third record.

We have now constructed a machine to extract and process the information we need. I have called it the Genesis Machine, for it is the beginning of our new future. Most importantly, the Genesis Machine streamlines the process of obtaining organic energy—

"Hey!"

At Will's yell, Rita whirled around. The scientist pushed him away and made a break for the door. It slid open and the guard turned with wide eyes. He drew his gun just as Will fired above the scientist's head. He dropped to the ground as the guard fired back, but Will's next shot hit his gun hand and sent the weapon flying.

Rita dashed forward and caught it, and as the guard turned to face her, Will caught him in a chokehold from behind. He struggled but went limp.

The unconscious guard slumped to the ground and Will let out a long breath. "That was bad."

Rita hefted the gun. "On the plus side, we're both armed now."

But the scientist was missing. He must have gotten away in the chaos.

"Is it too much to hope he'll just escape without telling anyone about us?" she asked.

A shrill alarm pierced the air, and red lights began flashing.

She sighed. "I knew it was too much to ask."

Alarms blared as they raced through level B4 en route to Misha's cell. Breaking through the deepest layer of security wasn't easy, especially since they'd already lost the advantage of surprise. The covert approach was impossible now; all that remained was to get in and out with as little damage as possible. Rita's heart pounded. At least she managed to divert Hawke and most of his forces, but there was no telling if she'd be able to complete her mission at this rate.

"Tell me you have a plan this time," Will said.

"I have a plan this time."

He let out a sigh of relief. "What is it?"

"Telling you I have a plan so you don't panic."

"*What?*"

"I can't leave my colleague imprisoned here," she said. "Once we rescue him, we'll figure out the rest."

"Isn't it more likely that we'll all die?"

She shook her head. "Don't be such a pessimist."

Will glanced at her. "Please give me just one reason to be optimistic."

"Fine. Hawke probably assumes this is the last thing I'll think of doing."

After all, the interrogation meant his greatest association with her was through the recounting of her fabricated memories. False Rita always put the mission first and considered other things later. Even once Hawke realized he'd somehow been deceived in regards to Will's treachery, he'd still likely assume she would prioritize destroying the weapon—or rather, the Genesis Machine, a name which suggested Hawke's delusions bordered on a god complex.

They rounded the corner and the cell door came into sight. The guard at the door straightened and raised his gun.

Rita shot faster.

He dove to the ground to dodge the shot, but Will closed the gap and tackled him. He knocked the guard out before he had a chance to shout.

"Not bad," Rita said.

Will grinned. "I have my uses."

His mood certainly improved. Maybe he realized there was still room for optimism after all. Rita grinned back at him and crouched alongside the unconscious guard. He didn't have any keys, but a security card in his pocket looked just the right shape to fit into a slot alongside the door. She pushed it in.

The door made a clicking sound, and Will pushed it open.

Misha was imprisoned in a large metal pod, hands shackled to the sides and wires attached to him via electrodes and needles. They crisscrossed behind him to give the impression of a spiderweb with Misha at its center. He was unconscious, and a bruised bump on the side of his head just visible under his thick blond hair made Rita wince in sympathy, but he appeared healthy enough. He'd certainly endured worse before. A computer hummed alongside the pod, with a display screen similar to that in the lab.

"More gifts from their visitor?" Rita asked under her breath.

Will glanced at her. "What?"

"Did you read those records we found in the lab? Hawke's getting information from someone else that let him build all of this. He credits this 'visitor' with their technological advancements."

"So it's... someone from the government?"

A government official leaking advanced technology to a loose cannon like Hawke, that was all they needed. "Maybe."

"We need to get out of here," Will said.

"Just as soon as I free Misha."

"Do you know how?"

"Well..." She looked at the machine. "I have good news and I have bad news."

"I'll take the good news," Will said.

"I'm an expert with electronics. Give me a machine and I can figure out how it works."

He brightened. "That *is* good news!"

She sighed. "The bad news is that it usually involves pressing random buttons and sometimes kicking things, which I can't very well do with my buddy attached to it."

Will winced. "Then what are you going to do?"

"I'll figure something out."

"How?"

"Watch the hall," Rita said.

Mercifully, he didn't comment on her lack of an answer to his question.

Maybe he realized she was relying on good luck and a prayer. Gun in hand, he slipped out into the hallway.

Rita looked at the pod. The shackles were easy enough to figure out, but for all she knew, just ripping him free of the wires would kill him. She glared at the machine as though she might make it release him through sheer willpower, then walked to the computer screen instead. At least its controls matched those of the computer in the lab, so she had more experience with it by virtue of having used such a computer exactly once before.

The screen displayed Misha's vital signs, as well as another continual feed that suggested the output of energy. From what she'd seen in the lab, it appeared as though this device was one component of a larger machine.

If she was reading the output correctly, it was draining something from Misha and feeding it into whatever the central node on the diagram represented. *What* this machine drained from him wasn't entirely clear. It didn't appear to be anything physical. The screen called it life energy, which was at once unhelpful and alarming. She frowned at the readings. Misha's heart rate dipped, and the values fluctuated before his heart rate gradually returned to normal. So the computer was monitoring him and sustaining him to keep him alive at the same time.

Ripping him free might kill him if she didn't disconnect the wires in the right order.

She gritted her teeth. She'd found Misha alive, more than she hoped for when she started the mission. She wouldn't come this far only to let him die. They would get out of here together.

Rita took a deep breath and studied the screen again. First, she had to shut down the part that was draining his energy. She tapped the data output, and it brought up the diagram she'd seen in the lab, but with a focus on Misha's node this time. There were several different buttons on the screen, one of which said *shutdown*.

She said a silent prayer and tapped it.

The machine powered down with a low roar, and the room dimmed as the lights on the pod went out. The shackles around Misha's wrists clicked as though they were unlocked. Breath held, Rita brought up the main screen again.

Misha's vital signs remained active. She let out a slow breath. So far, so good.

She pulled the needles from his skin first, eyes on the screen in case anything changed. Then she disconnected the electrodes, one at a time. Soon the computer had no way to monitor him anymore, but she held her breath and continued her work.

Footsteps from the hall alerted her a second before the door flew open. "They're coming!" Will whispered.

Rita clenched her jaw and unfastened the shackles. They snapped open, and Misha fell forward. She caught him and staggered as the unconscious man's weight hit her.

"Oof." She tried in vain to steady him. At six feet tall, her colleague was a big enough man that she couldn't exactly carry him around. "Misha! You with me? Wake up!"

He stirred with a delirious mumble, but he didn't look like he'd be walking any time soon.

Will ran to her side and slung one of Misha's arms over his shoulders. "We need to get out of here."

"You're telling me." With Misha supported between them, they left the cell. From the left came sounds of their pursuers. Going right would take them toward the central node and the other cells, but it didn't look like there was any way to double back. They'd have to pray they could reach the stairs, or that there was another elevator that she hadn't noticed.

"How many are coming?" she asked.

"Noah and at least six others."

"Armed?"

"Do you *really* want to take the chance that they're not?"

From the tone of his voice, he worried she might. Rita bit her lip. Seven against two—technically three, but Misha didn't count until he regained consciousness. And considering they had to support him, they didn't quite count as two. If she considered each of them half a combatant, that made it seven against one.

She turned right. "This way."

Heading toward the central node might be a stroke of luck. Maybe she'd be able to find out what Hawke was constructing and shut it down after all.

Or maybe it was something so dangerous, they'd be better off taking their chances in a fight.

With a known threat behind them and the unknown ahead, they headed deeper into the facility.

The sounds of their pursuers grew fainter as they continued until at last they no longer heard them at all. That was either a good sign or a terrible one. When they saw the empty cell, they might have concluded they already made it to the elevator. On the other hand, it could be that Hawke assumed no one was stupid enough to head deeper in.

The silent hallway at last opened up onto a large chamber. It looked like a monitoring room similar to the one in the lab. Machinery along the walls hummed quietly, but the window was shuttered.

Misha groaned and stirred.

"Misha!" Rita and Will helped him over to the wall and eased him down into a sitting position.

He rubbed his head and blinked up at her. "Rita?"

"In person," she said.

"Had to rescue me, huh?"

"How many times is that now?" she asked.

"Twice."

"Four times."

"It does *not* count as rescuing me when you crashed a meeting I had perfectly under control."

"Oh yeah," she said, "that's why there were guns pointed at you."

"I keep telling you, that was part of the plan."

She waved her hand. "Fine, but you can't discount the time I saved you in Peru."

"That was when *I* rescued *you!*"

Will cleared his throat. "Uh… could you two settle the score when we aren't in immediate danger?"

Rita held up her hands. "Sorry. You know how it is."

He furrowed his brow.

"Who's this?" Misha asked.

"Will," she said. "One of Hawke's boys, but he decided he'd rather work for the good guys."

"Although I still haven't found proof of what he's doing," Will said.

"What about you?" Rita asked. "Did you get any evidence before being captured?"

Misha rubbed his head again and looked around. "Where are we?"

"A bit further in than the cell where we found you."

"Oh no."

"I'm guessing that's bad?" she said.

"Everything about this place is bad. Hawke is playing with fire, and I don't know what his endgame is. But he sees himself as a prophet or savior, which doesn't bode well for the people who stand against him."

The hallway at last opened up onto a large chamber.

"Does he have the firepower to back up his words?" she asked.

"If not now, he will soon."

"Thanks to his visitor?"

Misha stiffened. He glanced at Will.

"Don't look at me." Will held up his hands. "I was never high-ranking enough to know any of this stuff."

"We found references to the visitor in Hawke's log," Rita said. "But I don't really follow any of this. Why does the visitor know so much? How are they getting so much information that they need a computer to process it? And what's up with that cell we found you in?"

"I don't even know where to begin." Misha's roaming gaze landed on the shuttered window. "Then again, it looks like you brought me to the right place after all."

Rita nodded and tapped her head. "You can always count on me."

Will frowned. "It was a coincidence, and you know it."

"Instinct."

"Open the shutters," Misha said. "There should be controls nearby."

Rita stood up and walked over to the shuttered window. There was no major computer here like in the lab above, but one section of the quietly humming machine included a control panel, as well as a small screen alongside it that displayed the machine's diagram. She studied the panel for a moment, then pressed the button marked "View."

With a soft *whir*, the thick metal shutters lifted.

Beyond the window, the walls of the facility gave way to dirt and stone. On the map, the central node appeared to be outside the facility; that must be the area it referenced. Wires and tubes led from below the window toward the center of the cavern, where they connected to…

"What is that?" Rita whispered.

"The one they call the visitor."

It stood at least ten times higher than a human, though the numerous wires held it partly suspended, its body as limp as Misha's had been in the pod. Its skin was a deep sapphire blue, so dark as to almost blend in with the shadows cast by the facility's observation lights. Its suspended arms ended in long, vicious claws. At least two sets of closed eyes and curling horn-like appendages took away from its humanoid appearance, and on its back—were those crumpled shapes *wings*?

She backed up to get a better view and then turned to Misha. "That's the visitor?"

"They're not constructing a weapon here at all," Misha said. "At least, not yet. After an initially friendly relationship, they used the creature's knowledge against it to build this so-called Genesis Machine. Through their advanced technology and the life force of their prisoners, they have developed a way to forcibly extract knowledge from its mind."

Rita thought back to her interrogation. Hawke must use the serum when the information he wanted wasn't worth the effort of using this machine. Still, the possibilities were ghastly.

And that was only what they had so far.

All that data being produced by the computer up above, a constant stream their computer sorted through for them to examine and put to practical use. The advancements they already made, with their underground facility and the Genesis Machine itself. It all came from the creature out there.

Will stared at the thing slack-jawed, apparently too stunned to speak.

"What *is* it?" Rita asked again.

"The visitor is an entity from another planet," Misha said. "Hawke made contact with it by accident and came to understand the possibilities it held. He then captured it to satisfy his thirst for knowledge and power. That's all I was able to learn before I was captured myself and…put to use." He waved his hand out at the control panel. "So, can our resident electronics expert handle this?"

She sauntered back to the control panel and smirked. "They haven't made a machine I can't master. Plus, I can kick this one."

"Just don't free the visitor by mistake."

"Why not? I feel bad for it."

"I doubt very much it will distinguish between us and Hawke's men if it goes on a rampage."

"Good point," she said.

Ideally, they'd free the creature, have a good old human-alien heart-to-heart, and take down Hawke together. But Misha was right; even if it could communicate with them, it might very well see all humans as the nasty little nuisances that captured it. It didn't feel right to let the visitor be a casualty of Hawke's schemes any more than the people he'd imprisoned, but there was no way around it.

With a silent prayer for the poor creature, Rita examined the control panel. The small screen alongside it showed the four nodes. One previously marked "Stable" now displayed a big red X instead, no doubt because she'd saved Misha.

She looked at the other two nodes. One stable, and one unstable, both almost certainly prisoners whose life forces sustained this diabolical machine in its efforts.

"Monstrous," she whispered.

Will looked like he was going to be sick.

She returned her attention to the control panel. There seemed to be a shutdown process, with buttons to disconnect each node and then turn off the entire machine. This section appeared much more primitive than the lab above. It must have been one of the first pieces built when they discovered what they could learn from their "visitor."

Rita shut down the remaining two nodes and then hit the primary shutdown button. The machinery made a loud *whirring* sound, and then everything went silent and dark. "Nailed it!"

Above them, a mechanized voice crackled out of a loudspeaker. "Emergency shutdown detected. Facility will self-destruct in thirty minutes. Please evacuate immediately."

Her heart leaped in her throat. "What kind of failsafe is that?!"

Will found his voice at last. "Self-destruct? Are you kidding?"

With a groan, Misha staggered to his feet, although he leaned against the wall for support. "Are you *really* about to blow up the building?"

"Don't blame me; blame Hawke for designing it!"

"Isn't there anything you can do?" Will asked.

Rita kicked the machine.

"Not what I had in mind!"

"All right," Rita said. "Don't panic. This is just like when I saved you in Peru."

"*I* saved *you*," Misha said, "and yes, as I recall, that also involved you blowing up the building."

Will gave him an alarmed look. "Does this happen often?"

"She's an electronics genius and one of our best agents, but also chaos incarnate."

"I heard that," Rita said.

"I wasn't trying to keep it a secret."

She scanned the control panel and tapped a few buttons in the vain hope that it might end the self-destruct. Yet it seemed like once the option was activated, there was no way to reverse it, at least from there. Hawke was an absolutely deranged madman, and if they both survived this, she was going to kill him. Who built a machine designed to self-destruct if it was turned off?

"Looks like it's time for Plan B," she said.

"What's Plan B?" Will asked.

Rita drew her gun and started for the door. "Running as fast as we can."

Despite Will's dismayed protest, the three of them hurried to the door they came from. Rita burst into the corridor. Her gaze met that of Hawke at the end of the hall a split second before his group started firing.

She ducked back inside. "Bad idea!"

"What now?" Will asked.

At the other end of the room, a second door led to a different corridor. She looked at it and hesitated.

He followed her gaze. "Won't that lead us even deeper in?"

"Right now, it's the only way that doesn't involve bullets."

"We're on a thirty-minute deadline!" he shouted.

"Do you have a better idea? There should be a stairwell in that direction."

Gunfire destroyed the edge of the door as Hawke's group approached. Misha scowled at them. "There's no time for debate. We have to go with her plan."

She grinned. "Knew I could count on you, partner."

They edged toward the other door, staying behind cover while it lasted. Gunmen behind them, a corridor that may or may not have stairs in front of them, and thirty minutes before the whole place would be blown sky high… "Look at the bright side," Rita said.

Will glanced at her. "There's a bright side?"

"Things can't possibly get any worse."

A thunderous roar shuddered through the facility, intense enough to make the ground tremble. It drowned out the blaring alarm and the gunshots. On the other side of the window, the imprisoned entity ripped one massive arm free of the wires that bound it.

"I hate it when you say things like that," Misha said.

They raced down the corridor together, although Misha lagged due to his injuries. Rita hated pushing him so soon after he'd regained consciousness, but they didn't have many other options. According to the diagram, they should be on their way toward the other two nodes—the cells for the remaining prisoners connected to the machine.

Behind them, the sound of pursuit quieted. Hopefully, that wasn't because Hawke decided they'd doomed themselves.

Up ahead, the smooth metal wall dipped into an alcove. No, not an alcove—

"The stairs!" Will shouted.

They reached it together and looked up. The stairwell was empty and unguarded. Either everyone had already evacuated, or they took another path.

"This almost feels too easy," Misha said.

Another roar shook the facility, and the walls caved in as something struck them from the outside. A second blow revealed one of the imprisoned creature's hands, apparently strong enough to rip apart the whole facility if it wanted to. And it definitely wanted to. Another strike tore through the corridor, and debris rained down upon them.

"That one's all on you," Rita said to Misha.

He snorted.

"Can you manage the stairs?" she asked.

"Under the circumstances, I don't seem to have much choice."

They started up the stairs together, forced to adopt a slower pace due to Misha's struggle. As the facility trembled around them, Rita closed her eyes. This wasn't going to be easy.

"What are you thinking about?" Misha asked between strained breaths.

She opened her eyes. "Just planning our escape."

He frowned but didn't press her on it.

"So," Will said, as they passed the door for the floor above them and continued up, "how did you two end up paired together, anyway?"

"I'd rather not talk about it," Misha said.

"Excuse me," Rita said, "but the story of our partnership is sweet and heartwarming."

"For you, maybe."

Before she could recount the tale, their progress brought them to the next door up, which burst open to reveal three armed guards.

For a moment, the two groups stared at one another in shock.

Rita moved first, raising her gun and pointing it at the three. Instead of surrendering, however, one reached for his own gun while the other two dove to the side. She fired at the man's gun hand, and he flinched back with a shout, but Misha grabbed her arm.

"Don't fight, just run!"

"Can you do that?" she asked.

He managed a pained smile. "It's better than the alternative."

He was right; while fighting would allow them to take more time for his sake, it wasn't as though they could afford to delay. She and Will supported Misha between them, and they took off up the stairs together as fast as they could manage. At last, they reached the uppermost floor and burst into the hallway. It looked much the same as all the others Rita saw when they first infiltrated the facility.

Above them, the alarm blared from the speakers that they only had twenty minutes left.

She looked at Will. "Tell me you know where we are."

"I know where we are." He moved ahead to take the lead. "Just follow me, and we'll—"

The creature's enraged scream shook the building again, and its massive hand punched a hole through the wall. It slammed its arm down, and the floor cracked.

Rita waved her arms. "Hey! We come in peace and with goodwill!"

"That's what the alien is supposed to say," Will said.

She frowned. "Then what do the peaceful humans say?"

"How should I know?"

Misha glared at them. "Is this *really* the time?"

Rita cupped her hands over her mouth. "Welcome, friend! We hate Hawke!"

The creature ignored her attempted overture of peace and slammed the floor again. Its claws ripped a massive chasm open in the floor between them and safety.

"Oh no!" Will stared at it with wide eyes.

Gunfire rang out somewhere in the distance, and the creature shrieked. Its hand withdrew.

This was it. Rita's heart hammered. "Jump!"

"What?"

"You can make it—then Misha will go next, and then me."

Misha narrowed his eyes. "Why are you going last?"

"You'll need help with the jump," she said.

"Then have the kid jump last."

"What," she said, "you'd make a lady catch you? How unchivalrous."

"I don't know what you're up to—"

"We don't have time to argue about it," Will said. "Let's just do it the way she suggested, okay?"

Then he leaped across the chasm.

For a heart-stopping moment it looked like he might not make it, but then his feet hit the ground and he stumbled forward before turning to face them again. "Ready!" He crouched and held out his hand.

Rita looked at Misha. "You have to go next. You know you do."

He sighed. "Fine."

She helped him run to the edge and did her best to propel him toward Will when he jumped. In his weakened state, his jump was short of the goal even with help, but Will stretched out and caught his arm before he could fall. He hauled him up.

Relief crashed over Rita. Will knew the way to the surface. He'd get Misha out. "Okay, you two get to the exit. I'll meet you there in, oh"—the warning alarm hit fifteen minutes—"fifteen minutes."

Will stared at her. "*What?*"

"I knew it." Misha shook his head and clenched his hands into fists. "I knew when you insisted on being last that you were up to something."

"There are two more prisoners," she said. "I doubt Hawke cares enough to evacuate them."

If she'd mentioned it earlier, Misha would have insisted on helping. She couldn't risk that in his current condition. Now that she was confident he would reach safety, she could return for the prisoners.

"Wait!" Will cried. "How are you going to get out?"

She winked. "I'll find a way."

Then she turned and raced back in the direction they came.

No one troubled her as she ran back to the stairs. Everyone was trying to evacuate and therefore didn't care much about someone running in the opposite direction even if she did look out of place.

The stairs were still intact, thank God. She raced down as fast as she dared run with the building still shaking from the creature's attacks. As she ran, she thought over the blueprints. Finding the other prisoners shouldn't be too hard. Getting out would be the tricky part.

Metal screeched somewhere on the other side of the wall, and the stairs collapsed beneath her as she neared the final few feet. She stumbled forward with a yell and managed to reach the bottom without falling.

She wouldn't be returning that way.

There was no time to worry about it. She took off at a run to the next cell. It was unguarded now, and the door opened in response to her stolen keycard. Inside, a woman hung in the pod-like Misha had been, but the machine was silent and malfunctioning, her shackles already unlocked.

Rita disconnected her from the pod as fast as she could and tugged her forward. "Hey, wake up! Can you hear me?"

The woman breathed in short, shallow gasps, but remained unconscious.

Great. This was probably the prisoner marked "Unstable" on the diagram. Rita gritted her teeth and slung the woman's arm over her shoulders. She hauled her out of the room and continued down the corridor to the next cell. Once again, her keycard opened it.

She came face to face with a young man who blinked at her in confusion. The pod was empty, and he rubbed his arms. He must have regained consciousness on his own after the machine shut down.

"Good," she said. "Help me with her."

"Who—"

"It's a long story, but the short version is we need to get out of here before the building blows up."

He stared at her.

From the loudspeakers, the mechanized voice informed them that they had ten minutes left.

All the blood drained from the man's face, and he stumbled to her side. He caught the unconscious woman's other arm and helped support her, which let Rita set a brisker pace out of the cell and back down the hall.

They passed the collapsed stairs, which Rita cast a regretful look before continuing.

At least the creature's assault on the corridor had ended before it ripped apart the floor completely like up above. With the prisoners in tow, Rita headed back through the central monitoring chamber. Despite the urgency, her gaze went to the window.

Hawke's "visitor" was completely free now. It thundered through the cavern that imprisoned it and glared around—probably looking for its enemies unless it didn't understand how to reach the surface.

The conscious prisoner made a garbled sound, and Rita hustled them out the other door as fast as she could. No sign of any of their enemies on the other side of the chamber. The whole facility felt empty and abandoned. She reached the elevator and let out a long breath.

She pressed the button.

It sparked, and she withdrew her hand with a yelp.

So the elevator was also broken.

"This is fine," she said out loud.

"Is there a second elevator?" the prisoner asked, his voice desperate.

"Not as far as I know."

"Then—"

"This way!" She pulled him and the unconscious woman back down the hall.

One shard of hope still glimmered in the growing darkness. On the map, this floor was symmetrical. There were only three cells for prisoners, but a fourth room marked "Emergency." She couldn't think of anything that qualified as an emergency much more than this.

They passed Misha's old cell and reached the fourth room. Rita pushed her keycard into the slot and prayed it wasn't just another cell.

She opened the door. It was a small room, but there was an open hatch with a ladder leading down.

Down. Great. She'd been hoping for *up*.

"This won't be easy," she said, "but it's our only shot." She shrugged off her borrowed lab coat. "Help me get her onto my shoulders."

The other prisoner looked like he was on the verge of hysteria, but he helped her get the unconscious woman onto her shoulders.

"Use the coat to fasten her onto me."

"Are you kidding?" he asked.

"It's better than nothing."

A coat was no substitute for a proper harness, but together they managed to tie the sleeves around them to provide at least partial support.

Rita let out a long breath. "Okay. I'll start down, and you follow as soon as you can. I'm hoping this will be our way out, but if it isn't, being so deep underground might at least provide us with some protection from the blast." Unless, of course, the entire facility was set to blow instead of the self-destruct being centered on the machine, but he didn't need to know that.

He nodded, lips tight with worry.

Slowly, awkwardly, Rita started down the ladder.

Five minutes left.

Rita finally stepped off of the last rung onto solid concrete. She turned around.

This chamber was only partly complete. Far out in front, it opened up onto the cavern—with the night sky visible above. Starlight shone down on the cement floor of…

A hangar.

Three planes occupied the underground hangar. One took off even as she stepped forward. The other two appeared to be unoccupied. How this wasn't visible from above was a concerning question, but she'd deal with that later.

The plane soared toward the open sky, but then wheeled about. Rita had only a moment's warning to guess the pilot's intention—she jumped back behind cover as the plane fired on her. She untied the lab coat and eased the unconscious prisoner down. Behind her, the other prisoner reached the ground.

"On my signal," she said, "get to the plane on the… right." She shoved the unconscious prisoner toward him. "No matter what happens, head straight for the rightmost plane and get inside. Can you do that?"

He nodded.

Rita sprang out from behind cover. "Now!"

She raced toward the plane on the left side of the room. Bullets ate up the pavement around her. As long as the prisoner trusted her plan, this should buy enough time for them to get to the plane.

The plane in the air stopped firing at her and aimed for the leftmost plane instead. The pilot thought that was her goal, and he intended to take away her escape even as the self-destruct loomed. It felt like the thinking of a fanatic—was Hawke in that plane?

A roar announced the attention of the creature, who lumbered toward them. The ground shook as it found the hangar.

Rita tumbled to the ground, then scrambled to her feet. She veered to the right to reach the other plane even as the creature tried to knock Hawke out of the air. All the same, he fired at *her*; she drew her gun and fired back, enough to buy just a little more time.

She reached the plane and scrambled into the cockpit. The dashboard made her freeze. This was some sort of advanced vehicle from the visitor's information, not the sort of plane she trained with.

"Do you know how to fly this?" the prisoner asked. Both of them were securely inside.

"They haven't made a machine I can't fly," she said.

She hit the screen and blinked as it lit up with numerous controls.

Two minutes left.

Engine? Liftoff? She tapped around the screen until she gained some familiarity. The controls might be new, but it was still a plane. At last, it trundled into motion.

The noise drew the attention of the creature. It turned toward her, and

Rita's breath caught.

This was the same design as Hawke's plane, so there had to be guns somewhere. She scrolled through the controls desperately as the plane lifted off and the creature lumbered toward her. Gunfire from the side forced her to veer away, and Hawke—visible now in his cockpit—fired relentlessly.

The creature turned toward him.

One minute left.

Rita gritted her teeth and gunned it, hurtling toward the open sky as the creature Hawke had betrayed ignored his enemy's plane to corner him instead. A fiery explosion consumed the facility, and she glanced back in time to see the brilliant flames swallow up Hawke, his opponent, and the Genesis Machine in a sea of fire, crimson against the white snow of the mountains.

She made a slow circuit of the area and then flew toward safety.

"This was an unorthodox mission, to say the least." Simmons rubbed his forehead. "You understand that this has to remain top secret, especially everything in regards to the 'visitor' Hawke had found." He shook his head. "This is going to be quite a report..."

Rita stood with Misha in front of his desk. The two of them had reported back immediately, as soon as she located him and Will in the mountain clearing.

"Anyway," he said, "despite the obstacles you faced, you both performed admirably."

She straightened. "Thank you, sir. I even rescued Misha."

Misha gave her a wry grin. "Next time, I'll be the one saving you."

"We'll see."

"I saved you in Peru."

"That doesn't count," she said. "You saved me from my own explosion."

"That's not a point in your favor!"

Simmons cleared his throat, and they both faced him again. "This might have serious consequences. We need to determine the full extent of Hawke's organization and track down the survivors. We'll also need to assess the situation with the 'visitor,' although the initial survey suggests the entire facility and everything in it was lost in the explosion. The two prisoners are recovering, but we'll need to deal with both them and the man who switched sides."

Personally, Rita had hopes Will might join them since he joined Hawke thinking it was a government project, but she wouldn't blame him if he chose to stay a civilian instead, especially given how young he was.

"But for now," Simmons said, "take some time to relax and do whatever you want. You've earned it."

"Great!" Rita started toward the door. "I've got a lot of work to do."

"Work?" Misha asked. "Already?"

She faced him again and held up her hands. "Did you forget?" She winked. "I've got a radio station to manage. Who knows what happened to it without me?"

"It probably didn't blow up, for one thing," he said.

"You say that like buildings regularly explode when I'm around. It's only happened twice."

"Which is two times too many."

"Are you inviting me to join you for a vacation?" she asked. "Is that what this is all about?"

"*No*, I'd like to relax on my vacation, thank you very much."

"Hmph, you'd be lost without me and you know it."

As they argued, they left the office and headed down the halls of the building known to the public only as Reports & Accounting. Soon, the reports from this mission would indeed be accounted for—keeping the Hand of the Law's secrets from all but those who already knew.

THE END

Essay

When I learned about *The Adventures of Radio Rita,* I thought the concept was fantastic—Airship 27 would take an original character, give writers a few basic details about her, and let each one come up with their individual interpretation of this character for a new collection. I loved the idea and soon envisioned a spy story's basic details.

Now, I couldn't write about a character named "Radio Rita" and not include the *radio* part in some way. At first, I thought Rita might coordinate events from a radio station to keep other agents in contact with one another and give reports on their activities, but I discarded that idea since it meant the starring character wouldn't actually be involved in the action.

Instead, I switched to the idea of the radio station being used to send coded messages, after which Rita would leave on her mission.

I worked out the basics—the radio station, the secret headquarters, the village in the mountains, and the secret lab—but then I ran into a problem. Rita wasn't interesting.

I'd written her as a straightforward hero, heading out to stop the bad guys and save the day, without much more to her personality than that.

So I paused the draft and went back to spice things up a bit. This new version of Rita liked making quips and had more of a reckless "never tell me the odds" attitude. Her scenes became much more entertaining, especially as she got a little quirkier, and I resumed writing up until Rita teamed up with Will and they infiltrated the base.

At that point, I hit another problem. For a supposed action story, the plot was proceeding at a glacial pace. That was when I decided to completely change the setup to what we have here. Rita has already been captured when the story begins. The opening scenes are flashbacks while she's being interrogated under the effects of a truth serum. While writing the story in this new direction, I then asked myself how Rita could even get out of this if the villains knew everything. So I added my favorite twist of the story: she's fabricating certain false memories in order to feed her enemies inaccurate information and give herself an advantage.

I went back and forth on how to show this a few times. In one version, the story began with the interrogation, so the reader would know from the start that she'd been captured. That was exciting, but ultimately I felt it made it too confusing to understand which memories were real and which were fake, short of retelling the whole sequence of events afterward. In the end, I chose not to start with her capture, and instead to use specific cues to signal the interrogation (scent of pine) and the false memories ("grave danger"). While you might wonder at those things being repeated the first time you read those scenes, it should be easier to follow in retrospect after the reveal.

With the new direction set, I continued writing… until the story started to drag once again. At this point, the villains were still building a super-weapon, but that just wasn't working.

When in doubt, fall back on what you know—a quick shift in the then-unnamed villains' true goals meant they were now secretly *trying to awaken an eldritch abomination sleeping deep beneath the earth!*

(To date, more than half of my stories for Airship 27 were briefly cosmic horror at some point in the process, which probably says something.)

I happily continued the story in this manner, despite having promised a friend that my new story was definitely not horror. But wait! Rita is a pilot,

F-94 Starfire

and this was supposed to be an action story. I shifted gears again at the end for an action-packed conclusion and a desperate escape by plane.

My first draft was complete. It was a mess.

I went to a couple of my writer friends—who also helped as beta readers for this story—and explained my problem: I had written something that began as a 1950s spy story, suddenly introduced a high-tech underground base, and briefly became cosmic horror before concluding with a dogfight.

One of my friends responded jokingly with the "aliens" meme image.

And I said to myself, "Wait."

That might actually work.

If the creature in the climax was an imprisoned alien… If the villains intentionally had advanced tech because they stole it from their prisoner… If that was the truth of the machine they were building…

All the pieces started to come together.

Other details still needed to be ironed out, like naming the bad guys now that I'd figured out their goals, and naming the *good guys* since I hadn't bothered with that for the

first draft—a bit of research online convinced me that instead of giving Rita's organization a cool acronym, it was better to give them an innocuous public name and a more casual name used internally, and so "Reports & Accounting" became the outward face of the Hand of the Law.

These revisions were fairly extensive, and of course, my beta readers found many more things I had to adjust, from the villain's name going through three different variations without me noticing, to glimmers of hope glimmering, so my ever-present tendency to skip over description. I can't thank them enough for their help in bringing this story to life.

At last, all I needed was a title.

I went through several different ideas ("Radio Rita in Grave Danger" was half-seriously tossed about quite a bit), but none of them seemed to fit. Then I remembered I'd never given Hawke's machine a name. And being the sort of man who renames himself Noah and calls his organization the Ark, he was bound to pick a melodramatic and grandiose name for the machine he thinks will allow him to create a new future.

And so, "Radio Rita and the Genesis Machine" was born.

It was a strange feeling to step back after the end and realize that "my" Rita's story was over, and that there were other versions of her out there who would likely be very different. I grew attached to these characters as I wrote their adventure—and I hope you also enjoyed your time with them.

SAMANTHA LIENHARD - has been writing for most of her life, especially in the fantasy and horror genres. She graduated from Mansfield University with a B.A. in English and a minor in Creative Writing, and then from Seton Hill University with an M.F.A. in Writing Popular Fiction. When she isn't writing, she can usually be found playing video games. Her publications include a comedy novella called *The Zombie Mishap*, a Lovecraftian horror novella called *The Book at Dernier*, a Lovecraftian horror novelette called *It Came Back*, the pulp fiction story "The Domino Lady Takes the Case," and several short horror stories. She also writes for video games and has worked on the scripts for several indie titles, including *Ascendant Hearts*, *The Trials of Olympus III*, *Two Till Midnight*, and *Eternal Radiance*.

Information about all of her work can be found at her website: http://www.samanthalienhard.com

Frequency
by Gene Moyers

The tall, lean woman slipped into the briefing room and sat on one of the rickety wooden chairs. She was dressed in a khaki shirt and trousers, her long red hair tied back and hanging down beneath the back of her battered Bronx Dodgers baseball cap. Like the rest of the buildings of Squadron 13's Caribbean base, this one had a thatched roof and large, shutters that were folded back to catch the gentle, early morning breeze, prelude to another hot Caribbean day.

Ron Forster, "Captain Ron" as he was known, nodded as she entered, "Rita."

Rita nodded back. As she did, Squadron 13's youngest pilot Mike Baxter entered. He took a seat, and smiled, "Morning, Sparks." Rita smiled at the common nickname although she quietly rebelled at being thought of as just the radio operator.

"Lots to do, so I'll make things quick."

Rita turned her attention to her new Boss. Ron Forster cut a trim and dapper figure in his khaki shirt and trousers tucked into knee-high boots. He was of slim build and medium height. His brown hair was worn short, military style, his mustache neatly trimmed. To Rita's eye, he looked every inch the former naval aviator he was.

Squadron 13 was an independent outfit that did survey, mapping, transport, and security work. It had been formed by Forster and his long-time friend Rob Davidson. The two flyers had met when both had volunteered for Lighter Than Air training. When the Navy had de-emphasized LTA flight after the *Macon* disaster the two had transferred over to other duties. Two years before both officers had resigned and formed Squadron 13. Scuttlebutt among the squadron's pilots said that both had connections to Naval Intelligence and much of the business thrown the squadron's way had the smell of Washington on it.

Rita had been a pilot for a couple of years. She was a gifted flyer but had trouble finding anyone to take her seriously. Hearing of Squadron 13, she tracked down its commander. Forster had been doubtful at first. He had a full complement of pilots and was skeptical of the young aviator. Rita had made a call to her father, asking advice. He had been supportive but non-committal. Suddenly, Forster had changed his mind. She suspected her father had made some calls but was unsure. Whatever the reason, Forster had taken her on as their communications officer.

Rita had snapped up the position, sure that she could prove herself as a pilot if given the chance. She had caught up with the squadron three days before as they were setting up this forward base on a small island in the US Virgin Islands. They had been sent here to investigate a series of mysterious ship sinkings and disappearances in and around the Caribbean.

The summer of 1939 was a dangerous time. The Spanish Civil war had ended but the rest of Europe was on the brink of war. Captain Ron had briefed the squadron that the suspicious sinkings might be by a foreign power but more likely the international criminal organization known as *Viper* was behind them. Little was known about *Viper* except that it was powerful and involved in smuggling, piracy and arms trafficking. Even less was known of its mysterious leader, known as the Copperhead.

Rita focused her attention as Forster continued, "Rob, Nick, and Jake are ferrying the last three A-12s in from the mainland. They should be in by dark. 'Wish' is flying the Orion in from Puerto Rico this afternoon. Rita, keep an ear out for them. They may need a radio fix if clouds build up. Once we're fully equipped with the new birds, we'll set up better patrol patterns.

"Today, Mike and I will fly a search pattern to the southwest. After refueling, we'll fly another patrol to the southeast. Rita, maintain radio watch. Listen to the international distress frequencies. It's been a week since the last ship went missing. We're overdue for trouble. Any questions?"

"Just how are these ships just disappearing?" Mike, asked.

Ron shrugged, "Unknown. Could be mines, sabotage, or even armed stowaways. But it's getting important people worried enough to help grease the skids and get us these surplus attack planes."

Rita and Mike nodded. The A-12 Shrikes had been introduced only five years before. Then, they were cutting-edge equipment. With American re-armament gearing up, they were now being replaced by the new A-20s. Mike asked, "Do you think *Viper's* behind it all?"

"Maybe. It's the kind of chaos they like to create. All right, let's go."

Rita watched the A-12 off the dusty airstrip and climb out of the pattern. At two thousand feet, Ron circled patiently. When Baxter reached altitude, he fell in on Ron's wing and the two aircraft headed southwest. Rita watched them out of sight before heading off for the radio shack.

Shack was a good description. The buildings on their new island base were all constructed of wood or corrugated tin. The sturdiest building was, not surprisingly, the hangar. Tools, equipment, and fuel needed to be kept dry from daily showers during the rainy season. Fortunately, it was the dry winter season. As she entered the shack and pushed open the large woven grass shutters, Rita could already feel the sweat beginning to soak through her khaki shirt back. Warming up the transmitter and the two receivers, she adjusted the frequencies and plopped herself down in the worn swivel chair in front of the radio equipment. Settling the headset over her ears she picked up the hand mike and called, "Airship Flight 1, Airship Flight 1, this is Base 13. Radio check, over." Rita flicked the transmit switch over to receive.

Moments later Ron's voice came through tinnily in her headset. "Airship Base, this is Flight 1. You are coming in 5x5, over."

Rita flicked back to transmit and replied, "Reading you clearly as well. How's the weather look, over?"

"Visibility unlimited. High clouds to the south, over."

"Roger. Check in as scheduled. Base out."

"Wilco. Flight 1, out."

Rita pushed one side of the headset off one ear so she could hear around her and began the morning's watch.

The morning passed slowly. Rita kept in regular voice communication with Flight 1. She also received a morse code message from Aloysius "Wish" McGonigle in Puerto Rico. Notifying her he was delayed by cargo loading but would still arrive before dark. She made a note of this for Captain Ron.

Ron and Baxter landed back at the airstrip just before noon. She had someone relieve her and headed for the mess hall. Over sandwiches and semi-cold drinks, she asked how the morning patrol had gone. Ron took a long drink of his coke and eyed it. "Ya know, what we really need down here is a decent icebox." Mike Baxter grunted his assent as Ron answered Rita, "Routine. We patrolled out about two hundred miles southwest, came around for almost fifty miles northwest, and then headed back home over St. Croix. We saw a couple of freighters and several fishing boats, but nothing suspicious."

"Not that some of those fishing boats couldn't be spotting for a Viper outfit," Ron added. "But nothing we could confirm. How about you? Any unusual radio traffic?"

Rita shook her head. "Nope. Nothing suspicious. Just routine messages. Although I did pick up some French traffic. It was distant but military, I think."

Ron nodded. "Their big naval base is down on Martinique but they also have stuff on Guadaloupe southeast of here. I'm surprised you picked anything up at that range."

Rita shrugged, "Radio reception is funny. You never know how far signals travel. Must have been good reception today. So, southeast this afternoon?"

Ron nodded, "When the rest of the squadron gets in tomorrow, we'll be doing multiple patrols in all directions every day. You'll be busier then, coordinating all the traffic."

Rita, smiled, "I'm ready."

After that, the conversation turned to other things. Finishing his sandwich, Mike asked, "How did you get into radios, Sparks?"

Rita shrugged, "Came by it naturally. My Dad was an electrical engineer. He did a lot of work in radiotelegraphy. Invented some components, even. He worked for RCA for a long time. I grew up around radios and he taught me a lot. He was into amateur radio when I was a kid. I remember sitting on his knee as he talked to people in Canada and Mexico."

Ron looked interested, "He sounds like quite a guy. Is he still with RCA?"

Rita shook her head, "No. He took a position several years ago working for some rich millionaire back east. He and Mom moved back to New York over eight years ago."

Mike whistled softly, "Sounds cushy. What's he doing, helping start a new company?"

Rita frowned, "I'm not exactly sure. He just says he's in charge of private communications for this reclusive millionaire. I've been curious myself, but he doesn't talk much about it."

Mike sipped the last of his lukewarm coke as he eyed the attractive radio operator, "You said your folks moved to New York. Where are you from?"

Rita replied, "California. Burbank; I grew up there."

Mike frowned, "Burbank? Where's that?"

Ron put in, "Just north of L.A. It's where Lockheed builds aircraft."

Mike nodded, "Well, it's good to have somebody on the radio who knows his…uh her, uh knows what she's doing." He colored slightly at his fumble. Rita just smiled

Afternoon was a repeat of the morning. Radio watch; listening, changing frequencies, and listening again. She also monitored the progress of

Rob and the rest of the squadron. They were refueling in Puerto Rico and still due in by dark. By five o'clock, Rita was hot, tired, and ready for a shower and a lukewarm beer. She had just taken a report from Puerto Rico that "Wish" McGonigle would be landing in an hour or so.

Leaning back in her chair, her legs propped on the bench, Rita reached overhead, stretching her stiff shoulders. She reached out and slowly moved the big frequency dial of one of the receivers. As she passed over an open frequency, she heard in her left headset earpiece, "—day, repeat—" Something about the tone caught her attention. Leaning over, she carefully spun the dial back and heard, "—station, any station! Mayday! Mayday! Request immediate—" The broadcast was cut off as Rita, trying to get her feet down off the bench, reach for the mike, and the volume control all at once, fell out of her chair. Landing hard on the dusty floor, Rita cursed and quickly scrambled up. She pulled her chair under her and sat down while grabbing the microphone. Firmly seated, Rita tweaked the dial until the unknown voice came in clearly, "Mayday! Mayday! Is anyone receiving, over!"

Flipping to transmit, Rita held the mic up and called out, "Unknown station, this is uh…" She hesitated. Ron had made it clear that their presence was to be kept as low-key as possible. She continued carefully, "This is a commercial base near Puerto Rico. We have received your Mayday. What is your emergency, over?"

"This is the *SS Donegal*. We've had a serious explosion forward. We are taking on water and down by the bow. Captain has ordered abandon ship. Can you help us?"

Rita took a deep breath and transmitted, "*Donegal*, what is your position? I can get search planes out very soon, over."

There was a pause. Rita wondered if in the confusion they could even get an accurate position to her. Holding the mic, she pushed her rolling chair down the bench to the other receiver. She adjusted the frequency dial and flipped a couple of switches as *Donegal* transmitted again. She pressed the headset against one ear to hear clearly, "This is *Donegal*. We are approximately one hundred miles north of the island of Anguilla."

"Roger that, *Donegal*," Rita said into the mic as she stood up and reached for a metal wheel that protruded down out of the roof. The wheel was connected to a moveable antenna on the roof. By moving it around, Rita could get an exact compass bearing on the broadcast. She spoke into the mic, "*Donegal, Donegal*. We are dispatching aircraft to your position. Please continue broadcasting as long as possible for us to get a bearing on you. Repeat, continue broadcasting, over."

"Roger, we will stay on the air as long as possible."

Rita transmitted, "*Donegal*, say again your damage. What kind of explosion?"

There was a short pause before the reply came, "Captain says it was external. Somebody said it felt like a mine or torpedo against the bow, over."

Slowly turning the wheel, Rita felt a chill. Mine? Torpedo? That was not good. One eye on the compass degrees painted on the inner roof, the other scanning over the radio panel she continued turning the wheel. Her mind raced. Ron would be returning soon and so would Wish. She transmitted again, "*Donegal*, do you have any casualties, over."

The answer came back quickly, "Yes, several injured and several missing. Wounded are away in the lifeboat. They're having trouble launching the other one." There was a pause, then, "Going down faster now. Bow nearly under. May have to shut down soon."

Rita bit her lip as she turned the antenna. There! Bearing 065 degrees, true!

As she was about to transmit again, the *Donegal* beat her to it. The lonely radio operator came on once more, "Down by the head. Ship going. Shutting down and abandoning ship. Thanks for your help."

That quick, he was gone. Rita sat down and let out a breath. In a few minutes, everything had changed. She had heard a ship die. Rita angrily pushed herself up out of her chair. She had to do something. She walked over to a faded map of the Caribbean tacked to the wall. She bent forward. Anguilla was about one hundred fifty miles due east, where the Lesser Antilles chain of islands bent south. It was British-owned. From there many islands, Dutch, French, and British stretched nearly all the way to South America. North and east of Anguilla was nothing but the broad expanse of the Atlantic, broken only by a few reefs and small uninhabited islands near the Antilles.

Rita looked at her watch; five thirty. Sunset in an hour and a half. The distance to the sinking ship was one hundred seventy miles. An aircraft could reach it in an hour. They would have ships and pilots back soon, but they would need to be refueled. That would take time. Finding survivors after dark would be tough. Rita chewed her lip; she needed to notify the skipper. She picked up the mic and adjusted the transmitter back to the Airship frequency, then stopped.

She set the mic down, turned, and walked to the door of the radio shack. The sun was low in the west. Shadows from trees and buildings stretched long across the airstrip. In front of the hangar sat the newly re-painted

A-12. Rita's mind raced. The survivors had to be found before dark. Relays of aircraft could then orbit overhead directing rescue ships in. But someone had to go now.

Deciding, Rita ran across the airstrip to the A-12. The mechanics looked up at her in surprise. Running up to them she asked, "Is she ready to go?"

The blond-haired mechanic nodded, "Yep, fueled and ready for tomorrow's flight."

Rita eyed the aircraft. Gone were the bright yellow tail and wings. Gone were the red, white and blue rudder stripes. The entire under surfaces, including the wheel spats were now a very pale blue. The upper surfaces were olive drab broken up by large swaths of brown. From the air, she would blend in perfectly with ground foliage and from below she would be hard to spot at altitude. Under each wing two medium-sized bombs hung on shackles. They gleamed evilly in their metallic black paint.

Rita looked at the mechanic and asked, "What about the guns?"

"All loaded; six hundred rounds each."

"And the internal racks?"

The mechanic answered, "Not loaded. The captain's orders were only for the external racks."

Rita spoke firmly, "All right, get some help. I want you to push her out to the end of the strip. Warm up the engine, I'm taking her up."

Both men looked surprised. The first one said, "But Sparks, are you authorized to uh, fly this…"

Rita cut him off. "I am now. There's a ship out there sinking. It just came over the radio. I'm going out to locate them. The rest of the squadron will follow when they return."

"Well, maybe we ought to wait until…"

"We're not waiting! I want you to get that six-man life raft and bring it out here. Get some help and pull that outboard, starboard bomb off. Get some rope and tie that raft securely to the empty bomb shackle. Rig it tight. I don't want it falling off until I'm ready. Got it?"

"Yes but…"

"No buts! Get moving! And bring me out a box of those waterproof flares. Go!"

Leaving the two men standing there open-mouthed, Rita turned and jogged toward the shacks that served as quarters for the squadron. As the only woman in the squadron, she was accorded the luxury of her own hooch. Inside she threw open a footlocker at the end of her narrow cot. She quickly selected what she wanted and stood up. She quickly shrugged into her shoulder holster. Reaching under her pillow she pulled out her Smith & Wesson revolver. She quickly flipped open the cylinder and peered at it. Six rounds gleamed back at her. She spun the cylinder and closed it up. Under her left arm it went. She then looped the yellow life preserver over her head, picked up her leather flying helmet, gloves, and goggles, and jogged out the door.

Across the airfield, she heard an aircraft engine cough to life. It quickly built up to a loud roar. Back inside the radio shack, she sat down and adjusted the frequency. She flipped to transmit and picked up the mic, "Flight 1, flight 1, this is base, over."

Moments later Captain Ron's voice came back through the headset she held to one ear, "Airship base, this is Flight 1. What's up, over?"

"Flight 1, we have received a distress signal. A ship, *SS Donegal* is in trouble. She has struck a mine or been torpedoed and is sinking fast. Her position is approximately one hundred seventy miles east, northeast of base on a bearing of 065 degrees. There are survivors in the water, and she is requesting assistance."

Ron came back immediately, "Right. Good work, Sparks. We are increasing speed. ETA is thirty minutes. Have you heard from Wish, over?"

"Flight 1, yes he should be landing within the hour, over."

"Good. Have the mechanics stand by. As soon as we're down we'll refuel and go out to find this ship, over."

Rita took a deep breath and spoke clearly. "Flight 1, there are men in the water. Every minute counts. I'm taking up the A-12, It's warming up now. As soon as you can, follow me out. Hopefully, I'll have the survivors marked with flares and we can stay overhead until we can get ships in, over."

Ron came back quickly, "Rita, listen! You aren't trained or experienced in this kind of thing. Wait for us, we'll be back soon! Repeat, you'll have help soon, over!"

Rita was suddenly very calm. She remembered a story her father had told her. Blowing loudly across the microphone, she then tapped it loudly with her fingertip several times and shouted, "Flight 1, your last transmission garbled. Time is of the essence. Airship Base, out."

Setting down the mic, she turned and jogged to the idling aircraft. Up close the huge radial engine made a terrific racket as it idled, the nine-foot propeller a blur. The mechanic climbed out of the cockpit and met her on the ground. As she buckled her life preserver around her, the mechanic bent and pulled open a small wooden box. He scooped out a double handful of parachute flares.

Rita nodded as she pulled on the leather and cloth helmet, tucking her long, red hair up under it. She climbed up on the wing and crabbed forward. Throwing a long leg over the side of the cockpit she settled into the seat on top of a parachute. The mechanic climbed up beside her. Taking the flares from him she stowed them along the seat. Reaching down, she pulled heavy web straps up over her shoulders. The mechanic helped her buckle it correctly and pull it tight. She looked into his worried face and gave him a "thumbs up" gesture. He nodded. Rather than try to make himself heard over the racket of the radial engine just feet away he mouthed, "Good luck!" then turned and slid off the wing to the ground.

Peering around the strange cockpit, and remembering she was not checked out on the A-12, Rita thought, It's going to be a quick flying lesson. Everything seemed in the green; oil pressure, manifold pressure, RPMs, engine temp, although the last was climbing. She looked around and pulled the goggles down over her eyes. Time to go.

Rita pushed the throttle forward. The engine noise increased as she fed fuel to the 670 horsepower engine. The aircraft rolled forward. Tapping the brakes, she carefully steered the big ship out to the end of the runway. As she did, she searched for and found the flap crank. She had never flown a ship with full-length flaps but knew what they did; unsure of the exact setting she cranked in half flap and hoped for the best. At the end of the strip, she paused momentarily. Gripping the stick in her right hand, she shoved the throttle all the way forward.

The engine noise rose to a howl as Rita let off the brakes and the aircraft rolled forward. It gained speed quickly. Trees and building rushed past in her peripheral vision. In seconds she was doing over sixty knots and she felt the tail start to come up. She had never flown anything with this much power. She stayed calm and held the stick forward.

Speed increased. Seventy knots. Eighty knots. Rita felt it as the A-12 lifted gently from the dusty strip. She did not pull back on the stick. Instead, she let her speed build as she lifted gently over the trees at the end of the airstrip and was immediately over water.

Only then did Rita let the ship rise gradually. She smiled widely behind her goggles. Boy, did this ship have some power! That big Wright Cyclone engine had nine cylinders and was made for military aircraft. It thrilled Rita to feel the vibration of it through the stick. This was what she lived for.

Setting a course of 065 and continuing to climb, she gently felt the ship out. She knew the Curtiss had leading edge slots and was interested to see if they gave an advantage at low speed and high angles of attack. Raising the flaps, she pushed the pedals and moved the stick gently back and forth. The A-12 was light on the controls for such a large ship. She was very steady but rolled slowly when the aileron was applied.

Rita was feeling better about handling the big ship as she reached five thousand feet. Leveling off, she sped northeast at 130 knots. The sky was clear and visibility was good, but the sun was low behind her and she could see the sea darkening below.

Nearly an hour later Rita looked at her watch. It was almost six thirty. A glance behind her showed the sun just touching the horizon. Pulling the throttle back, Rita lost altitude and began a wide circle. Gradually the sea darkened below her.

Then, off to starboard a flare arrowed upward. Reversing her turn, Rita pulled the stick over and orbited right. Almost immediately she saw something light-colored in the water. She throttled back more and dropped toward the sea. In the last rays of the sun, she saw an open boat with men in it waving as she overflew them.

Rita reached down next to her and pulled out one of the parachute flares. She pulled the ring and tossed it over the side of the open cockpit. Circling, she watched it sink downward. It illuminated the dark sea and Rita could clearly see the single lifeboat. She also saw debris scattered across the sea, then she realized that some of the 'debris' were the heads of men swimming in the open ocean. Rita watched the drift of the flare. Judging the wind, she circled, waiting for the right moment then rolled the big ship directly toward the lifeboat. Rita flipped the master bomb switch and as she passed over the lifeboat, toggled the starboard outboard shackle.

She didn't see the lifeboat hit and begin to inflate thirty yards from the lifeboat but by the time she had climbed away and dropped another flare, she could see men swimming toward the bright yellow inflatable.

Rita circled the survivors. Daylight was fading fast. It was nearly seven o'clock, Captain Ron would have ships in the air heading her way. Dropping another flare Rita again widened her circle looking for stray swimmers.

She was two miles southeast of the lifeboats when something caught her eye on the dark sea. She could see a bright green, very straight line on the dark surface of the ocean. Surprised, Rita cut her throttle and settled lower. Overflying the green line, she could see it ran northwest-southeast and was fading gradually at the southeast end. She finally realized she was seeing some kind of phosphorescence on the surface of the sea. Rita knew certain microscopic sea creatures generated light similar to fireflies. The scientists

She saw an open boat with men in it waving as she overflew them.

called it 'bio'...something or other. It was also generated by the wakes of ships at night. She realized it must be the wake of a submarine just below the surface of the ocean.

Rita circled back over the line of phosphorescence and tossed another parachute flare over the side and watched it sway beneath its small parachute. There! In the glare of the sinking flare, she saw a straight dark line sticking up out of the sea at the northwest end of the glowing green line. It could only be the periscope of a sub.

This must be what sank the *Donegal*. But, whose sub, was it? Some European power? Or as she suspected, *Viper*. She had accomplished the squadron's mission. But what now? There had to be squadron aircraft on the way by now. She reached for the radio switch. Time to call in the clans.

As the radio warmed, Rita hesitated. This sub might be legitimate. It might even be American. She needed to get it to the surface and identify itself. She would call the skipper when she had proof. She pulled her goggles down over her eyes and pushed the stick over.

Reversing her turn, Rita cut power as she dropped toward the wake of the sub. Airspeed down to one hundred ten knots, she leveled out a hundred feet. In the dying light of the parachute flare, she could see the periscope sticking about four feet out of the water. As she swept over the unknown sub, she toggled the outboard port bomb.

Seconds later, it exploded as Rita was climbing away. She could see the white column of water thrown up fifty yards ahead of the sub, cascading down in the last of the flare's light. Tossing another flare over the side, Rita came around again. On the dark sea, she saw only the fading phosphorescence and the periscope disappearing beneath the waves.

Angry now, Rita bore in for another run. The sub was diving away. That was an admission of guilt if she had ever seen one.

Sweeping in at a hundred feet, Rita toggled her second bomb just ahead of where she thought the sub's position would be. Crossing her finger for luck, she again put on power and circled around. A minute later in the light of the flare she saw a boiling of white water on the ocean below and the triangular bow of a sub surfacing. Rita shouted in delight. She'd done it!

Circling she looked down over the portside. It was hard to see in the slanting light of the flare but she could see the sub was dark, if not black in color. It was low on the sea with only the conning tower amidships and what appeared to be some kind of deck gun forward to break up the low, silhouette. To her eyes, it looked sleek and sinister.

As she watched, dark forms spilled out of the sub and onto its deck. Rita tossed another flare out as she passed over the sub at a thousand feet. Picking up the mic, she pressed the call button and sang out loudly to be heard over the engine noise and rushing wind, "Any Airship Squadron aircraft; this is Radio Rita. I have pursued and forced an unknown submarine to the surface southeast of *SS Donegal's* last position. Am dropping flares to mark the bandit and am requesting assistance, over."

There was a pause and then a distant voice replying tinnily in her earpiece, "Calling Rita. This is Airship commander. Repeat. Did you say unknown submarine? Over."

Rita could not keep the smile out of her voice as she spoke into the mic, "Airship commander. That is a roger. I have the bandit submarine surfaced below me. I believe he may be damaged. What is your position? Over."

"Rita we are nearing *Donegal's* last known position with two aircraft. Others are spaced out behind me. We can assist soon. What is your exact position? Over."

"Airship commander, I am…" Rita's reply was cut off as a line of red tracers arced up from the submarine toward her. Rita dropped the microphone. She shoved the throttle to the firewall and horsed the stick hard over. The line of glowing red balls seemed to travel faster and faster as they arced toward her. Concentrating on her tight turn and the tracers, she didn't see the second line of tracers lancing up from the sub's deck. The first line of tracers passed just under her. Rita reversed her turn and felt rather than heard the second trail of bullets carve into the rear of her fuselage. The stick vibrated under her hand, feeling as if someone had thrown a handful of gravel against the metal skin of the aircraft.

This was the first time Rita had ever been shot at. She found herself surprised rather than scared. The idea that someone was actually trying to kill her seemed rather shocking. She pulled back and climbed for altitude, the lines of tracers reaching after her. Rita shook her head. How dare they! Angry as much at her own shock, as at the enemy, Rita gritted her teeth. All right… if those pirates wanted to play, she was ready.

Rita grabbed her next to last flare and tossed it over the side. Then skidded around in an S-turn. The sub was still on the surface. Rita had heard the Airship 13 pilots talking about the A-12. They claimed it was one of the best ground attack aircraft in the world. Those pirates below were about to find out just how good it really was.

Keeping her speed up, Rita lost height and came in low behind the sub. She estimated its speed at about ten knots. She closed from the rear at 150 knots. At five hundred yards she pressed the fire button on the stick. Instantly, lines of tracers lanced out as the four Browning .30 caliber machine guns mounted in the wheel pants opened up. Her fire was short but she closed the range and a second later her fire reached the stern of the submarine. Head down, attention split between the target and her altitude, Rita didn't see the lines of tracers reaching out toward her from the conning tower of the sub.

The bullets chewed into her wing and across her cowling. The windscreen starred and she felt glass slice her chin. Wind whistled around her as she held the stick as steady as she could. She was closing the sub with frightening speed. Her tracers walked along the deck of the sub; bullet hits sparkling as bullets ricocheted off the iron conning tower. Her plane shuddered as more fire thudded into her fuselage. She felt the jarring through her stick. Ignoring everything but the target. Rita reached for the bomb panel and toggled her last bomb as she swept over the sub's stern. Immediately, she pulled the stick back, clawing for altitude. It was then that the second machine gun on the foredeck tracked along her fuselage in a long burst that walked from her engine back past the cockpit and halfway to the tail.

The stick was well back and Rita pounded on the throttle for more speed as bullets hammered the aircraft. Two tore through the instrument panel shattering gauges. Another cut through the cockpit side, just missing her. She clamped two hands on the now badly vibrating stick.

In a steep climb and losing speed, Rita checked her gauges; most were shattered. Her ears told her the engine was running rough and she knew she was nearing a stall. Easing the stick forward, she slowed her climb. The vibration eased off as she gained lift under her wings. She felt the leading-edge slots deploy trying to keep air flowing over the wings. The oil pressure gauge was out but she could tell from the climbing oil temp that she was losing pressure.

Easing the throttle back, Rita came around gently to the south. She figured she was at about a thousand feet. Below her, the last flare went out. Rita had no trouble spotting the sub though. Off to starboard, she could see the bandit dead in the water. Multiple flashlights were in use forward and a spotlight suddenly clicked on from the conning tower, illuminating the crew swarming around the bow.

Her last bomb had missed but must have done some damage. Busy trying to keep her wounded Shrike flying, Rita had no time to celebrate. The engine temp was climbing toward the redline. She knew she didn't have much time left. She wanted to throttle back but needed altitude. Altitude would buy her time.

Reluctantly, Rita groped for the microphone. She took a breath and transmitted, "Mayday, Mayday, Mayday. This is Radio Rita. I've been shot up by an unknown submarine approximately one hundred miles north of Anguilla. Engine hit…am going down. Repeat, Mayday, Mayday. Going down north of Anguilla."

Dropping the mic, she listened hard as she leveled off. She heard a garbled voice replying but could not understand the words. She craned around trying to see the tall antenna behind the cockpit but couldn't tell if it was still there. The engine was misfiring badly, and the temp was off the scale. She knew the engine would seize soon. It must be pouring oil out somewhere.

As Rita reached out to pull the throttle all the way back, she saw the first flames. The propeller slowed. She killed the fuel pump and the prop stopped. The silence was deafening. The nose of the aircraft staggered as her speed fell off. Rita pushed the nose down slightly to keep flying speed up. This only fed air to the flames now licking back toward the cockpit. She ignored this and brought the Shrike around more to the south. Right now, her goal was to get as far from the enemy as possible. She would get little mercy from those pirates if rescued.

Smoke now began to leak into the cockpit. She coughed at the smell of burnt oil. Realizing she wasn't going to get the chance to ditch, she craned her head over the side. The sea below was a black void. Rita gritted her teeth. The flames were lengthening. They were now streaming back and licking toward the windscreen.

Checking the altitude, she found she was dropping past eight hundred feet. She needed to get out now. Airspeed was down to one-twenty. She pulled back gently on the stick to slow her speed and cranked down the flaps to "full' with her left hand. She wasn't sure of the stalling speed of the A-12 but figured with those leading-edge slots, it must be down around eighty knots.

Not much time left. Her heading was due south. She had never had to 'hit the silk' before. She had heard that the exit could be rough. Flames were licking back along the fuselage and smoke was filling the cockpit. Suddenly she remembered a story from an old army pilot. He had claimed the easiest way out of an aircraft was to roll the ship on her back and unbuckle your belt. Biting her lip, Rita threw the stick over to the left.

The burning ship fell off to port as the ship rolled. In seconds the A-12 was on its back. Rita reached for her belt, her other hand on the D-ring of her chute. She closed her eyes and pulled the buckle. Gravity took her and Rita fell out of the aircraft into the black night.

She exited cleanly except for her ankle brushing the edge of the cockpit. Spinning in the darkness, Rita pulled hard on the D-ring. There was a fluttering in the dark above her and a second later a loud "Pop" and sharp jerk as the chute opened. Suddenly it was very quiet as she hung in the harness. All around her was darkness.

Looking around she saw a streak of light below her. Her burning ship was going down almost vertically. She heard nothing when it hit the sea. The burning wreck quickly sank leaving only small fires burning on the surface of the sea.

Otherwise, the darkness around her was unbroken. No lights were visible. Looking down, she was still surprised several seconds later when she hit the ocean. She went under without time to take a breath. For a second, she almost panicked. She had to get out of the harness before she was dragged down by the collapsing chute. She found the buckle and twisted hard. It popped open. Holding her breath, she shrugged out of the harness and stroked for the surface. She came up under the silk chute and had a bad moment until she submerged again and swam from under it. Finally, she was in the clear floating on the ocean. She was being pulled under by her clothes but now had a chance to inflate her life preserver. It inflated and lifted her head out of the water.

Rita took a breath and looked around. It was totally dark around her. She didn't have the foggiest idea of her position; other than she was somewhere south of where the *Donegal* had gone down and somewhere north of Anguilla. Somewhere out there, Airship fliers were searching for the survivors and her as well. But there was no way to signal them and no hope of quick rescue. She tried to relax and not think of the immense ocean beneath her.

Floating in the warm water, Rita quickly grew bored. She lifted her left wrist and tried to read the time, but it was too dark. She had been drifting for what seemed a long time but certainly was less than an hour. She was hungry and thirsty but could do nothing about either. This thought made her mad. Rita did not like bobbing around doing nothing. The more she thought about it, the angrier she got. It was all the fault of those pirates. She swore that if she ever got out of this mess, she would make somebody pay.

Eventually running out of things to worry about, Rita realized in addition to being hungry and thirsty, she was very tired. The gentle swells of the ocean were making her sleepy. She didn't fear falling asleep, but she wanted to stay alert. Her life jacket would keep her head above water. This was her final thought as she yawned widely, and her heavy eyelids closed.

Rita jerked awake with a start. She had fallen asleep. She was bobbing around gently, and it was still dark. Only not as dark as before. Looking up she was surprised to see a half-moon rising. She was pleased, then concerned. How long had she been out? Frowning she tried to remember when the moon had risen the night before. She wasn't sure but it seemed like it was near midnight. Had she really slept for several hours?

A bit of light didn't help much. She could now read her watch but it had stopped at 10:22. It must be later than that. Who knew how many more hours until dawn? Rita sighed.

She dozed here and there but the rest of the night passed so slowly that she felt disoriented. At one point she decided she was dreaming. After a seeming eternity, she realized the moon was setting. And there was the faintest lightening of the sky on the opposite horizon. Splashing, she turned herself that way and waited. Time passed as the sky gradually lightened.

Soon the sun rose, and Rita's spirits rose with it. As expected, there was little to see from her position down in the water, but it sure beat the hell out of the darkness. An hour later, she wasn't as happy. It wasn't even eight o'clock and the sun was already glaring in her eyes. She constantly pushed herself around in the water to keep her face out of the sun that was growing hotter every minute.

The ocean swell had picked up as well. By mid-morning Rita was regularly being lifted gently up as waves passed under her. Then she would slide down into a trough with a wall of green water rising up on each side of her. The wind was almost non-existent. Rita decided that she had drifted into some kind of current. The question was, where was it taking her? With no landmarks to give her perspective, she didn't even know what direction she was drifting.

As the day wore on Rita's thirst grew. Her tongue felt swollen, and her face was hot even though she regularly splashed water on it to cool her from the hot sun high overhead.

The swell gradually increased, raising her up and dropping her down. Finally, on one of the peaks above the surrounding ocean, Rita saw something. As she dropped down into the trough of a wave, she couldn't decide if it was a mirage or just her imagination.

She paddled to turn herself in what she thought was the right direction. The next wave lifted her and this time Rita was sure she saw something out across the water. Another cycle of lifting and sinking confirmed her vision.

There on the horizon was a smudge of land. From the position of the sun, she decided it was to the south. Was the current carrying her toward it or away?

The answer took time. An hour passed before she decided the dark strip of land on the horizon was gradually growing larger. The sun was off to her right so the island was south of her. Her eyes crusted with dried salt and her mouth so dry she could barely swallow, Rita tried to stay alert but found her eyes closing.

Rita woke with a start. The sun was low behind her. Weakly, she pushed at the water to turn herself southward. Her vision was blurred and she swiped at her eyes with her hand to clear them. It was then a sound came to her. To her hazy brain, it sounded like a periodic roaring gradually getting louder. She realized that her rise and fall was also quickening.

A wave taller than the rest raised her high enough to see some distance. It was then she realized the roaring sound was waves breaking on a shore. The island was very close now. Excited, Rita tried to swim in that direction but quickly found that life jackets are made for floating not swimming. She considered discarding it but knew in her exhausted condition she would quickly slip beneath the waves and drown.

As the waves began to pile up in the shallows Rita was tossed back and forth. She concentrated on keeping her head up and swallowing as little water as possible. Nearly exhausted, a large wave broke over her and pushed her underwater. She could feel herself being spun around in the translucent water. She held her breath. Her head finally broke water and she spit out water but before she could suck in fresh air she was spun, turned completely upside down, and hit something hard flat on her back. Stunned, she was tumbled through the surf and across rough sand and gravel.

Rita came to rest face down in hot sand. She lay there stunned, too exhausted to do anything but breathe. She could feel water washing over her feet and legs. All she could see was sand. With a groan, she got her arms under her torso and lifted her chest off the ground. Blinking several times, she could make out a green wall ahead and above her. Dropping back down she groaned. She had made it.

Mustering her strength, Rita rolled over on her back. She was surprised not to be looking up into a blazing hot sky. It took a moment to realize she was in shadow. She rolled over onto her left side and stared up the beach. The sun was low in the sky, dipping behind trees twenty yards west of her where the small beach disappeared.

Sitting up, Rita assessed her situation. She was alive. But she wouldn't be if she didn't find some water soon. She was badly dehydrated. With a groan, she rolled over slowly and pushed herself to her knees.

She got a foot under her and pushed herself upright. She swayed and nearly fell but somehow stayed on her feet and staggered toward the tree line. Under the cover of the trees, it was much cooler. There Rita found a solid tree and leaned against it for support. A few deep breaths later, she reached up and unbuckled her shoulder holster and let it drop at her feet. She shrugged out of her khaki shirt and wrung as much water out of it as she could. She then used it to wash the salt off her face and out of her eyes. That revived her somewhat and she peered around curiously.

She was just inside the tree line about thirty feet from where the waves were breaking on the small beach. Sunlight over the sea was coming in so low it was turning the ocean into a sea of red lava. The sun would be down in minutes. Tropical twilight would be short. She must try to find water before it was dark. Rita shrugged into her damp shirt, picked up her holster, and set off in a southerly direction.

The sand under her feet soon turned to dirt. The undergrowth was not too heavy but low-growing trees obscured her vision. Plowing ahead, Rita stopped periodically to lean against trees to get her breath back. She tried not to think of the thirst that was making her vision swim in and out of focus. She pushed onward, her shirt hanging open and her holster dragging from her hand.

She had gone what seemed like miles when a sound penetrated her consciousness. Her head came up as she listened to the alien yet familiar sound. It was the sound of an aircraft engine racketing to life. She listened for a moment surprised then opened her mouth to shout in joy. Instead, only a rough croak came from her parched throat. Angry, Rita took a breath and pushed through some bushes toward the welcome sound. Distance was hard to tell through the trees but it was loud enough to not be far off. Darkness was falling and Rita stumbled on a rock. Somewhere ahead the engine suddenly cut off. Rita continued on. It was dark now and she could see very little ahead of her. A minute later she pushed through some bushes and fell flat onto open ground.

Her face in the dirt, Rita spat and raised her head. It took a moment for what she saw to make sense. Across a cleared strip of ground was another wall of trees. On that side of a clearing that ran north and south, some kind of netting had been set up. Under this camouflage, an aircraft illuminated by lanterns was parked. Two men were closing up the cowling of this aircraft and talking to each other. Rita moved her head creakily to the right, farther south on the makeshift landing strip another camouflage netting was set up, and under it sat another aircraft. This bird, although illuminated by a lantern hung from a tree seemed deserted.

Rita was tired and dehydrated so it took a moment to sink in. She was too far to recognize the language, but those men weren't speaking English. The only people that could be running a secret airbase on a deserted island had to be *Viper*.

Rita knew she was in a lot of trouble. This island was probably crawling with *Viper* men and she was trapped here alone. Hell, maybe the sensible thing to do was surrender and beg for some water. Lying there in the dirt this sounded like a pretty good idea. Instead, Rita wiggled her way back into the brush.

Deciding she still had some fight left, she buttoned up her shirt, picked up the holster, and pulled out her revolver. She wiped it off with her shirttail and using just feel opened the cylinder and spun it. It seemed to move freely. Bringing it up to her face she blew as hard as she could around the open cylinder, trigger and hammer. She thrust it back into its holster and shrugged into it. She had no idea if it would fire or if the ammo would even work after being in the water so long but at least she was armed.

Using the trees, Rita worked her way down the west side of the airstrip using the lanterns for reference. A hundred yards south, the clearing ended. She worked her way across this end carefully. She could see and hear nothing from the area around the closest aircraft. Moving north along the trees she soon reached it. A wide area had been cut out of the trees. Netting covered it, held up by trees surrounding the ship. Rita studied the plane but did not recognize it. It was a large, single-engine, parasol monoplane. With an open cockpit under the wing and another cockpit behind it. Behind the parked ship was a tent, open on the side facing the strip and aircraft. It was in shadow but she could see what looked like a table or bench inside. Pulling her revolver out, Rita staggered toward the tent.

The only light came from a lantern hung in a tree near the nose of the ship, so the tent was shadowy. Rita could see a bench with what looked like tools and parts on it. Stacked nearby were rectangular metal cans. She rushed to them praying they were water cans. Pulling the flip lid on one open she was met with the smell of gasoline. Disappointed, Rita stepped back. As she did, she staggered with weariness and put out a hand to steady herself on the center tent pole.

Her hand struck not the pole but something metal that clanked against it. Frowning, she reached out again and touched the swaying object. When she realized it was a metal canteen hung from a strap, she dropped her revolver and scrabbled at the life-saving container with her fingers. Praying it was full she wrenched the canteen loose and pulled the cork. Lifting it up, she poured water over her waiting face and into her mouth.

The water was warm and stale but tasted like champagne as it flooded into her bone-dry mouth. Rita tried to swallow but couldn't. Her throat was closed up. Instead, she spit out some of the water and swilled the rest around in her mouth wetting her mouth and throat. Gradually the dry tissues absorbed moisture and soon Rita was able to swallow the precious liquid. She lifted the canteen and drank again, sinking to the ground with a sigh.

Rita sat there for some time, sipping and resting. Her head was rapidly clearing. She wasn't ready to take on *Viper* just yet, but she wasn't going to pass out in the dirt either. She pushed herself to her feet. Bending down she groped around and found her much-abused revolver. She thrust it back into its holster and was lifting the nearly empty canteen again when she froze. The sound of whistling came to her ears.

Her gaze darted around. Where to hide? She had no idea where the whistling was coming from. The only safe direction was to her rear. Getting down on her knees she crawled under the bench. She groped out her revolver and waited.

The whistling grew louder. Into her vision walked a single man. He was dressed roughly in workman's trousers and a khaki shirt. Over his shoulder hung a rifle. The sentry paused by the nose of the monoplane pulled out a cigarette, lit it, and glanced casually around while he breathed out smoke. Satisfied that all was quiet, he left heading north toward the other aircraft, whistling to himself.

Rita breathed a sigh of relief as she crawled from beneath the bench. This secret *Viper* base was probably where the submarine was operating from. What had happened to the sub? Was it here somewhere? She had to find out more about this base, but she also had to stay out of *Viper*'s hands.

Draining the canteen, she took the time to study the aircraft in front of her. It was about the same size as her belated A-12 with a radial engine and fixed landing gear. Somehow, it seemed trimmer and more graceful than the big A-12. The fixed gear was enclosed in streamlined fairings and almost delicate struts compared to the huge wheel spats of her Shrike. Rita put a foot on the step and pulled herself up to the cockpit. Leaning over the edge she peered around. The cockpit looked normal. She felt around carefully, finding the throttle and other controls. She also came up with

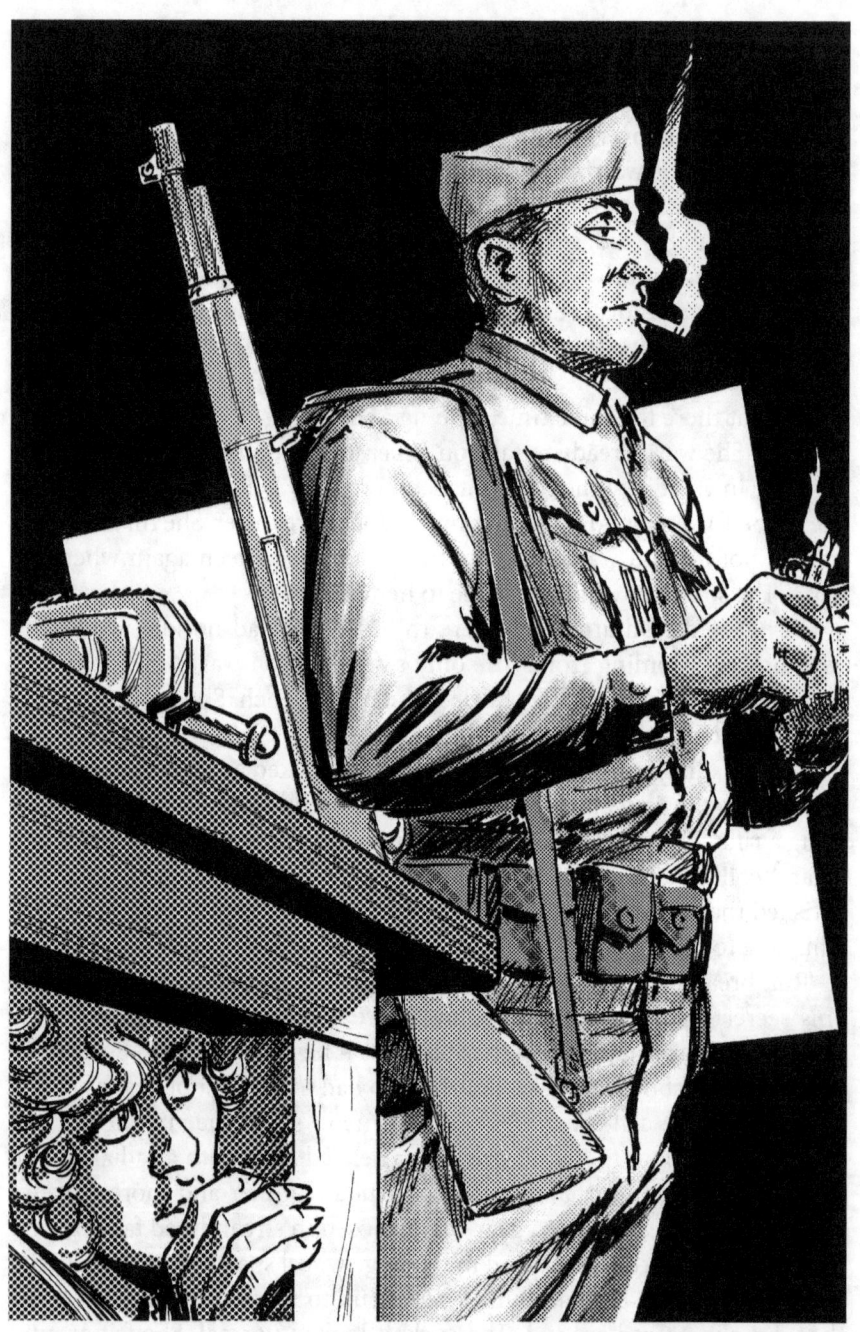

The sentry pulled out a cigarette, lit it, and glanced casually around...

a small flashlight. Delighted, she shielded it with her hand and carefully shone it around the cockpit. Surprisingly, the labels attached to the instrument panel were in German. She found the fuel gauge and noted that it read "Full." She clicked off the light and climbed down. *Viper* was certainly well equipped, Rita thought as she ducked around the nose of the ship. To the north, she could hear the muttering of voices. She could also see the sentry standing in front of the farther ship smoking a cigarette.

Nearby was an opening in the trees. Rita chanced a quick flash of her light. A dark path led eastward. Using the flashlight sparingly, Rita set off down the dark path. A few minutes later, she emerged into a large, cleared area. She ducked back under the shadow of a tree to observe.

Rita was surprised at how much better she felt after a little water. She was still weak and hungry, but her head was clearing fast as she observed the secret encampment. Underbrush and most trees had been cleared for some distance. Several large trees had been left to provide shade and cover. She could see netting strung from tree to tree to help conceal rough buildings built below the cover. She could count half a dozen buildings from where she stood. Some were dark. Several larger ones were illuminated by what she guessed to be lantern light. She could hear voices and occasional laughter.

Rita's attention was soon drawn to a small party of men walking through the camp using a lantern to light their way. She ducked as the three made their way to a small building set off by itself to the south of the main camp. As they neared, she could see two armed men escorting a third. The unarmed man was ushered into the small building and the door appeared to be locked behind him. The guards slung their rifles and departed, leaving the lantern hanging outside the prison building on a hook.

A prisoner? Rita was intrigued. A prisoner might have information about the base and its occupants; he was also a potential ally. She was tempted to speak with him but instead settled down behind the tree to watch. She was feeling better, but the growling of her stomach reminded her of her hunger. A half-hour later she heard voices behind her. Soon three men coming from the direction of the airstrip passed her. They were conversing in what sounded like Italian. They headed toward one of the larger buildings a hundred yards away.

Rita soon noticed things. One was the drone of a large engine somewhere on the other side of the camp. From the sound, it must be large diesel of some kind. A generator? Or perhaps the sound was the diesel engines of a submarine or other vessel. From the same direction, she could see a glow of light over the buildings. This was not the soft glow of lanterns but brighter electrical lights. She became convinced there must be some kind of dock or ship mooring in that direction.

Nearly half an hour later, a wandering guard came by the prison hut. He used a flashlight to shine through an opening in the door. Satisfied he moved on. Rita relaxed and continued to wait and watch. It was nearly an hour or more before another guard came by and checked on the prisoner.

Rita judged it was sometime around nine o'clock. Too early to make a move. She would rest here, watching and waiting for the camp to settle down. She wriggled around against the base of a tree until she found a comfortable position. She yawned. It had been a long day night and day. She need sleep but knew she was too wound up to doze off. Her eyes were heavy though and soon drifted closed.

She woke with a start. She froze wondering where she was and then the horrors of the battle and ocean came flooding back. Glancing carefully around, Rita heard very little; the night call of a bird, then a distant whistling tune. The camp was notably quieter. Rita cursed her dead watch, wondering what time it was. She must have slept for a while. It was still dark and quiet, but she knew the night must be fading. The good part was she felt refreshed. Her stomach protested its emptiness, but she felt better than she had since she had ditched her ship in the ocean. Standing up she looked carefully around. She saw no sign of movement.

Slowly, she crept out of the underbrush and slipped over the small prison hut. The door was dimly illuminated by a glass lantern hung alongside it. The door was roughly made but solid, as were the log walls. Good news, it was locked only by a metal bolt. A small, barred window about eight inches across was head high in the door. Standing on tiptoes she looked through but saw only blackness. Lifting down the lantern, she cautiously pushed the bolt back and pulled the door open.

Stepping in, the lantern in front of her, Rita looked around. To her left against the wall was a crude stool. On it sat a half-burned candle and a ceramic jug. Near it, rolled in a rough blanket was a man-sized figure; soft breathing came from the prisoner. She stepped forward and toed the sleeping figure. It jerked, turned over, and began to snore. Irritated, she kicked the figure less gently. It jerked and groaned, "Whaddya want?"

Rita was surprised to hear English. She leaned down and whispered loudly, "C'mon! Wake up! We haven't got much time!"

"Unhhhh..." the figure threw back the blanket and rolled over. Lifting himself up on one arm, the man held up his free hand against the light and squinted, "Who are you?"

In the lantern light, Rita got a look at the prisoner. What she could see looked good. His uncombed, brown hair hung in his face, but he had a strong jaw, covered in a rough beard. She couldn't tell the color of his eyes, but she could see intelligence gleaming in them. She decided he might be good-looking with a shave and a haircut.

Rita stepped back and said brightly, "I'm the rescue party." She pointed, "Is that water?"

The man looked confused, "What? Uh, yeah, water."

Rita set the lantern down turned and grabbed up the earthenware jug. Lifting it she drank deeply of the lukewarm water. Trickles of it ran down her cheeks. Finally, she lowered the jug and wiped her lips. Meanwhile, the captive had scrambled to his feet and picked up the lantern. Rita turned. On his feet, the former prisoner was tall and lean. His tee shirt was stained and torn. His rough work pants were equally stained. One knee showed through a rip. He wore worn sneakers bursting at the seams.

For his part, the lean man raised an eyebrow at the sight before him. He saw a tall redheaded woman dressed in the remains of what once might have been a khaki uniform. What he could see of her was pleasing, and he could see a great deal. One sleeve, torn at the shoulder, hung down to her elbow and her shirt gaped open. Her trousers had seen better days; they were filthy, and one leg was split from her thigh down nearly to her ankle showing an alarming amount of pleasantly shaped leg. A large revolver hung from a shoulder holster under her left arm. He shook his head and said, "Rescue parties sure have changed since I've been away."

Rita was surprised at the man's clearly American accent. Curious she asked, "Who are you and what are you doing here?"

The man essayed a tiny bow and smiled, "Bradley Monatague Cooper the third, at your service. And, I've been here ever since these pirates sank my ship and captured me, the bastards! But who are you and what's a wom-an doing on a rescue party?"

Rita frowned, she hesitated to tell this stranger too much about the Squadron's mission. So, she smiled brightly and said, "I'm Rita. Uh...Rita Burbank. And I'm just a scout. I followed their submarine here but was shot down. The rest of my people are looking for me though and they'll find this place soon. Right now, we've got to get out of here. C'mon."

Cooper's face showed surprise, then doubt, and finally acceptance, "Sure. Where are we going?"

"Well, I kinda thought since you've been here a while you might know a bit about the island," Rita said this with as much aplomb as she could while realizing how weak it sounded. Cooper looked askance at her before saying, "Well, we can figure out a plan later. Right now, we better get out of here before the guard makes his rounds."

"Uh, when is he going to be back?"

Cooper frowned, "How should I know? I've been asleep. Don't you know?"

"Well, uh, I was watching but I fell asleep and now it's late, and I uh. . ." she trailed off.

Bradley rubbed his chin through his beard, "They usually come by every hour or so when I'm awake. I don't know what they do this late. What time is it?"

Rita felt her face redden, "I'm afraid my watch has stopped."

Cooper mulled this over for a moment. He looked her up and down. And said with a smile, "Hmmm…I've got an idea. Here's what we're gonna try." As he whispered Rita frowned, then finally nodded.

Twenty minutes later, Rita heard low-voiced singing coming closer. She was crouched behind a tree stump about thirty feet from the front of the prison. Moments later a flashlight came into sight around the corner of a large building. Singing softly to himself the sentry sauntered toward the prison, flashlight leading his way. When he was close, Rita stood up and let out what she hoped was a startled squeak. The sentry froze and swung his light around. It swept past her, stopped, and swung back until she was fixed in its glare. Caught in the light, Rita made sure her bare leg was forward, moreover she had unbuttoned the second button on her shirt; the top one had ripped away. The sentry was swinging his rifle off his shoulder but stopped cold the weapon dangling from his arm, shocked to see a good-looking woman in ripped khakis spring up from the darkness. His mouth dropped open and he gasped out, "Gott in Himmel!"

The sentry was so fixed on the vision in front of him, he never heard Cooper creep around the corner of the prison, a solid tree limb in his hand. The sentry slumped silently to the ground never knowing what hit him.

Cooper grabbed the sentry under his arms and dragged him to the prison. Rita ducked ahead of him and opened the door. As Cooper dragged him inside, she grabbed up the rifle and flashlight. Five minutes later, Rita closed and bolted the door. The sentry tied and gagged with strips of his own clothes lay inside. Whispering to Rita, Cooper said, "Follow me." Carrying the rifle, he moved quietly toward the trees south of the camp. Rita followed her pistol in hand, hoping it would fire if the time came.

Safely inside the tree line, Cooper turned and asked, "What now?"

Rita thought a moment, "You know there's an airstrip here?"

"Sure, I've heard the planes land. I don't know where it is, though."

"It's west of here. It runs north-south. There were two light aircraft there earlier today."

"Great! Let's go see if we can steal one of those planes and get off this sand pile!"

Rita wanted to do just that but had thought a little further along, "Well, the thing is, I'm not sure if any of those aircraft have radios and I really need to get word to my squadron."

She could feel Cooper eyeing her, "Just who are you, and what kind of 'Squadron' has a girl flying for it? And just how did you happen to run into their sub?"

Rita frowned, "You've seen the sub?"

"Up close, they fished me out of the water and brought me here on it."

"Where's it anchored?"

"A lagoon on the east side of the island, on the other side of the camp."

Rita mulled that over. Cooper then said sarcastically, "I suppose you want to go see it."

"Not right this moment. There must be a radio around here somewhere. I need to get a hold of my people. If they know about this place, they can send help right away."

"All right, give. Who are you flying for and just what are you doing out here?"

Rita spoke carefully, "I'm flying for a private squadron. They're down here looking to find out what's happening to all these missing ships."

"Hmmnn…military?"

"Not exactly. We're kind of a private company that works for the government sometimes."

Cooper nodded, "Kinda like some of the groups fighting over in Spain. Working for their governments but on the sly."

He was uncomfortably close to the truth. Rita changed the subject, "Uh, sort of. Look, we really need to find that radio. Do you know where it is?"

"Sure. Their big radio is in the command bunker. Headquarters, actually."

Rita didn't like the sound of that, "Can we go there? I need to see it."

Cooper shrugged, "It's your funeral." He turned and pushed around a tree toward the camp. Rita followed. The two crept into the clearing and toward the shadowy buildings. They moved cautiously from building to building staying in the shadows. Only once did they glimpse movement. It was a guard moving among the buildings using a flashlight. They waited quietly until he had disappeared. Near the center of camp, they reached a large open-sided building. Creeping under the palm frond roof, they took cover behind some packing crates. Cooper gestured with a thumb and slowly lifted his head to peer over a crate.

The two were in deep shadow but could clearly see a building about forty yards away. To Rita's eye, it seemed like a low hill until she realized the large building was sunk halfway into the ground. Earth had been piled against the sides nearly to the roof. More earth was piled on top. Shallow, shuttered windows ran around what little vertical walls were visible. Light leaked through cracks in the shutters. The whole thing was concealed from above by netting strung from trees. A tall, metal antenna pierced the netting and reached twenty feet into the night sky. She realized why Cooper had called it a 'bunker.' It was bulletproof and bombproof save for a direct hit. The throbbing of a generator came from somewhere on the other side of it.

Cooper nudged her and pointed. Peering through the gloom, Rita finally made out what looked like the top of a door by the light leaking around it. Leaning over he whispered in her ear, "The door is sunken. I haven't been inside but every time I've been marched past it, people were coming and going. They must have someone in there on radio watch now."

Rita nodded and whispered back, "If we can get inside, I can send a message to my squadron. They have an advance base a hundred miles west of here. Once they know where to go, they'll have a squadron of attack planes overhead in an hour. After we send the message, we head for the airstrip. When our boys get here, their attack will give us the distraction we need to get a plane started and get away.

Cooper nodded and whispered, "I love a woman who has connections. But we're going to have to get inside there without raising an alarm."

"Got any ideas?"

"Well, it worked once…" Moments later Rita nodded. She shrugged out of her shoulder holster and handed it to Cooper. She stood up, ruffled her hair, and again unbuttoned the second button on her shirt. She took a deep breath, "Okay, here goes."

Stepping out into the moonlight, she walked boldly across open ground to the bunker. Sure enough, there were four steps dug into the ground leading down to a roughly built wood door. Light leaked around its edges. Rita stepped down to the door and pushed it open. Giving out a low cry of distress, she took two steps into the bunker and sank down in an apparent faint. As she crumpled to the hard-packed earth, Rita caught a glimpse of the startled face of a young man at a side cabinet.

The young, dark-haired mercenary knocked over his coffee cup as he turned in shock at the sight of a tall, beautiful redhead tumbling through the door of the command bunker. Setting down the pot he jumped forward calling out, "*Mon Dieu!*"

He knelt beside Rita, touching her on the bare shoulder and saying, "Mademoiselle?"

There was a soft thud. He looked up in surprise but all he saw before the night burst into fireworks was the butt of a rifle about to hit him in the nose.

Rita sat up and pushed the limp soldier off her as Cooper held a finger to his mouth. A voice from deeper in the bunker called, "Alain? Ques e passe -til?" He lunged up next to a doorway that led to an inner room. Rita got to her feet and stepped in front of the unconscious guard. As she did a figure appeared in the doorway. He stopped short at the sight of Rita. She held up her hands in apparent fright and he stepped through the open doorway.

Cooper prodded him with the rifle barrel and said something in a foreign language. The guard froze and slowly raised his hands. Cooper smiled and said, "Rita, darling, you're in the wrong business. You ought to be out in Hollywood. Better close that door before somebody walks by." She turned and quickly pushed the outer door closed.

"Good, now find something we can tie these two yahoos up with."

Rita looked around. The room contained a small camp desk, the side cabinet on which were a hot plate and spare cups, a bench, and an empty weapons rack. Ahead was the doorway through which the second guard had come. To her right was a darkened doorway. She brushed past Cooper into what turned out to be good sized room. It was dominated by a large table. Several maps adorned the rough walls: the Caribbean Sea, the Lesser and Greater Antilles, Cuba, and Puerto Rico. To her right was a lighted doorway.

Rita entered this room and found it. The room was dominated by a bench holding two complete radio set-ups: receivers, transmitters, a morse key, and microphone. In front of this was a battered roll-around chair much like the one back in the Squadron radio room.

To her right gaped a darkened doorway. She entered this and groped for a light switch. She found one, flipped it, and found herself in the office of whoever was commanding this *Viper* unit. There was a desk, chairs, and a battered file cabinet. A door led out to the entry room. She could see the body of the guard on the floor.

Rita longed to search the room. There would certainly be crucial information here about *Viper*'s activities in the region. Unfortunately, there was no time. Shaking her head, Rita ducked back into the radio room. Rummaging around she found a roll of black electrical tape. She grabbed it up and ran back to where Cooper was holding the guard at gunpoint.

"I found some tape; best I could do."

"Okay, tie up sleepyhead first. Look in his pocket for a knife." Sure enough, Rita found a pocketknife in the unconscious man's pants pocket. Using it, she cut lengths of tape and quickly bound his hands and feet. Next, she tied up the standing guard. Lowering his rifle, Cooper nodded at her work, went to the side cabinet, and began searching. He asked, "Find anything interesting?"

"I found the big cheese's office and the radio room."

Cooper grunted positively and came up holding some towels which he proceeded to tear into strips, "Can you work it?"

"I think so."

"Good, crank it up while I get rid of these two." He then began gagging the prisoners. Rita ducked past into the radio room. Sitting down in front of the bench she looked things over. The equipment was modern with labels in German. She picked up a headset and reached for the frequency dial. She paused as she heard a muttered curse behind her. Through the doorway, she could see Cooper rolling a body under the table.

The set was already warm. They probably kept a radio watch twenty-four hours a day here. Fitting the headset over her head, Rita was ready to transmit when Cooper appeared at her shoulder. "Can you make that thing work?"

"With this set, I can talk to anybody." She pulled the morse key over in front of her and tentatively tapped the key twice. Cooper asked, "Morse? Can't you reach your people with voice?"

"Not sure. Don't know the range of this set so Morse is a better bet. More range."

"Okay. But whatever you do, do it quick. Have you seen the time?"

Rita half turned to her partner; he pointed. High on one wall a clock ticked away silently. The time read 4:45. Rita said, "Sunrise in an hour and a half. But it'll be getting light in less than an hour. You need light for take-off."

"So, it'll be a couple of hours until we can expect your pals?"

Rita chewed her lip, "An hour flight time at full throttle…yeah, close to that."

"Okay, that'll give us time to get over to the airstrip and scout out a plane. We'll have to gamble nobody finds these two birds for a while. Send your message and let's get going. I'm gonna watch the door."

Hefting the rifle, Cooper gave Rita a smile and faded away through the doorway. Turning back to the set Rita took a deep breath, reached for the key, and began tapping, "Squadron 13, Squadron 13. Do you read me, over?" Only silence answered her. Rita minutely adjusted the frequency and tapped again, "Squadron 13, Squadron 13, please respond."

Moments later clicking sounded in her headset. Rita grabbed up a pencil and took down the fast morse words, "This is Squadron 13. Who are you and why are you using this frequency? Over"

Rita tapped out, "This is Rita. Trapped on secret *Viper* base. Request immediate assistance. Is squadron leader available?"

There was a slight pause then came, "Wait one."

Rita let out a whoop! Most likely they were fetching Captain Ron. From somewhere out of sight Cooper's voice came, "You wanna hold it down. This is Indian country, y'know."

"Sorry, but I raised the squadron. I knew they'd be listening for me!"

"Good. Hurry it along. We need to get out of here soon."

Moments later quick morse sounded in her headset, "Unknown station, say again your identity."

She tapped, "This is Rita, radio operator for the squadron. Was shot down answering *SS Donegal's* distress signal. Is the captain there?"

The answer came quickly, "Standing by. What is your situation?"

Elated, Rita quickly tapped out the signal she had rehearsed, "Shot down by enemy submarine. Washed ashore next day on small island. Located HQ of *Viper* operations in this area. Island located somewhere south of *Donegals'* last position and somewhere north of Anguilla Island. Submarine damaged and under repair here. Hidden airstrip and considerable troops and equipment located here. Request immediate air support."

A pause and then, "Wait one."

Seconds ticked by and Rita fidgeted. Cooper was right. They were on borrowed time. Finally, tapping came to her ears, "Squadron ready. We're coming for you as soon as we can. Island not found on our charts. Can you send constant signal for us to home in on?"

She sure could! Rita grinned and tapped out, "Roger. Will continue sending. This is Radio Rita calling, one two three, four, five. Fix on my signal. Repeat, Radio Rita calling one two, three, four, five."

A whispered voice came from behind her, "How we doing, darling?"

Fiercely, she whispered back. "They're coming! I'm sending a signal for them to home in on."

"Great!"

Rita kept tapping out her signal as she looked up at the clock. Nearly five o'clock. The squadron couldn't take off until first light but at least they were coming.

Ron Forster stood on the edge of the darkened runway. Around him, powerful radial engines were roaring to life. Men carrying flashlights and lanterns darted among the shadowy aircraft. A tall, strongly built man ran up to Forster and half saluted, "Ships are ready, Ron. All we need is some light."

"Full fuel and bomb load.?"

"Yep. Loaded to the gills. Can Rita hold out until we get there?"

"Don't know. But we're not waiting." He pointed with a flashlight, "Get some of the mechanics with lanterns and station them down the runway. And get somebody to build fire at the end of the strip. Use rags and gasoline. We need something to give us perspective."

Twirling the end of his magnificently waxed mustache, Davidson's eyes twinkled, "You got it, Ron." Turning, he raised his voice calling for help as he jogged away. Forster used the flashlight to illuminate his watch. It was nearly five a.m. An hour's flight away. He would cut that time once in the air if he could. No telling if Rita could hold out where she was. He turned and jogged toward one of the idling aircraft calling out orders as he went.

Rita kept up her steady morse, tapping out "Radio Rita calling," every few seconds. Finally, she heard morse code in her headset, "Have your di-

"They're coming! I'm sending a signal for them to home in on."

rection fixed. Squadron taking off now. Find cover away from vital targets. Keep your head down. Help is on the way. Good luck."

Rita sighed with relief. The squadron was on its way. She quickly tapped out one final message, "Wilco. Am abandoning this position. Will take shelter near airstrip and try to capture an aircraft. Shutting down. Radio Rita, out."

Reaching out, she spun the dial off the Squadron frequency, then flipped off the power switch. As she stood up, a drawer in the underside of the bench caught her eye. Jerking it open she found pencils, paper, and a revolver. She grabbed it and ducked through the now-darkened conference room. The outer room was also dark. It took a moment to locate Cooper. He was next to the partially open outer door peering into the night.

She crept up next to him and whispered, "We're good to go."

"It's about time! Who were you talking to, your aunt Martha?"

"Very funny! They had to get a fix on my transmission. They got it and said they're ready to take off. They'll have to wait for enough light but the important thing is, they're coming. And they know we'll be hiding out near the airstrip. We'll be safe there."

"Good. What time is it?"

"A little after five. Is the coast clear?"

"It was a second ago." Cautiously, Cooper pulled the door open enough to get his head out. He looked for several seconds, then suddenly pulled his head back and closed the door softly, "Oh, no! A wandering guard. He's stopped to have a smoke." Rita's heart jumped into her throat. A few seconds later Cooper cracked the door and peered out. He watched carefully for a couple of minutes and Rita finally hissed, "What's happening?"

Cooper waved her off with his free hand and kept watching outside. A couple of minutes later he leaned back and said, "Okay, the guard's moved off. Let's go. Say, where'd you get the pop gun?"

Glancing down at the borrowed revolver, she said, "Found it in the radio bench."

Handing her back her holster and gun, Cooper said, "Good. It might come in handy."

Cooper pulled open the door and slipped into the night. Rita quickly followed pulling the door closed behind her. The two crouched down on the sunken steps, their heads just at ground level. Peering around she whispered, "The airstrip is west. Which way do we go?"

Cooper looked up at the sky and pointed toward the moon, now low in the sky shining through tall trees, "That way." He stood up and took the steps to ground level, Rita right behind him. Suddenly there was a shout in the darkness ahead of them. The two froze. A second later an answering shout came.

Cooper spun around, "Get down!" he hissed. He dropped down on the steps. Rita jumped down next to him, "What is it?"

"Somebody must have found the guard we left tied up."

They lay there quietly. Soon flashlights could be seen among the buildings and more voices were heard.

Cooper whispered, "We'll never make it past the guards, now. We're stuck."

"What do we do?"

Cooper shook his head, "I guess we hole up here and hope the Cavalry gets here in time." He gave her a weak smile, turned, and ducked back to the door behind them. Rita followed and pushed the door closed. Cooper was pulling on the end of the cabinet, "Gimme a hand!" Between the two of them, they pulled the heavy cabinet up against the back of the door. Quickly they lifted the camp desk atop it. The bench followed.

"C'mon." Grabbing his rifle, Cooper ducked through the door into the conference room. He laid down where he could point his weapon through at the entry door. Rita took up a place beside him.

"There's no one supposed to be in here but the radio guy. No reason to search in here," Rita said hopefully.

"They'll go wake up the commander and alert other guards but sooner or later they'll come a knocking."

Minutes later the door rattled. A questioning voice called out in a foreign language. Cooper put a finger to his lips. A moment later the voice shouted louder through the door. Then someone began pounding on it. This ceased after a moment. Minutes later something hit the door so hard it rattled in its frame. The door was hit again. They heard a board splinter. Cooper lifted his rifle and fired through the upper door. Rita raised her revolver and fired as well. The hammer fell with a click. She swore and pulled the trigger again. The cylinder rotated and the second cartridge fired. Meanwhile, Cooper had worked the bolt and fired again. Rita continued pulling the trigger. Two more rounds fired, while two more were duds. She was surprised that any had fired at all after all day in the sea. Rita holstered her gun and picked up the liberated weapon.

Cooper had ceased firing. The two waited. There was silence from outside. Cooper fed cartridges into his rifle. He whispered to Rita, "It doesn't look too good, does it?"

Before she could answer, a voice from outside yelled out; in German, Rita was pretty sure. Whomever it was waited a minute and yelled out in English, "You in there; throw out your guns and come out. If you don't, we'll open fire."

Cooper laid a calming hand on Rita's arm and whispered, "Shhhhh!"

After another minute another voice yelled out, in Spanish this time. Cooper yelled back in very good Spanish. There was a pause before the voice replied. Cooper and the unknown voice called back and forth for a couple of minutes before Cooper finally whispered, "They seem confused about who we are. I'm stalling."

"Good. Help's on the way."

Time was running short though. There was a shout outside and a dozen guns opened fire outside, the bullets tearing through the door and windows.

Taking off in the dark with only a few lanterns for light had been exciting, to say the least. But everyone was now safely in formation at five thousand feet. A glance to starboard showed the running lights of two A-12s. The other two were off to port. Forster didn't like the lights but formation flying at night was dangerous. He couldn't risk a mid-air collision or someone getting lost. He looked down at his gauges, illuminated in the dark. Course 071. Speed 150 knots. He leaned forward and pushed on the throttle trying to get more speed out of the ship. Behind him, he could hear his gunner swinging his gun around and cocking it. A glance at his watch showed it was five twenty. He cursed silently, willing the aircraft to go faster.

Fortunately, only the top two feet of the walls were visible above the banked earth. Rita and Cooper were flat in the conference room doorway. The bullets screaming through the upper walls and long, narrow windows were safely above them. Splinters and dust spun through the air. After a couple of minutes, the fusillade tapered off. The shouted voice came to them clearly through the now splintered shutters. After a moment Cooper shouted back a brief answer. Rita asked, "What did you say?"

"Nothing printable. Get back. They'll try something else now." Rita wiggled back and then thought of something. She quickly crawled toward the radio room. It was the only room with any lights on. Reaching the bench, she stood up and started flipping switches. Suddenly Cooper was at her elbow pulling her, "What are you doing?' Get down!"

"I wanted to warn the squadron we're under attack here."

"It's too late for that. They couldn't help if..."

Suddenly, through the shattered window above the radio, a round metal shape flew. The grenade bounced off the bench to the floor. Rita recognized it and, without thinking, kicked out wildly with the side of her foot and sent it spinning into the darkness of the Commander's office. This happened as a second grenade coming through the window bounced off the top of the radio and right at Cooper. He caught it and flipped it back through the window to the outside.

The grenades went off almost simultaneously. The explosion outside came with a scream. The one in the next office filled the bunker with a cloud of papers, dust, and debris. Rita felt herself jerked backward. She ended up on her back coughing, dust in her face. It was dark and her ears were ringing slightly. She felt Cooper shoving her and bumped into a wiggling warm body. Realizing she was under the conference table, she felt around for Cooper. Not realizing she still had a gun in her hand she was surprised when he yelled out, "Oww! Watch it with that thing!"

"Sorry."

Rita could see almost nothing. She coughed, spat and was going to ask a question when there was a crash against the barricaded door. This was followed quickly by another crash. Cooper fired his rifle. He worked the bolt and fired again. Rita crawled up next to him and fired the liberated revolver. She fired again. Cooper as well. Seconds later silence fell over the bunker. She felt Cooper move next to her and heard clinking. He whispered, "Seven rounds left. How about you?"

"Three. You know a lot about guns."

"Yeah, picked it up in Spain."

Rita raised an eyebrow, "You fought in Spain?"

"Yeah, I was with the Lincoln Brigade for nearly two years."

"So that's why you speak Spanish."

"'Fraid so. You know, I'm sorry your friends didn't make it in time. I'd like to tell them what a great gal they have flying for them."

Rita thought this over for a moment, "I'm sorry too. What do you think they'll try next? More grenades?"

"If it was me, I'd blow the door with explosives."

"Oh."

At that second the door blew inward with a tremendous bang! Debris and shrapnel flew through the front room. On their stomachs and back in the conference room under the table, the two were shielded from the blast. Rita was still coughing as she heard Cooper fire next to her. She got her head up and saw men spilling down the steps and pushing past the ruins of the door and cabinet. Cooper fired again. So did she. Silhouetted by flashlights they were easy targets. The attackers were firing as well and bullets crisscrossed the outer room. Rounds came through the conference room door but far above the two defenders.

Suddenly the attackers stopped coming. In the silence, they could hear men groaning in pain. Rita shakily whispered, "Last round."

Cooper leaned in and whispered, "Two rounds left. I guess this is it. It's been nice, Rita. Wish I could take you to dinner somewhere nice in Baltimore. Mom would love to meet you."

Impulsively, Rita leaned in and quickly kissed Cooper. She pulled back but was still shoulder to shoulder with him, "It's been a pleasure rescuing you Bradley Montague Cooper."

"The third," Cooper said with a smile.

Before Rita could reply, there came a shout from outside. She brought her revolver up and aimed at the lighter opening of the door. Then a distant roar of thunder came to her ears, low but rapidly growing louder. More shouts came from outside followed by a flurry of shots, but not at the bunker.

Beside her, Cooper muttered "What the hell—" he was cut off as the bunker filled with the roar of machine guns and a radial engine screaming overhead. A second later the ground shook as an explosion rocked the bunker. This was immediately followed by more ground-shaking explosions. Rita got to her knees screaming, "They made it! That's Squadron 13. Yay!!!!

Jumping to his feet, Cooper grabbed her by the arm and yelled to be heard over the noise, "We have to go! C'mon Rita, before your friends kill us." Pulling the remains of the cabinet out of the way, they stepped over and across bodies to climb the blood-soaked steps. Rita realized the sky was lightening with false dawn. All around them was chaos. Buildings were burning. Explosions were going off everywhere. Men were running in all directions. Overhead another Shrike roared by at fifty feet, its machine-guns spitting into the camp. Standing up Cooper pointed and yelled, "That way!" He pushed Rita and the two took off running through the camp.

They passed men running chaotically here and there. They were totally ignored; everyone concentrating on their own survival. The *Viper* base had been taken completely by surprise. Two minutes later, Rita and Cooper reached the western tree line. Most of the action was behind them with aircraft flashing past overhead. Smoke drifted everywhere and the crackling of fires burning was a background to explosions and gunfire. It took a few moments to locate the path through the underbrush but soon they were plunging down the narrow path. Suddenly the jungle shook to an explosion. The two skidded to a stop and looked at each other, "Did that come from the airstrip?"

Rita gritted her teeth, "Maybe. We better go carefully." The two continued carefully up the shadowy path; soon the trees opened up. To their right, a pillar of black smoke spiraled up from the burning *Viper* aircraft. As they watched, a squadron Shrike screamed across the runway west to east firing at the camp behind them.

Rita turned south and jogged down the edge of the trees, Cooper next to her. They quickly reached the aircraft that Rita had seen the night before. Pushed back in the trees under netting it had not been spotted by the raiders, "Thank God," Rita said with relief and started forward under the wing.

At that moment, a man in rough clothing appeared around the tail of the aircraft. He had a pistol in his hand. Rita brought up her revolver, remembering it had only one round left. The man did the same. Before either could fire, a rifle cracked from behind her and Rita stared as the *Viper* mercenary was thrown backward off his feet, his pistol flying away.

Shocked for an instant, Rita stared as Cooper yelled, "Rita! Get this thing started. We gotta go!"

Rita threw down the revolver and jumped for the aircraft scrambling up its side. She grasped the edge of the parasol wing and dropped into the forward cockpit. As she reached for switches, she could see Cooper pulling the wooden chocks away from the wheels.

Master switch on. Fuel pump on. Throttle to half. Mixture to rich. Rita was just reaching for the starter switch when a head appeared next to her shoulder. Cooper, standing on the lower footrest, hung on the edge of the cockpit. Rita looked at him and said, "Here goes!" She pushed the starter button and held it. A whine built up; the propeller started turning slowly. It spun faster, then coughed and slowed. The engine backfired and the propeller spun faster as the engine caught with a roar. Airstream from the prop rushed over them. Rita grinned at Cooper, "Need a ride?" Cooper grinned back and scrambled up the side and dropped into the second cockpit behind Rita. She did not have a flying helmet or anything to hold her hair back and it whipped around as she buckled her seat belt. Or a parachute, she thought as she quickly pushed the throttle. The aircraft rolled forward. As they reached the rough runway, Rita stood hard on the right brake. It locked and the ship's tail came quickly around until the ship was pointed north down the strip.

Rita shoved the throttle to the firewall, and they rolled forward. Quickly gaining speed the tail came up and the ship lifted off cleanly after less than four hundred yards. Keeping the stick back Rita concentrated on gaining altitude. She felt a hand pounding on her shoulder as she reached a thousand feet. Looking back, she saw Cooper pointing frantically over his shoulder toward the tail.

When Rita looked back. She was startled to see one of the squadron's A-12s coming right at her. It was closing the distance quickly and Rita suddenly realized it thought they were *Viper* pilots escaping. She pulled the stick hard over to the right, quickly leveled out, and began rocking the stick side to side. This had the effect of waggling her wings. She stuck her free arm up as far as she could and waved. Behind her, Cooper had his arms up waving as well.

The A-12 bored in. Rita waited for the flashing of the machine guns. Three seconds later the A-12 screamed overhead; it did not fire. A minute later the squadron ship fell into place off Rita's port wingtip. The pilot waved. Rita returned the wave and felt herself relax. She was back with the squadron.

The next morning, Rita stood on the edge of Squadron 13's advanced airstrip. Thirty yards away the Lockheed Orion transport sat, passenger door open, engine idling. Rob Davidson stood near it. Rita turned to Cooper standing next to her, "Rob will have you in Puerto Rico in a couple of hours. You should be able to catch a Pan Am clipper back to the mainland in a few days. Where are you going when you get home?"

Cooper looked off into the distance, "Home. Maryland. I'm sure Mr. and Mrs. Cooper will be glad to have their prodigal son and heir home safely. It's been a couple of years after all…"

"Heir?"

"Yeah. Didn't I tell you that I'm kind of rich? Or will be someday when Bradley Montague Cooper the second heads for that great silver mine in the sky."

Rita was annoyed, "No, you didn't tell me that. But I'll bet it's a heck of a story."

"Kind of. I'll tell you when you come and visit me. I still owe you a dinner."

"You certainly do."

Cooper smiled and swept Rita up in his arms. Surprised, Rita stiffened, but melted as Cooper pressed his lips hard to hers. Time faded for a bit. Finally, he dropped her back to her feet. He stepped back and fondly said, "You are one heck of a woman, Rita Burbank. I'm gonna miss you."

Rita was at a loss for words for a moment but finally nodded, "Thanks for everything Coop. I have to say, you really know how to show a lady a good time. I look forward to our second date."

Smiling as he turned to jog toward the Lockheed, Cooper called out, "So do I."

Reaching the ship, Rob said to Cooper as he turned to wave one last time, "Our Radio Rita is some gal, isn't she?" Stepping up into the transport, Cooper said, "She sure is."

Having given the two friends a moment, Ron Forster stepped up next to Rita as she watched the Orion taxi out and line up for take-off. As the transport gathered speed, Ron said, "Seemed like a good man."

"He is that. I'll miss him."

"Uh, huh. Say, what was that Rita Burbank stuff?"

"I wasn't sure how much to tell him about the squadron or our mission when we met. And, I hesitated to give him my name. So, Burbank was the first thing that popped into my mind. It's something my dad said once."

The two turned and walked toward the squadron buildings. Ron said, "Things have gone pretty good for us Rita, and you were a big part of that."

"Thanks, skipper."

"It seems a shame to waste the talents of a pilot as good as you. So, even though we're an aircraft short until we can get a replacement flown in, I'm putting you into the flight rotation."

Rita stopped dead in her tracks, "What?"

"But, you're still in charge of communications."

"But, but."

"That's right. Radio Rita will now be a pilot as well as communications officer." Smiling at the surprised look on Rita's face, Ron continued, "Now, let's go take a look at that captured Henshel. I'm interested in how *Viper* got its hands on modern German equipment like that. Grinning widely, Rita fell in step with her commander.

The End

Radio Rita Calling...

I'm used to writing characters I did not create. Geez, I'm a pulp writer for pity's sake. That's what they do. And, I am actually proud to name myself a pulp writer. I see myself in fine company and carrying on an honorable tradition. Still, the latest assignment I took on was unique as far as I know, even for the pulps.

It happened this way…Airship 27 has quite a following online. I'm not too involved with this as I avoid online stuff as much as possible. Why? Well, for one thing, the internet is not and never will be safe. Also, I'm a rather private person. I tend to keep my private life (and ego) off the internet. So, I am often not on top of all the strange things that happen online. Thus, I was somewhat surprised when Ron Fortier started talking about some mythical personages that somehow got created for the Airship. Soon there were even some character sketches floating around. All well and good, I was amused by them but not too interested until Ron decided that he needed to flesh one out and actually wanted stories written about her. He even proposed an anthology with four adventures written for someone dubbed Radio Rita.

Now, here's where it got very interesting. Ron wanted four different writers to make up a pulp adventure featuring this mythical Airship 27 character using nothing but the briefest physical description. The story could be set anywhere and in any time period as long as it featured the attractive, young flyer. The writer was to make up everything else about her, including her personality and back story.

Curtiss A-12 Shrike

This was enough to make me set up in my command chair and stare at my computer screen. Hmmnnnn…an intriguing idea. As I have said, I'm used to working with other people's characters and I'm used to making up my own. But this was something different. And, I would actually be working simultaneously with other writers doing the same thing with none of us knowing what the others were writing. It took me all of about thirty seconds to decide, "I'm in."

I quickly wrote Ron and he graciously accepted my proposal and I joined a talented group of writers working away on bringing Radio Rita to life. That's right; she doesn't even have a last name. This was going to be fun!

One of the things that tipped me over to committing to this project was the fact that Rita is a woman. I love writing women characters and have had some modest success with Domino Lady and some of my original female protagonists. So, lots of ideas for Rita came immediately to mind. I quickly decided a couple of things; First, I wanted my Rita to be fixed firmly in a classic pulp time frame and story and it had to have lots of classic pulp feel. This meant the nineteen-thirties or at least the forties. And second, since Rita is a homage to Airship 27, I wanted it to have a personal feel for Captain Ron and Chief Engineer Rob.

With that decided, I went to the bookshelf and pulled down an old copy of Frank V. Martinek's Don Winslow of the Navy and re-read it for the first time in many years. It confirmed my thoughts as to a storyline and away I went. I said earlier that this was going to be fun and the writing of it was. It was getting to the writing that was the problem.

When Ron threw this proposal out for grabs, I was knee-deep in another writing project. I dropped everything when Ron picked me and worked hard on a detailed outline. Normally the more detailed my outline the faster the actual writing goes. Mine was nearly two thousand words. Satisfied, I longed to dig in right away but trying to be at least somewhat organized, I reluctantly went back and finished my then-current story. Back to *Frequency*, or so I thought. Unfortunately, I now found myself running up against another deadline that took priority. Finally, nearly two, months later, I was ready and began writing.

I would like to say it was easy work from there, but I got off to a rather slow start. The intro and character development were tricky, and I had to do more research. I wasn't totally satisfied with the first thousand words or so but once past that, things smoothed out considerably. Most of *Frequency* is flying and action scenes and this I do very well. Writing then moved along quickly and I had a lot of fun writing Rita in action. A couple of weeks and I was through it and fairly satisfied.

Every story needs revisions… at least mine do. I then got to go back and smooth out that intro and a couple of other rough areas, along with the usual grammar errors, (Who wrote this stuff?). But the story was solid and came together nicely. I also had to pare the story down by over three thousand words. Yes, I'm afraid I got carried away with our lovely aviatrix's adventures. But it's now a better story than when I started.

From the beginning, one of my goals was to make Rita's story very much part of Airship 27. She is after all a creation of Airship fans and creators, so I worked hard to integrate some familiar figures into it. I hope I succeeded, and I hope you enjoy *Frequency*. While writing it, I had lots of fun dropping hints and leaving clues for

Brad Cooper

you Airship fans as well as all you classic pulp aficionados. Ten bonus points for those figuring out Rita's true background.

Is this the last we will hear about Rita? Only Captain Ron knows for sure. Maybe he will be back soon with even more authors' views of the Airship's lovely heartthrob. Speaking of that; I am terminally curious as to my fellow authors take on our unofficial Airship pinup girl. Ron is playing his cards close to the vest on this topic and I have no idea what the other writers have in store for our lovely heroine. Can't wait to read this new anthology. It should be quite a ride.

Take care and I'll see you next time loyal airmen (& women).

GENE MOYERS - studied European and Medieval history at the University of Oregon. He is also a U.S. Army veteran. He worked in the high-tech industry for some time and is also a licensed massage therapist.

An avid military gamer and roleplayer, his favorite game was Daredevils a pulp-based roleplaying game set in the 1930s. His love affair with the 1930s and pulps in particular stem from his first time reading a Shadow novel as a boy. Although interested in writing since a teen he did not turn to serious writing until 2000.

He is the co-author of GURPS Crusades published by Steve Jackson Games. He has written several stories for Airship 27 including stories published in all of the Purple Scar volumes, all of the Domino Lady volumes, Mystery Men and Women vol.5, The Phantom Detective vol.1, Moon Man vol. 2, Dan Fowler vol.3 and The Legends of New Pulp Fiction. He has also written a story published in Alternative Air Adventures for Pro Se Publications and one published in I.V Frost Scientific Detective for Moonstone Books.

When not working on various new pulp projects, he is busy writing alternate history stories or horror adventures for his occult investigator, the Dream Master. Safe from Covid-19 in his hidden sanctum deep in the forests of the Great Northwest, Gene currently continues writing, carefully watched over by his wife and two lazy dogs.

Operation Rocket Man

By Mel Odom

"Burt," I drawled laconically, "what does a girl wear to her kidnapping? This *is* my first time to be kidnapped, you know."

Me getting kidnapped was the first leg of the mission the generals were calling Operation Rocket Man. I thought the name was dumb, but I didn't name these things.

Despite the devil-may-care attitude I put on, I'd admit to a smidgen of uneasiness at the prospect of being kidnapped. But I wouldn't admit to any more than that. A girl must maintain appearances after all. And I'd never admit any uneasiness whatsoever to the man in my dressing room.

Burt Kimble, secret agent to President Roosevelt himself and standing near the doorway to the tent where I was presently ensconced somewhere in France, stopped twirling his fedora on his forefinger and frowned at me. There was something about his dark gray eyes that hinted at a stormy nature and violence. I'd been around him long enough to see the violence, and he was never a mirthful guy.

He had what I'd heard called a *lupine* face, and he looked like a wolf. A nice wolf, though, not one of those guys who just wanted to put his hooks on a girl. He was of medium height and lanky, the kind of guy most people, certainly those of the feminine persuasion looking for a guy with class and money, would overlook if they passed him on the street and didn't bother to look straight at him. He didn't smack radars as handsome or loyal. Maybe he wasn't much to look at by some women's standards, but he was the most loyal guy I knew.

Not that there were any streets to pass him by on where we currently were. I, and the other entertainers of the United Service Organizations at the camp, had been brought in by an Army truck from a barely-there airstrip that had me respecting the pilot's skills a lot more after the landing than I had during takeoff. He hadn't had much to work with on the ground here, and he'd put us down with hardly a bump in what looked like the countryside.

In fact, I didn't know *where* we were. I had no real clue other than it was somewhere near the front in France. And if I had known our location, I couldn't have told anyone because I was "under orders." USO entertainers, like Bob Hope, Dinah Shore, and my personal favorite, Marlene Dietrich, were considered part of military operations while we were on the Foxhole Circuit. Which was practically within spitting distance of the war. As Bob often joked, on stage and in private, we were "in the army now."

"Don't try riling me up about this," Burt growled. He was a little more prickly than usual. "I'm already none too keen on this cockamamie *scheme* the brass has cooked up."

I looked in the mirror in front of me and brushed powder across my cheeks to give me that freshness that was in all my pin-up posters. This close to the front, with the bombing going on "right down the road," so to speak, nights weren't always restful. That expected freshness came out of a jar these days.

"I thought you said this was the best plan *they* could come up with," I said.

"The best plan they could come up with," Burt growled. "I didn't say it was the best one *I* could come up with."

I glanced at his reflection in the mirror. "You think you could come up with a better plan?"

"Give me five minutes."

I smiled at him, in support, not to poke fun at his self-aggrandizing claim. Burt Kimble was a smart man. While working behind enemy lines in Europe, he'd saved my life a few times. Of course, I'd saved his too. We were probably pretty even on that score, and we'd been together long enough that we no longer kept count of who saved whom.

We'd both lost people in this war, though, and that remained constantly in the back of our minds. We just made it a point to never talk about those losses. Time to time, when we split a bottle of wine or whiskey, we got quiet, and we both knew why.

"I'm sure you had five minutes while they were going over this plan." I put my powder brush back in my makeup kit. I put on confidence with the makeup. It was always like that for me. Having time to take care of myself was important. "If you'd have thought of something, you'd have told them, and we'd have been doing that. We're not doing something else, so we're doing this."

I looked in the mirror. My fiery red hair tumbled down to my shoulders in big curls in the best way possible. I had good cheekbones, a generous mouth, and lips I'd covered in a good shade of red that complemented my hair and fair complexion, and I had emerald green eyes that Edward G. Robinson had told me were the prettiest he'd ever seen. I'd believed he'd meant it at the time. I still did.

I looked good.

Especially for as nervous as I was. Oh, I wouldn't let Burt know I was worried because that would only worry him more. When I acted like bullets would bounce off me like Superman, he didn't like it too much. He didn't like those times I thought I was cleverer than Felix the Cat much either. Where I was headed, straight into the jaws of possible death, I could have used Felix's Magic Bag of Tricks.

"You can always say no," Burt told me.

I swung around on the ammunition crate I was using for a vanity chair and smiled at him. "When the big man asks me to do something, do I ever say no?"

The "big man" was what we called President Roosevelt so no one who was listening in would know whom we were talking about.

Burt sighed, and those gray eyes looked less stormy and a little sadder. "No, you don't."

"You don't say no either," I told him. "You could have let someone else work with me."

"That's not happening," he growled, and the storm was back in his eyes. "Ever. You and me, since we teamed up back in Los Angeles, that's how it's going to be. If you're out in the field on an operation, I'll be right there."

"Well okay then. Right back at you."

We were uncomfortably quiet for a moment in that cramped canvas tent the camp commander had given me to use as a dressing room. I was lucky. Since I was the only woman on the USO team who'd landed here, I had my own space. The four guys had to share a tent that was probably the same size as this one.

The space was big enough for me, but it would have been tight on them. Especially since Tony Beeson was with them. He was a one-man-band and a comedian. His instrument rig with the drum, the accordion, two horns, and the harmonica was bulky.

"Knock, knock," a young male voice said at the tent's entrance. The effort was silly, but there was no door, and the speaker was ultra-polite.

"Come in," I said. "Everybody's decent."

Lenny Webster, the young corporal from Omaha who had shown me to my "quarters" shortly after my arrival to the camp, stepped into the tent and immediately looked away from me. His face flamed and he pulled nervously at his wool jacket over his OD 3 uniform.

Dressed as I was in a large, fluffy green robe to relax before showtime, I was comfortable and, in my mind, perfectly presentable. That robe reached practically to my knees, and I knew the pin-ups young Corporal Webster had seen of me revealed a whole lot more than my shapely calves. I thought I was dressed appropriately, but maybe people did things differently in Nebraska.

"Begging your pardon, Miss Rita," Corporal Webster said, and he made sure he didn't look directly at me, "but they wanted me to let you know you're on in five minutes." He cut a quick glance at me, then looked away again. "I can tell them you'll need more time."

"Why would you think I needed more time?" I asked innocently.

"Because—well—you're not—" the young corporal squared his shoulders, "—just in case you did, ma'am."

A little incensed because I was keyed up over how "defenseless" I was going to have to pretend to be during my "kidnapping," and because I had been ma'amed much too often since reaching the camp, I stood. "It's *miss*, not *ma'am*, Corporal Webster. I am not old enough to be your mother. For all you know, we're the same age. In fact, you're probably older than I am."

I thought I had him by a couple of years, but I worked hard not to show those years, and that work was going to be acknowledged, darn it!

"Yes, ma'—yes, *miss*."

"Tell everyone I will be there exactly on time."

"Yes, miss." Corporal Webster saluted smartly and headed back through the tent flaps like he was glad to be going.

"You didn't have to be so hard on the kid," Burt observed. "He's got all of Hitler's army waiting to do that in a few days."

"I didn't do anything to him. My hands are clean. He didn't have to call me ma'am."

"Actually, I think he did. He's a soldier boy. They have rules for everything, from how to get up in the morning to how to go to bed at night. Probably have a few new rules for how to handle pretty pin-up girls since this war started and the USO created the Foxhole Circuit."

Burt Kimble had never been anybody's boy, and he'd never been a soldier either. I still didn't have his whole story, and it wasn't from a lack of trying, because I had attempted to get it so many times. He'd avoided spilling the beans on several occasions, and even under the duress of social drinking. He was a killer. In Manilla, while we were on another operation, I'd seen him take out three armed men in as many seconds. None of those men had survived the encounter.

Of course, to be fair, Burt didn't have my whole story either. No one did. President Roosevelt came the closest to knowing everything about me, and even he didn't have it all.

I stood, all five-feet-eight of me, probably a couple of inches taller than young Corporal Webster, and at least as tall as Burt, and walked behind the changing screen in the corner of the tent. I slithered out of the robe.

Burt wasn't a gentleman. He stared at me from the other side of the changing screen like he could see through it and watch me dress. All he could see was from my shoulders up, but they were good shoulders. Definitely worth a look.

I ignored him and stuffed myself into the modified army soldier's uniform that consisted of a tight-fitting olive blouse, a loose brown jacket, and a short olive skirt that would not have passed the Army's rigid dress code. I kept my modesty, but only just. I slipped into a pair of military boots and carried the regulation M1 helmet by its chin strap.

I stepped out from behind the changing screen and struck the "what-am-I-doing" pose Gil Elvgren had made so famous in the calendar I'd been in as Miss January 1942. That painting had been a rush job after Pearl Harbor was hit. I'd been doing some photo shoots for other artists, and Elvgren popped by and immediately asked me to model. I agreed.

The calendar publishers got the image into the calendar by kicking out the previous Miss January 1942 and earning me an enemy for life. After a year spent as a part-time pin-up model, I became an overnight star. That success spun out into an excellent cover for the spying and guerilla work I did for FDR.

In the two years since I'd worn several looks, many of them ridiculous and highly improbable, accompanied by several "accidents" that nearly revealed much more of me than the skimpy clothing because that was how Elvgren and the other pin-up artists liked to paint their models. In many of those paintings, I'd been less dressed than I was this evening.

"Well?" I prompted.

Burt grinned at me, but the humor he showed didn't light those stormy gray eyes. "You make me want to sign up and fight for my country, soldier."

"You already are fighting for your country." I crossed to him, bussed his stubbled cheek, smelled his cologne to perk up my own desire to fight—or, in this case, get kidnapped—for my country, and walked to the tent flap. I stopped and turned to face him. "You've got to let me get kidnapped. That's the only way we're going to get to *Standartenführer* Harald Fischer and maybe Doctor Albrecht Richter."

He nodded reluctantly. "I know."

"I mean it. There's a lot riding on getting some information on Richter's work."

"I know, I know." Burt nodded again, obviously irritated. "I don't have to like it. When the time comes, make sure you get out of there in one piece."

I smiled at him. "I always do."

I went out into the bright light of the afternoon because I didn't want him to see how nervous I was. He would never have let me go. And I probably would have let him keep me there.

The USO team performed out in the open, under thin clouds that drifted across a bright blue sky. Eagle-eyed sentries farther out from the stage kept watch for German bombers or the new rockets they were using with such devastating effect in Britain, Belgium, the Netherlands, and here in a few places in France because this country was divided by the war.

The soldiers had set up the stage we'd flown in with us as cargo. It was a postage-stamp-sized affair made of aircraft plywood, which I knew was made of mahogany, spruce, and birch layers glued together. Hey, a girl got bored flying from one show to another, and when I'm not doing the flying, I don't sleep so well on a plane. Not that I slept while I flew.

The stage was the same material that made up several fighter aircraft, including the De Havilland DH-98 Mosquito, which was also called the Wooden Wonder. I knew that from flight instructors I'd had, and who had maybe romanced me a little. I liked having a social life. Sue me.

The stage measured twelve feet across by eight feet deep, which was an awkward size, and small, but we'd learned to work within the space over the last couple of days, and there had been smaller stages in other places. Set back among a thicket of trees on the north end of the campsite, the stage was decorated with gaudy canvas curtains that hung from ropes strung from nearby trees.

Scattered among the trees, more than two hundred soldiers sat on the ground in front of the makeshift stage. They didn't have any chairs because chairs would have made a mad scramble for cover more difficult. Some of the soldiers looked bruised and battered, others wore bandages, and all of them were tired and exhausted. But they watched the stage with rapt attention. They were a captive audience, trapped by their own boredom and need for a distraction from the war and the fear that came with it.

Our receptions were like this everywhere we went on the Foxhole

Circuit. Our boys were banged up but vigilant, and they were starved for entertainment, something that would take them away from the war for a couple of hours. I was always aware of that and felt pressured to constantly try to deliver more, but I always met the task head-on. I was that way with everything I did.

Sure, I used the pin-up career as a cover for clandestine activities sanctioned by President Roosevelt, but I never forgot about the guys ducking bullets and fighting the good fight. What I did covertly helped the war effort, but what I did while I was on those stages helped the men.

I'd never begrudge them that entertainment, no matter how many silly costumes I had to wear or how many inane jokes I had to set up for the comedians. Or how much ogling some of the soldiers did. The singing was all me, though, and I loved that.

Tony Beeson, heavy-set and sweating ferociously, occupied the stage and played a frenetic medley of patriotic songs that included his closer "Boogie Woogie Bugle Boy." Even without the Andrews Sisters, or words for that matter, the one-man band made the music work. He always did. He was a true artist in his medium.

When he finished, he bowed as much as he could while wearing all the instruments he played in his act. Then he flung a hand in my direction and flashed a huge smile.

"I appreciate all you fellas bein' so patient and puttin' up with my cauterwaulin' and makin' a mess of the Andrews Sisters' beautiful song, but I know you've been patiently waitin' for the real star of the show."

The soldiers' heads followed his hand, and their eyes drank me in. Immediately, the soldiers cheered and whistled.

I stifled that wave of butterflies that filled my stomach the way it always did. I knew I'd never be able to live up to all their expectations. Thankfully, I didn't have to. All I had to do was put on a show I'd put on dozens of times, and they would do the rest. I'd get better with every retelling they delivered.

And I had a date to get kidnapped sometime after that. That made things a little more interesting.

"So here she is," Tony went on in his patter, "all the way from Los Angeles where the stars are always out at night, in the best gin joints of course—"

The crowd laughed and hooted.

"—the lovely, the vivacious, the girl of every man's dreams, Miss Rita Walker."

Smiling, I trotted up the rickety stairs that took me to the stage level, and, as I crossed the stage, I waved at all the soldiers like I owned the joint.

"Thank you, Tony," I said.

"My pleasure, Miss Walker." He walked offstage on the other side.

I turned to the audience and waved goodbye at Tony. "Wasn't he great, boys? The Andrews Sisters could benefit from him!"

Applause and hooting followed. Several soldiers called out my name. It never went to my head. They were ravenous for entertainment and the company of a woman. Several of them were missing their sweethearts back home.

"Good afternoon, boys," I greeted in that sexy contralto I'd learned to use professionally. I was good with voices, not as good as Mel Blanc, but I could change voices as easily as I changed hats, and I changed hats a lot. "They tell me I have to do this bit with Carson Evers, the ventriloquist, who is one of the most obnoxious men I know."

I waved a hand at Carson.

He stood on the ground on the other side of the stage. He was tall, dark-haired, and slender, and he wore a Clark Gable mustache that—I was glad to see—never quite worked for him. It looked fake even though he'd grown it himself. When he smiled, as he was doing now, his lips curled up more on the left side than the right side, and the expression gave him a smart-aleck appearance that offended me on some primitive level. He thought that smile came with a bank account filled with charm. It didn't have that. At least, I wasn't a customer.

His dark red suit and black shirt were always clean and freshly ironed no matter where we were.

In his left arm, he carried his ventriloquist dummy, Ace, a shaggy brown and white mule with a broad face and long, pointed ears on either side of an unruly forelock. As usual, Ace was dressed in a tuxedo and top hat.

"One of them is a mule," I said, "and the other is a jack—" I deliberately paused, "—of all trades."

Carson hated that bit. I'd adlibbed it a couple of months ago, and it had stuck. He'd wanted the gag stricken, but the show director, Joe Michel, wanted it left in. The crowd loved it, of course. They always did. Maybe Carson, or, more likely, Ace, was funny, but they didn't care for the ventriloquist. I'd wondered how that went over for Carson's ego. Having a thing made of wood, paste, and fabric—especially when you'd created it—outshine you had to be hard.

Carson slipped on one of his best fake smiles, and boy, he was good at those, and took the stage with me. Despite my dislike of him, Carson was a consummate professional. We ran through our bits flawlessly. Carson and

I set up the jokes and Ace knocked them down like Joe Louis taking out sparring partners. The crowd ate it up with a spoon.

Afterward, I sang a few numbers, which always went over well because I could sing. Then we closed the show and signed autographs for a while. Burt Kimble stood in the back of the crowd and watched everything. Somehow, despite his keen interest, no one noticed him. When someone came at me, I wondered if he'd be able to keep from interfering.

I wasn't kidnapped then. Of course, we hadn't figured it would happen onstage. Burt and I assumed they would take me on the last night we were there two days from now. I hadn't let my guard down, but I wasn't at my best.

Maybe that was why everything happened the way it did.

A short while later, I was back in my dressing tent and was taking off my makeup. We were done for the day. Evening was coming on and there would be no lights to mark our position. After chow call, soldiers would return to their units spread throughout the woods. Then darkness would fall, the threat of the war would return, and we'd shelter in the night and hope none of the rockets came our way.

I'd lie wide awake in bed—again—and wish there was more I could do. When I wasn't active, that's how it was. Too many thoughts of my family and how they were lost ate at me. They were the reason I'd chosen to do what I was doing.

Becoming a pin-up model hadn't been part of my plan. That had been a happy accident while I was working in Los Angeles rooting out some fifth-column spies planning an attack in Hollywood at the Oscars. After I'd dispatched two of the spies and called in the local police and FBI to round up the rest of them, I'd gone to the Brown Derby for a cup of coffee and been "discovered" by an agent who insisted I had a future as a model. I'd thought it was a pickup line of the worst sort, but he'd turned out to really be a modeling agent.

I'd been working for Howard Hughes then. Tracking saboteurs who had struck the Hughes Aircraft Company had led me to the fifth column. Working with the information I got from them, I found another group whose goal had been to assassinate Eleanor Roosevelt at the San Francisco

Fair in March of 1939.

I'd been a little too busy to take up the agent's offer to introduce me to artists and companies, but after Hughes talked to me and recommended I do it because it would be a good cover, I had. Hughes was also the one who told Eleanor Roosevelt who had saved her from getting it in the neck at the fair. She had been immediately interested in me. Especially after she found out I'd known Amelia Earhart, who was a hero of hers.

Admittedly, and I loathe doing so, especially since calendar modeling kept track of the years, I was older than young Corporal Webster. I just chose not to look it, and I had the good genes to carry it off.

Eleanor, and I had permission to address her as Eleanor, talked with me and pointed out that the war was coming whether anyone wanted it or not. I agreed because I had first-hand knowledge of that fact. My missionary parents had been killed, murdered, actually, by German soldiers at the outset of the Second Italo-Ethiopian War in 1935.

I'd been nineteen at the time and had wandered around Europe gathering the tools I figured I needed to exact my revenge on the whole German army. When I set my hat to something, I had never been a gal who only went halfway.

I'd met Imi Lichtenfeld in Hungary and I spent a year learning from him how to fight. He had been a wrestler and a boxer, but he'd invented a new style of martial arts that he was calling *Krav Maga*. I'd been a good student.

Some of his other students were military men, and one of them, Terry Conover, had worked for Hughes as a pilot. Terry and I had been friends until his death testing experimental aircraft for Hughes. I'd done some flight testing too. Hughes had told me that I was one of the most gifted and natural pilots he'd ever seen. He'd introduced me to Amelia Earhart.

I pulled my thoughts away from all that. Thinking about the past was good to remember why I was doing what I was doing, although getting kidnapped was a stretch, but dwelling on losing my family was never good.

Burt was off to the mess to get us something to eat. I would have never made it through the crowd without being accosted several times. Before I reached the mess, I would have starved on account of my own politeness.

"Knock, knock."

The voice wasn't that of young Corporal Webster. It was Ace the talking mule, and I knew, since Ace hadn't learned to talk on his own, or even figured out how to walk, he would be connected to that overdressed, self-obsessed jack—

Hughes introduced me to Amelia Earhart.

"Hey, it's me," Carson announced in his own voice. "I'm coming in. Hope you're decent. Of course, I don't mind if you're indecent. Indecency works for me. In fact, I'm a fan of being indecent."

Even though I was wearing a blouse and a skirt, I scampered across the room and grabbed my longer house robe. An expanse of skin wouldn't have embarrassed the ventriloquist the way it had Corporal Webster. When it came to Carson Evers, I could never have enough clothes on to suit me. I tied the robe's belt at my waist just as he cleared the tent flap.

He looked at me and smiled. At that minute, with the way he made my stomach twist with just one glance, I really wanted that shower I'd been promised after dinner. Burt and Corporal Webster were going to stand guard to make sure I got the necessary privacy.

I crossed my arms and glared at Carson.

"What do you need?" I asked pointedly. I didn't feel like being friendly. After a show, I usually kept to myself, and tonight there were other things going on that I wanted to be ready for.

Carson shrugged with his one free arm. Ace went along for the ride on the other. "Just wanted to go over some notes for our show tomorrow," he said. "I thought maybe we could freshen up some of the bits."

The man was a prima donna. He liked rehearsing for the attention he got while he played at being a director. I was okay with rehearsing, depending on the company, but I really didn't need it. I could usually get my deliveries done right in one take. I was popular with the radio stations for that very reason. When I wanted it and had the time, I did a lot of commercial voicework for the programs and sponsors.

I frowned at Carson. "You want to rehearse now?"

He gazed pointedly around the room. "Do you have anything else you're doing?"

I glanced at the small pile of *Movie Mirror, Hollywood,* and *Silver Screen* magazines I'd brought with me. They were part of my cover because I'd rather spend my time looking over the notes on *Standartenführer* Harald Fischer and maybe Dr. Albrecht Richter and Richter's research, but I couldn't be caught looking through those when the kidnappers arrived.

Whenever that would be. I figured maybe the next night or the one after that. After the third night, the show would move on to the next location. At least before the kidnapping happened, I hoped I'd get to eat. I didn't want to get kidnapped on an empty stomach. Being hungry made focus hard and got in the way of thinking.

"We've got a few minutes," I said. "Burt went to get dinner for us."

"I thought I saw him leave." Carson walked over to me, too close for my liking. "He's your talent agent?"

"Yes."

"And he's fetching dinner for you?"

"He's also my friend," I said. "And my photographer. Burt takes shots that he puts in my portfolio. Stuff for pinup artists. Stuff for advertisers. Promo pieces for the USO."

"He's got a swell job." Carson leered at me. "If you ever need another shutterbug, I'm your guy. I'm terrific behind a camera."

I pulled my robe a little tighter. "What do you want to work on?"

Carson pulled a wad of folded notes from his jacket pocket and handed them over. I took them and unfolded them. His looping cursive handwriting covered the pages.

All I saw was the same old tired stuff Carson and I did every time. I looked up at him.

Ace flicked out his arm and light gleamed along the long needle hidden in his hoof. I couldn't help myself because I'd been surprised. I hadn't expected Ace to attack. I'd trusted that mule but look at the company he kept.

I tried to move, but I was too late. Ace nailed me and the needle sank into my neck. Warmth skated along inside my skin and boiled to the front of my brain.

I opened my mouth to call for help, but nothing came out. I managed one step, then my legs turned into oatmeal, and I dropped like a rock to the tarp-covered ground.

I struggled to breathe. Carson ducked back to the tent flap, opened it, and waved. Three men carrying a big black bag slipped into the tent. They leaned down and tied my wrists together, tied my ankles together, and fitted me with a gag.

Then they shoved me into the bag and blackness consumed me.

Carson, you traitorous jack—

When I came to, my head throbbed, and my eyes were so light-sensitive that even the weak light around me sent daggers through my head.

Two of the men I'd seen earlier, at least, I believed they were two of the same men, hauled me from the back of a jeep and carried me on a litter to a waiting truck.

I struggled just enough to let them know I was fighting back, but I didn't get free. I thought maybe I could have because I'd wiggled some slack into the ropes they'd bound me with, but I wasn't sure. Whatever that Mickey Finn was that I'd been given, my arms and legs felt five sizes too big.

They laid me in the back of the truck. One of them opened a small black case, took out a hypodermic, and stuck it into my neck. Warmth wrapped my throat and climbed into my head.

The other guy pulled a tarp over me and it billowed out, but before it ever touched down, I was gone.

I woke again, but I didn't know what time it was. My head felt like it had been stuffed with lumpy mashed potatoes. The back of my throat and my tongue were rough and dry, probably from the cloth gag wicking the moisture away, and reminded me of an old ashtray. Focusing was a struggle, but I listened as intently as I could.

Ambient light, as weak and cloudy as candlelight, peeked in under the corner of the tarp where the canvas material didn't quite meet the sheet metal flooring beneath me. I was still on the truck. The growling motor and the whining transmission echoed around me.

Whatever opiate they had been giving me filled me with deadly languor. I suspected the drug was morphine because that was readily available—when it *was* available—on the battlefield.

Voices from the truck's cab filtered back to me.

"You're headed into no man's land, buddy," a man with an East Coast accent said from outside the truck. He had to raise his voice over the engine.

"I know," another man said, and he sounded closer, like he was inside the truck. I got the impression he was the truck driver seated in the cab. "I got it to do, though. I just follow orders, same as every other man in this outfit."

"Wouldn't want to be you," the New Yorker said. "Those Nazis have a lot of the locals pulled over to their side. Some of these French, brother, they flip-flop sides every day."

"That's just people trying to stay alive."

"I know." The East Coast guy heaved a loud, tired sigh. "I'm not happy here on the front, but I figure I'm safer here than you are going into that area. If I was you, while I was over there, I wouldn't trust nobody."

"I won't. The paperwork all good?"

"Paperwork's jake. Good luck and keep your head down. Heroes usually get sent back in a box."

"Thanks. Hope I don't need the luck."

I shifted a little and tried to get a finger under the gag in my mouth so I could yell for help, but the movement was bigger than I thought because it must have caught the attention of my captors. At the moment, I was groggy enough that I was thinking about getting free, not that everything was going according to plan. Or that me hollering for help would have probably gotten whoever was out there killed. Thinking clearly was a problem.

I definitely hadn't thought about getting drugged up the whole way to *Standartenführer* Harald Fischer.

The needle bit into my neck again. My senses whirled away like water down a drain and the light creeping in under the canvas slipped out of sight.

When I woke again, two men were carrying me from the truck to a long black Mercedes-Benz W31 automobile. Carson and the third man walked beside us.

I didn't know all cars, but the three axles and six tires on the type G4 made the vehicle distinctive. The Wehrmacht had ordered those for the upper strata of the Nazi regime. The vehicles weren't used in ordinary circumstances, and the type G4's presence there told me I was closer to Fischer.

The car was gray and black, and it featured a closed saloon instead of the open touring configuration. The G4 sat quietly on one side of the narrow dirt road where the truck had stopped.

The driver stepped back to the rear door, opened it, and stood rigidly at attention beside it. A Mauser K98k bolt-action rifle hung over his shoulder and his gray greatcoat covered his uniform. He wore a *Stahlhelm* helmet that had the "coal scuttle" shape everyone in the United States recognized and loathed.

He saluted. "*Hauptsturmführer* Groener," he greeted in German. "Welcome back. I trust your mission went well." His gaze flicked to me.

"Thank you, Felix," a woman answered. "The mission went well indeed. Though I still cannot fathom the *Standartenführer's* infatuation with this... *woman*."

Surprised, I looked at one of the "men" who'd accompanied my capture. She took off her hat, shook loose a wild mane of blonde hair, and shrugged out of her bulky coat. She was slim and in her early thirties. Her face held beauty and cold cruelty. Moonlight revealed the cold fire in her blue eyes. She regarded me disdainfully, then she turned her attention back to the driver.

"Did you bring my uniform, Felix?" *Hauptsturmführer* Groener asked.

"Of course." Felix left his post and headed to the vehicle's boot.

Carson, without Ace on his arm for once, took out a silver case, popped it open, and removed a cigarette. After tapping the cigarette's butt against the case, he lit up with an American Zippo that I recognized as Tony Beeson's. The lighter had gone missing a month ago, not long after Tony had gotten it from his wife for their anniversary. Tony had been heartbroken and hadn't yet been able to tell his wife because he hoped it would still turn up.

The ventriloquist was an absolute snake.

Groener looked at the men who carried me. "Put her in the middle row. Make sure her bonds are secure. Guard her well."

"Yes, *Hauptsturmführer*," one of them replied.

The two men shoved me into the middle seat and sat me up, which was a definite change. I didn't know how long I had been out, but my body ached and was stiff. My bladder felt full, but so far, I was holding my own. The narcotics slowed down everything. I was glad because I was betting Felix hadn't brought me a change of clothing.

My temples pounded, and I suspected that the effect was from the morphine. Lethargy gripped me.

Still, I managed to turn my head against the window to an angle that permitted me to watch Groener behind the big car. I couldn't see her clearly, but I could see her well enough.

After she pulled her hair back and secured it into a bun, she stripped down to her underwear, then pulled on a black *Schutzstaffel* uniform. The jodhpurs and blouse had been tailored to fit her like a glove. The boots held no sheen to give her away in the night, but they had been carefully cleaned. A thick black belt cinched high on her body and a strap crossed over her right shoulder. A sheathed *nahkampfmesser*, a close-combat fighting knife, hung from the belt's accouterments.

She took a Walther P38 from the other set of clothing, checked the magazine automatically, then seated the pistol in the holster on the belt and tugged the flap down. From the car's boot, she took a big officer's hat with its high crown, dusted it with a quick forearm swipe, and sat it on her head. She slid the red armband onto her upper left arm and took out a riding crop to complete her outfit.

She looked grimly efficient and coldly lethal.

"Let's go," she told Felix.

The driver moved from his sentry duty at the rear of the car, held the door open, and leaned inside to tilt the seat beside me forward to allow Groener access to the vehicle's back row of seating.

Smooth as a pantheress, all skill and grace, she settled in behind me and threat oozed from her as thick as maple syrup. I was aware of the fact her claws were currently sheathed, but they were there, waiting and ready. After she and Carson got into the back seat, one of the guards who had carried me to the car took the seat beside me while the other sat in the passenger seat beside the driver.

The window roller and the release lever had been removed from my door. The distortion caused by the glass told me the glass was thick enough to be bulletproof to small arms fire. The only way out of the vehicle was through my captors. I worked the gag out of my mouth so I could breathe more easily, and so my throat wouldn't dry out so much. No one tried to put the gag back in my mouth.

Groener sat easily in the back seat and idly popped the top of my seat with the riding crop. *Pop, pop, pop.* The beat carried just enough steady rhythm to get on my nerves, but I made myself remain still.

"Did you enjoy the show?" she asked me in German.

Even as woozy-headed as I was from the drug, I wasn't going to fall for the bait. My knowledge of German was going to remain my secret. The second mouse always got the cheese.

"Look," I said in English, and I even managed to simper a bit, which I detested, "I don't know who you think I am, but you've got the wrong girl. I'm just a singer and a straight man for ventriloquist whose dummy is smarter than he is." I shot Carson a scathing glance. "I didn't know he was a kidnapper."

Carson grimaced, looked on the verge of saying something, and glanced at Groener. then returned his attention to his cigarette.

Coolly, Groener regarded me and spoke in flawless English. "I don't think you're anything at all. Just another tawdry tart. Miss January 1942." She sneered. "Unfortunately, I serve a man who is interested in you. He is a brilliant man, but, like all men, he has failings."

Was that jealousy I detected?

"You, Miss January," she continued, "are just another such a failing." Finished with her bellicose bile, she leaned back in her seat and crossed her arms. "But, as has happened with all the others before you, he'll soon grow tired and want something new and precious." She smiled. "Then it will be my pleasure to break you. I'm very good at breaking people I don't like, and I don't like you at all."

A chill flickered through me. I knew she meant what she said.

Carson laughed at that. Obviously, there was a streak of cruelty that ran through him, along with the treachery I hadn't seen. Oh, I owed Carson a big what-for if I got the chance.

I wondered what he was doing there. He could have stayed at the camp. Maybe he was worried that someone would remember that he'd ducked in to see me right before I disappeared. I bet Burt Kimble would swiftly put two and two together and would look into Carson at the same time he was searching for me. If we hadn't had our plan in place to let me get kidnapped, Burt would be hot on the trail.

Having Burt come to my rescue was a comforting thought, but not what we'd agreed to. I was quite capable of rescuing myself. I'd done it before.

Carson had blindsided me though. That was something to remember because I didn't want to get caught up short again. I'd thought Carson was a letch and a narcissist, and not too terribly bright. But, sister, he'd fooled me. Or he'd allowed me to fool myself. At any rate, I only had myself to blame.

I couldn't help wondering if all the information I'd read about Fischer was enough. None of it had mentioned even one word about Groener. The intelligence had filtered through men, and I figured they'd overlooked the *Hauptsturmführer*. They'd taken advantage of Fischer's weakness while not being aware of their own. That was what men did.

So, I had to assume what I knew about the trouble I was walking into was even less than I'd been led to believe. Groener wasn't someone who could be easily discounted.

However, I was supposed to be kidnapped. This was all part of the plan, right? At least I'd knocked that out of the ballpark. I'd figure out what I needed to do next as I went along. While under pressure, I had always been good on my feet. My batting average was perfect. I'd survived every mission I'd been sent on. Some of them had been close calls though.

Besides that, Doctor Albrecht Richter and his new rocket technology were still out there to be grabbed—or ended. I was in this soiree till the bitter end.

Felix switched on the car's headlights and lit up the dark forest around us. Tall trees lined both sides of the dirt road. An owl scudded across the quarter moon. The engine growled to life and Felix put the transmission into gear.

I straightened up, just a little, to try to get a better look at what lay ahead. The guy beside me plunged a hypodermic into my neck. He was slick, or maybe I was off my game. Either way, I didn't see it coming and that irritated me. When my neck went slack and I couldn't sit up anymore, my head thudded against the thick, bulletproof glass.

The last thing I saw was a pack of gray wolves running silently through the forest and matching pace with the car. Or maybe they were just an illusion created by the morphine.

Then my eyes closed.

Darkness filled the small valley ahead of us, but the full moon brought out many of the highlights. Luckily, I regained consciousness leaning against the window and didn't have to raise my head to see. No one in the car with me needed to know I was alert. The steep descent of the road leading to the castle on a high hill on the other side of the large valley was almost enough to tilt me forward.

For a moment, I thought Felix was driving right into a scene out of a Brothers Grimm fairy tale. Those stories had plenty of castles, princesses, and woods in them, and I'd always imagined them looking a lot like the edifice ahead of us.

A high stone wall surrounded the castle and some outbuildings. Outside the wall was a moat that must have been fed by a spring. Judging by the black-uniformed sentries standing guard along the crenellations, the expanse of water was at least thirty feet across and must have been fed by underground springs.

A couple of hundred years ago, archers would have stood watch there. Tonight I spotted three MG-42 machine guns along the wall. The American GIs called those weapons "buzzsaws" because of the high rate of fire they were capable of.

My throat tightened at the prospect of facing those.

A couple of hundred yards from the castle, a long strip that looked like someone had dropped a section of road into the middle of a cherry orchard ran a fair distance, probably just long enough for planes to take off and land. That was the airstrip that had been mentioned in the information I'd read.

Until three weeks ago, no one had known for certain where Fischer and the Reich had staged his research station. Most of the details had come from an English pilot who had been shot down while escorting a British Handley Page Halifax nighttime bomber headed toward Berlin.

The pilot's story had been scattered in pieces and told while heavily medicated. He'd suffered terrible wounds before and after ditching his plane, and he'd gotten more injuries while running for his life from Nazi pursuers. An American infantry guerilla unit, Easy Company, had been assigned to cut off German supply routes in the area had rescued the pilot and brought him back to a hidden Allied base.

Right after the British pilot had been rescued, German forces had invaded the area. The American generals' thinking had been that the Germans had moved to re-secure their supply lines.

That had been until RAF Sergeant Addison shared his story about a strange aircraft that had shot him down. According to the young pilot, the strange aircraft was the oddest thing he'd ever seen, like something from "one of the science fiction pulps all the lads are on about these days." I'd read the transcripts of his debriefing.

The comment about the science fiction pulps had caught everyone's attention. I'd modeled for J. Allen St. John for a couple of issues of *Fantastic Adventures*, and once for Margaret Brundage for *Weird Tales*. Seeing myself on alien worlds and menaced by supernatural creatures had been…different.

Easy Company had slipped back into the valley and set up an observation post over the castle and the airfield. They'd identified *Standartenführer* Harald Fischer and the German officer's recent infatuation with Miss January 1942 through pin-ups on his walls and had sent the information up the channels.

As far as officers went, Fischer was high up in Hitler's scientific division, but taking him out wouldn't have had much of an effect. However, Fischer had Richter, one of the *Führer's* rocket men. Richter was a target worth a lot in the eyes of the generals. They wanted Richter.

Knowing there was a chance of getting Richter's research and maybe even the prototype aircraft that had only been glimpsed a couple of times, President Roosevelt and the generals had quashed all ideas of a hard insertion and assassination, and they had sent for me, set the trap, and waited for it to be sprung.

I'd heard the sergeant of Easy Company was a solid, dependable guy, and he hadn't been any too keen on getting assigned to the sidelines. But, by all accounts, he was a good soldier who followed orders, and he did so now.

So, he and his unit were somewhere out there in the woods. The trouble was, if anything went wrong, they'd be too late to grab the research Roosevelt and the Allied generals wanted. Either Fischer would abscond with the research and Richter, or he'd destroy both the man and the materials.

Easy Company would also be too late to save me.

That was fine. I never counted on anyone to save me.

All of that passed through my mind in a flash. I was focused on the castle and the valley where it sat, and I was already looking for ways I could escape.

All of that depended on Fischer. The intelligence operators had discovered Fischer's predilection for women, and they'd even found out he was a fan of pin-up models. According to agents embedded in Germany, the Nazi commander was an unapologetic philanderer. Back in Berlin, Fischer had a wife, a longtime girlfriend, and he frequently was in the company of other women.

No one knew how many women Fischer had ordered escorted to his castle, but reports of a graveyard with hills of relatively fresh-turned earth had shown up in Easy Company's reports. No women had been brought in since Easy Company had settled in somewhere along the valley. I suspected the young sergeant in charge of the guerilla unit would have jumped the generals' leash if there had been. He had the reputation of being a straight-arrow guy.

"I know you've regained consciousness," Groener stated. "Your breathing pattern changed some minutes ago."

I called the she-wolf a few choice names in my mind, noted how observant she was, and I sat up. "Are you going to have Hans stick me with the needle again?" I nodded at the big man next to me. "I'd just as soon skip that if it's all the same to you."

Groener smiled, but the effort was as cold as ice. "No. *Standartenführer* Fischer insists on greeting you. To give you a proper reception. For that, you must be conscious." Her voice took on a threatening timbre. "And you must be on your best behavior. Foolishness will not be allowed." She rapped the riding crop against the back of my seat. "You will be docile and meek, appreciative even, and you will thank him for his kindness and hospitality."

Fat chance, I thought.

"Otherwise," she added flatly, "you will thank me days from now when I finally allow you to die."

The *Hauptsturmführer*'s threat cleared away the last of the cobwebs inside my head.

...and I was already looking for ways I could escape.

Standartenführer Fischer made a show of his hospitality. He had several, maybe even all, of the staff out in front of the castle even this late at night. Or maybe it was morning. I wasn't sure. The drug still buzzed in my system, and I'd lost track of time. It was dark.

A dozen men and women dressed in black uniforms stood at attention on the wide stone steps that led to the doors. The men were of various ages. The women were old or plump or both.

I wondered if all the young and good-looking women were now buried behind the castle. Or maybe Fischer didn't hire young women because his temptations would require a lot of replacing the help.

I quickly banished that thought because thinking like that definitely wouldn't help me accomplish my mission. I planned for success. Nothing less would work. I didn't intend to fail or die.

The car stopped in the circle drive in front of the steps. The driver got out and opened the door. The man guarding me slid out, then reached back in and hauled me out too. He freed my hands and my ankles from the restraints, but he kept a hand clasped around my upper arm tight enough to let me know I wasn't going anywhere without him.

Not without a fight. I wasn't prepared to give him one at the moment.

Groener got out next and moved flawlessly like she had extra joints. She climbed the steps to the house and walked between the staff members. The men and women kept their heads bowed like they were afraid to make eye contact with the *Hauptsturmführer*.

Resplendent in his black uniform and with a great cloak hanging from his broad shoulders, *Standartenführer* Harald Fischer stood on the covered landing in front of the two huge doors. A holstered Luger at his right hip balanced the polished, lion-headed sabre on his left hip. Ribbons and medals decorated his chest. The German army believed in handing out pretty little gewgaws to their officers. Especially if they were nobility.

If Fischer hadn't been a bone-deep Nazi, and a guy who buried women in his backyard, he would have been a handsome man. He was strong and virile, probably only in his late thirties, and had smoldering blue eyes, a neatly trimmed mustache, and dark hair.

He made eye contact with me and smiled broadly. He spoke in German. "Ah, Miss Walker! So pleased to make your acquaintance!"

I looked at him. "All I recognized was my name. If you're talking to me."

Groener took a step toward me and drew back her riding crop. Fischer raised a hand palm out and froze her in place.

I grinned at her. "Great. You're obedient and you perform on command."

Her dark eyes blazed, and I knew she wanted to deliver the blow that she'd readied. I prepared myself to take it because now wasn't the time for anything more than a show of rebelliousness to create breathing room for myself.

"Step back," Fischer commanded.

Groener returned to her previous position, folded her hands behind her, and stood stiffly erect. "Of course, *Standartenführer* Fischer. I only meant to punish this woman's blatant disrespect."

"In time, *Hauptsturmführer*, if needs be. Until then, she is my guest, and you would do well to remember that."

"Of course, *Standartenführer*. Please accept my apologies."

If Groener had known I understood German, I was certain she wouldn't have been so quick to ask for forgiveness. Or so obsequious about it.

Fischer looked at me and switched to English. "Miss Walker, despite the circumstances, I am quite happy to meet you."

"You mean the fact that you kidnapped me?" I glared at him. I didn't want him to think for an instant I was anything other than what he believed me to be.

"If I had asked you nicely," Fischer said, "would you have come?"

"Not on your life. You're an enemy of my country."

"See? That is where the problem lies. I wanted to meet you badly enough to set aside any political disparity, and to take pains to arrange this daring little invitation because I knew you would refuse me out of simple patriotic loyalty. Trust me, getting you here was most difficult, and I risked a lot to achieve that goal."

"You mean because you had to reveal your toadie?" I shot Carson a glare. By now I had those expressions stockpiled, locked and loaded.

Carson looked nervous. Maybe he felt vulnerable because Ace the mule wasn't there at the end of his arm to back him up.

Fischer cocked an elegant eyebrow. "You believe Mr. Evers has been compromised by his part in this little charade to get you?" The *Standartenführer* shook his head like a patient parent. "No. Clues were laid so that your companions will think Mr. Evers was taken by force the same way you were. Later, he will affect his escape."

Carson gave me a small, mocking salute.

Fischer had overplayed his hand. There was no plan to release me. Groener glanced at Fischer with narrowed eyes in silent admonishment, but the *Standartenführer* never noticed. Still, I took that unspoken rebuke as a tool that I could possibly use at some point. Groener acknowledged Fischer's leadership, but she wasn't happy with it. There was a division between them.

"I should feel flattered?" I shook my head and folded my arms. Most of the circulation had returned to my hands and legs. "Sorry. I'm not a guest. I'm a prisoner." I nodded at the big man who still clasped my upper arm. "My human anchor here only bears that out."

"Trust me, Miss Walker," the *Standartenführer* said smoothly, "by morning, you'll feel much better about your situation. You will find that you are an honored guest and will be treated as such."

"Except for the whole held against my will business?" I arched an eyebrow right back at him. He didn't have the market cornered on eyebrow-lifting. I could deliver a pretty mean eyebrow castigation myself.

Fischer frowned a little, then he turned and waved toward the doors. "Please. Enter my home."

I went because there were no other options.

I assumed the castle was French, but it might have had Germanic origins. We were east of the Alsace-Lorraine. That region had been passed back and forth between the two countries since the Franco-Prussian War. France had gotten the territory back after the First World War and now struggled to hang onto it again. Both sides wanted the mineral resources located there.

The castle was in good condition, solid and formidable. It was a good place to stage a military operation, especially since no one had known about it and had been doing exactly that until Easy Company had reported its existence.

The old, handmade furniture was solid and well-cared for, and personal effects revealed that people had lived there before the Nazis had moved in. From the way things looked and the shape the place was in, I was willing to bet Fischer and his goose steppers had moved them out.

I wondered where they were, then realized that was something I probably didn't want to know. Thinking about that just made me more determined to succeed in my mission. Hitler and his goon squad were going to pay for what they'd done.

The red flag bearing the Nazi swastika was proudly placed above the fireplace in the great room. A stone staircase with a handsome railing climbed to the second floor. Above that, another staircase led up to the third floor.

The castle was big and heating it during the winter probably took a whole forest.

"Elsa," Fischer said, "please show Miss Walker to her room."

One of the plump, older women curtsied slightly and spoke in accented English. "Of course, *Standartenführer*."

She joined me and my human anchor.

I looked at Fischer. "I don't suppose you could tell your gorilla to get his mitts off me."

Fischer smiled unctuously. "Miss Walker, I will see you promptly at eight o'clock in the morning for breakfast. Until then, sleep well."

I tried again to yank my arm free, but still couldn't get loose that way, and fell into step with the big man at my side. Elsa led the way up the staircase and to one of the rooms along the main hallway. She turned on the electric lamp on a bedside table and hurried the darkness from the space.

The room was lavish and large. The bed was neatly made, and the pillows were fluffed. Elsa fluffed them again. She showed me the gown hanging on the changing screen in the corner of the room.

"The bathroom is here." Elsa pointed to a door to the left. "It is fully stocked with soaps and shampoos. You'll find all the amenities there. It was fully modernized less than ten years ago."

She looked like she was going to cry. Her lower lip trembled.

"Madame Cizeron," Elsa went on in a voice tight with emotion, "took great pride in providing the best for her guests." She wiped tears from her cheeks with her fingers.

Freed from the big man's grip and compelled by Elsa's raw emotion, I crossed to the woman and put my hand on her shoulder. "Thank you, Elsa."

The woman recovered herself. "Of course, *mademoiselle*. Will you require anything further?"

"No. Thank you."

"Then I will bid you *adieu* and wish you a good night's sleep."

"*Adieu*," I said.

"I will deliver a fresh change of clothing for you in the morning." Elsa left and the big soldier followed her out.

The door locked solidly behind them. I checked it and confirmed I was locked in.

The room had one window. I wasted no time in dowsing the electric lamp and investigating the window. On the other side of the glass, the castle's rear abutments looked south out over a forest. To the west, I could barely make out the rectangular hangar that ran alongside the airstrip.

The steel bars set into the masonry were brutal, ugly things and didn't fit the window's aesthetics, but they were firmly implanted there. I'd need a hacksaw with a carbide blade and several hours to get through the bars.

Or a bazooka.

Since I had neither, and since I knew I needed to recover from the last day or two of constant drugging, I headed into the bathroom for a deep, relaxing soak. Then I was going to sleep as long as I could till they came for me in the morning.

I'd be more ready then, and I intended to do the job I'd been sent to do. If I got a chance to take out the *Standartenführer* along the way, that would be a nice bonus.

Despite the fact that I was usually a light sleeper and easy to rouse at a moment's notice, I startled awake the next morning at the soft hiss of door hinges and came up in the bed ready to swing.

Elsa froze in the doorway with her hands raised and looked apologetic. "Forgive me, *mademoiselle*! I knocked. Several times I knocked. I swear that I did."

I relaxed and sat back in the bed with my elbows resting on my knees. I blew stray strands of hair from my face. "No worries, Elsa. I'm sorry. I didn't hear you."

"When they brought you in last night, you were very tired." Elsa carried an armful of clothes over to the changing screen. "I brought a selection of clothing for you so you may find something suitable for wear."

All the clothing looked expensive and well-cared for. It also appeared to be all dresses and skirts. Not exactly clothing for a girl who might have to fight or run for her life. I suspected the shoes would be equally rancorous.

"I don't suppose there are any pants in there?" I asked.

Elsa looked apologetic again. The expression must have been a reflex for her or one that was ground in by Fischer and Groener.

"No, *mademoiselle*," she answered. "I am afraid there are no pants. The *Standartenführer* was most explicit about what you were to be given. He picked out the clothing himself."

"Seems like the *Standartenführer* would have more important things to do," I said.

Elsa almost smiled, but the sadness stamped into her features prevented that. "Yes, *mademoiselle*. You will discover that he is most demanding about these things."

"How many girls has he *invited* to the castle?"

Pained uncertainty lined Elsa's face and she hesitated.

I held up a hand. "Don't answer. That was a foolish question. You don't want to say, and me knowing won't help me now."

"I'm sorry, *mademoiselle*." Elsa eyed the clothing. "These are the *madame's* clothes." Her eyes grew wet, but she held herself together. "The *madame* was a horsewoman. One of the finest I have ever seen."

Was. That thought hung in my mind.

"When she rode," the woman whispered, "the *madame* enjoyed wearing trousers. I can locate a pair of those and bring them to your room."

I smiled at her. "That'd be swell, Elsa."

"Of course, *mademoiselle*." She stood a little straighter. "Will you need help getting dressed?"

"No, thank you," I said. "I've been getting dressed all by myself for years."

"Then I will leave you to that and wait for you out in the hall."

I got out of bed dressed in the gown she'd left for me the night before. "Is that big ape still hanging around?"

"*Ape*?" Elsa looked at a loss for a moment, then understanding dawned. "Ah, you mean *Unterfeldwebel* Kilcher. Yes, he is there. The *Standartenführer* gave him strict orders that he was not to enter the room unless there was a problem."

"No problems here," I said, and I sorted through the clothing. It was really primo stuff. Still, realizing what had probably happened to *Madame* Cizeron, I felt like a ghoul.

"I am glad, *mademoiselle*," Elsa said. "I shall wait for you outside. Breakfast will be ready. And even if I say so myself, Chef Henri has outdone himself this morning."

Probably because he had a pistol pointed at his head, I couldn't help thinking.

Elsa and Kilcher escorted me to the large dining hall where a massive oak table sat. Uniformed staff stood ready to serve.

Fischer and the other men already at the table, including Carson Evers sans Ace, stood smartly. Evidently, the *Standartenführer* was going to continue his show of treating me as his guest.

Groener stood too and hewed into the officer status instead of her femininity. Just one of the guys. With her hands behind her back, Groener stood at attention alongside the other men.

"Miss Walker," Fischer greeted from the head of the table. He smiled broadly like he was an old friend and was grateful to see me after a long absence. "Good morning. Allow me to say you look splendid."

I couldn't help wondering if the dark blue pencil dress with the peplum was his primary choice for me. The short, gathered skirt on the dress wasn't something I was fond of. I'd tried to pick something that wasn't what he wanted to see me in, but I didn't know him well enough to be accurate. And the choices had been limited.

"It's too late to not allow you to say that," I told him. "Allowed or not, you've already said it."

His smile cracked just a little. He didn't like being addressed so cavalierly in front of his men. I realized I wasn't ready to go on the offensive and decided to haul in my sails a little.

"I apologize, *Standartenführer* Fischer," I said. "I didn't get enough sleep last night, and when I don't get enough sleep, I can be catty."

"Of course," Fischer said. He stepped to the right side of the table to the empty chair there and hauled it out. "Please. You'll dine with me."

Not having any choice and not yet ready to throw another verbal hand grenade into the mix, I sat, and I even thanked him.

As it turned out, Elsa was correct about breakfast. It was exquisite. I didn't hold myself back and ate all I wanted. Each meal from this point on might easily be my last. At least, it might be the last at that table. Things would happen quickly. Of that I was certain.

After breakfast, I accompanied Fischer, Kilcher, Groener, and two other German officers on a tour of Citadelle de l'Ormasse. We took the G4 that had brought me in last night, or one like it, and Felix was at the wheel.

Fischer sat with me to his left in the rearmost seat. Groener occupied the middle seat and turned so she could watch me with the eyes of a predatory cat. She held her pistol in her hand and waited for an excuse to shoot me. I could only imagine her disappointment, but I took pleasure in it.

The *Standartenführer* waxed eloquently about the castle and its history all the way back to the seventeenth century. He liked the sound of his own voice. Many of the powerful men I'd met shared the same trait.

Most of the information he relayed sounded right and matched up with what I'd read in the sensitive documents I'd been given access to. I only halfway paid attention because I was taking in the terrain and the possibilities it offered. I have a good eye for battlefields, both in the country and in urban areas. Once on a mission, I constantly weighed and measured options.

Easy Company had provided a lot of clear, concise information, and the correlations from studying the materials I'd been given to what I was seeing was almost a perfect match.

Fischer's stormtroopers had hidden machine gun nests and constant man and dog-walking patrols during the night. Even as a squad of special guerrillas and veterans of past engagements, Easy Company would have been hard-pressed to manage a rescue operation here, much less a materials grab.

Getting the intelligence research I had been assigned to retrieve would have been impossible from outside the castle and Fischer's operations. Once attacked, Fischer would either escape with the research, or he would destroy it. If I could make this retrieval assignment work, my success would depend as much on skill and luck as it did on planning.

Fischer didn't talk about the Cizeron family or what had happened to them. If Easy Company knew about that family, mention of them had been redacted from the files I'd been given. Or maybe no one in the intelligence division knew. Information was a commodity that could often be in short supply. Especially on a rush job like this one.

"Do you like airplanes, Miss Walker?" Fischer asked.

I looked at him. "Given my preference," I lied, "I'd rather travel in a good touring car. Something like this one. This is a nice car. Solid and comfortable." I patted the seat between us.

"I like automobiles as well," Fischer said, "but this war will be won by aircraft."

That was a load of hooey. This war was going to be won by men who gave their all in every battle they fought. I knew those men, and I'd fought beside some of them.

"Do you not like to fly?" the *Standartenführer* asked.

"Flying is all right," I said, "it gets you from one place to another pretty quickly, but I'd rather be the one in control."

Fischer looked at me. "Do you fly?"

"Only when I have to. It's hard to get from America to Europe without flying."

"My mistake." He held up a gloved hand. "I thought you meant that you liked flying when you had the controls."

"No, but I don't like driving when I'm not the one holding the steering wheel." That was true, and when we were working together, my insistence on driving sometimes made Burt crazy. "I can drive, but, when I have no choice about flying, I leave flying to those who know what they're doing. I much prefer a parade of martinis while I'm in the air."

Fischer chuckled. Groener slitted her eyes in annoyance. Fischer *liked* me a lot, and it showed. That made the *Hauptsturmführer* hate me a little more. I could live with that. Sometimes it was the silent wars between women that were the bloodiest, and the most rewarding.

"I love a woman who knows her mind," Fischer said. "Perhaps I can persuade you to enjoy airplanes a little more. You've noticed that there is an airstrip over there."

He pointed to the hangar and the airstrip like I might have trouble recognizing what it was.

I shaded my eyes with a hand and looked at the airstrip. "I thought maybe that was a road you were putting in. The one we came along last night was pretty primitive."

"That road is kept primitive by design," Fischer said. "We don't get many visitors out here, nor do we want to encourage them. However, that airstrip is a solid piece of work."

"It's big for something out in the middle of nowhere. But even with the size, this isn't much of an air base. I suppose you're scouting troop movements."

"No," Fischer said. "This place was chosen because it was off the beaten path. We are not a direct part of the war effort. Out here, we develop new planes and flying bombs that will be used against those who oppose Germany."

The *Standartenführer* was trying to impress me with his importance, but I'd already been briefed on what Fischer was doing out here. And I knew whom he was doing it with.

Groener grew irritated enough to shift in her seat and she spoke sharply in German. "*Standartenführer*, discussing our task out here—"

"Is my business, *Hauptsturmführer*!" Fischer barked in the same language. "Don't forget yourself!"

Like a trained predator, Groener sheathed her claws, but you couldn't forget she had them.

"Of course, *Standartenführer*," she said in a tone that never quite reached meekness.

Somewhat mollified, Fischer returned his attention, and his language, to me. "Perhaps you would like to see some of what I am working with."

I glanced at Groener and grinned. I sold my response to her as a control thing, like I was showing her I had more of Fischer's attention than she did. Which, at the moment, whether I wanted it or not, I did.

If she'd even had a hint that I was interested in seeing the inside of that hangar for any other reason than to snub her, she might not have backed down from the *Standartenführer*. She was more protective of the base than he was. She recognized him as a problem. Still, I thought she was infatuated with him. Women didn't always get to choose whom they were infatuated with, but they were generally more selective than men.

"Sure," I replied. "I'd be happy to see it."

After all, I had to play up to him to stay alive. I wanted Groener thinking that was what I was doing.

The hangar, inside and out, was neat as a pin. The mechanics wore stained coveralls and worked swiftly, but based on the cleanliness of those areas not covered in grease and oil, their clothing had started out clean whenever they'd showed up for their shifts. The tools hung on pegboards on the walls, or they filled large toolboxes.

The building ran for a quarter mile, maybe longer, and was at least half that in width. The space held a handful of airplanes and another handful of the newfangled German rockets that had the Allied generals worried. Looking at those monsters, seeing them up close, I got worried too. So far, though, the threat of the rockets wasn't as bad as it could have been, but that was changing quickly this year because the German war machine was gearing up.

The V-2 rockets (that was the Germans' designation for the weapons, although they called them *Vergitungswaffe 2s*, which translated into English as "Retaliation Weapon 2") were nearly fifty feet long and were almost six feet in diameter. The rockets carried over a ton of explosives, tore down buildings, and left huge craters where they hit. I'd seen a few of those up close.

The Allied forces needed that technology. American and British scientists were struggling to reverse engineer the V-2 rockets they had recovered, but there just wasn't enough of the weapons left over to get a clear

Groener sheathed her claws, but you couldn't forget she had them.

picture of the original design.

I walked through the hangar at Fischer's side. Groener trailed us, and I couldn't help thinking she was like the medieval representation of Death that could be found in so many paintings of that time. The Renaissance painters liked to acknowledge that Death was waiting out there for everyone, even at the dinner table.

Groener was definitely waiting for me. One slip, or the instant Fischer grew disenchanted with me, and I was dead.

In her mind. Not in mine. I imagined a different outcome, but if she had a team with her, I wouldn't make it.

The V-2s were experimental models tricked out to carry different destructive payloads, including white phosphorus, which was one of the most destructive and horrifying weapons I'd ever seen. Some of the guys in the army called the munition "Willie Pete," to take advantage of the initials.

A few minutes into the tour, Fischer took me to a room built within the hangar, like one of those boxes within boxes that made up Chinese puzzles. More guards stood at the door, but they stepped aside at our approach.

Inside the room, seven men worked at drafting tables, at blackboards mounted on the considerable wall space, and with model rockets that looked sleeker and more lethal. Thin, flimsy cots lined one wall and a table held the remnants of a meal. Workroom and prison all in one convenient location.

Fischer raised his voice and called out. "Dr. Richter!"

A gangly man in his forties turned to face us. He wore a white lab coat and had a ratty beard that reached to his chest. Round-lensed spectacles covered pale blue eyes that looked like cobalt flames that had been nearly extinguished. He was gaunt and his yellowing skin hung loose on him as if he'd recently lost a good deal of weight.

Due to the weight loss and the haggard appearance, I almost didn't recognize Dr. Albrecht Richter from the photos I'd been given to review. The man in those pictures had possessed modest humor and decorum. This man didn't look far removed from a feral creature.

Richter struggled to haul himself erect, but his shoulders remained bowed, and his back was stooped from long hours spent working. He took off his spectacles and cleaned them with a handkerchief from his pocket.

"*Standartenführer*," Richter greeted woodenly. His shoulders hunched as though he expected a blow. A faded bruise showed on his cheekbone.

Then Fischer spoke in German. "A moment of your time." He smiled. "I have brought someone to meet you."

Confusion filled Richter's face. "Whatever for?"

I knew why. Even though Fischer didn't expect me to know who stood in front of us, the *Standartenführer* wanted to show off his prize to the captured scientist to emphasize his own importance. Maybe some women liked being shown off as a trophy, but I wasn't one of those. I masked my irritation with a practiced smile.

"Miss Walker," Fischer said, "I'd like to introduce my colleague, Dr. Albrecht Richter. He is one of the most brilliant minds I have ever met. Dr. Richter, this is Miss Walker. She is a highly regarded entertainer."

I offered my hand and, when Richter took it briefly, smiled warmly. My mother had made certain I had impeccable manners. I still used them on occasion under the right circumstances. I felt kindly toward Richter because I knew how he'd ended up with the Nazis. His wife and children had been killed by a British bomb.

Our intelligence source suggested that Richter placed the responsibility for their deaths on the Nazis, not the British. Hitler had started the war, and it was he who had brought the destruction to Germany. A lot of the Germans felt that way these days. Before his family had been killed, Richter had been taken from them by Hitler's troops to work for the German war machine.

"*Fräulein* Walker." Richter gave me a hesitant smile. "Any friend of—"

"Oh, I'm not a friend," I said. "The *Standartenführer* had me kidnapped and brought here."

From the corner of my eye, I caught Fischer's pained grimace.

Richter shoved his hands in the pockets of his lab coat. "I see."

"Dr. Richter is in charge of designing the latest weapon for the *Luftwaffe*," Fischer said. "Come. I will show it to you. You will be amazed."

He gowered at Richter, led the way out of the room, and took us to the back of the hangar.

As I was hauled away, I told Richter, "Goodbye. It was nice to meet you."

"And you," he said. He looked sad and worn standing there.

I walked at the *Standartenführer's* side.

We walked to the far end of the hangar, toward a monstrous aircraft that looked formidable. It didn't look like a conventional airplane. This latest creation had a triangular shape and was wider from wingtip to wingtip, probably just short of two hundred feet, than it was from nose to tail, which I estimated to be something over fifty feet. There were no propellers, no tail, and no fuselage that I could see. It was just a very large wing.

Even though I'd studied pictures of the aircraft, seeing it in the flesh, so to speak, was still shocking. Tailless aircraft were nothing new. Designers had experimented with that since Orville and Wilbur Wright had launched their plane from Kitty Hawk, North Carolina.

According to the experts, a flying wing was the lowest drag design possible, and an aircraft with that shape would be the fleetest. The design was also one of the hardest to pilot. If this one could do what Easy Company said it could do—

"This is the future of flying," Fischer declared proudly, "and the end to this war. Once we have these in production, Germany will first rule the skies, then she will rule the world."

I laughed. "First, you're going to have to put propellers on that thing. And without a tail, how do you plan on keeping it flying straight?"

Fischer reddened a little, but probably because he was in front of his men, he kept his anger admirably restrained.

"You don't know aircraft well enough to see what is before you," he insisted. "This aircraft doesn't have propellers. It is powered by jets that hurl it through the air faster than anything has gone before. Propeller-driven aircraft will be far out-classed. They will be sparrows before great German hawks."

Intelligence from Easy Company agreed with Fischer's assessment. They'd seen, and gotten photographs of, the aircraft they'd designated X-713 only a handful of times. Reports had been filled with awe and dismay. According to Easy Company, the flying wing was dreadfully fast, and it was capable of carrying a large payload of bombs.

"Do you know what jets are?" Fischer asked.

I shook my head and he proceeded to tell me. Men expected a woman to lack knowledge about things, then attempted to fill their heads with things they didn't think those women would understand or remember so they could feel important about themselves and the pittance they might know. It was an exercise in futility for women, and I detested the practice. Give me a true teacher any day. True teachers didn't talk down to their students.

Of course, I knew about jet engines. I'd gotten the chance, off book, to fly one of the two British Gloster Whittle jet prototypes in Britain last year. That had been exhilarating. Roosevelt had somehow learned of my experience, the man always knew more than I expected him to, and I suspected Eleanor had a lot to do with that.

My prior experience with jet aircraft had been mentioned at the briefing I'd received. It was hoped that my familiarity with the design would aid me in gathering information about Richter's flying wing. Being a woman, a pin-up girl, got me into Fischer's inner circle. Knowing aircraft, particularly jets, made me invaluable.

After a while, Fischer tired of talking about his "great experiment," or he ran out of what little he understood about Dr. Richter's creation. Maybe he just got hungry. We loaded back into the G-4 and returned to the castle for lunch.

That evening, Fischer decided I would "sing for my supper." He thought that was hilarious. He laughed, so his officers had to laugh with him, and it was painful to watch.

So, after the meal, never a good time for singing, by the way, one of the officers played the piano in a large music room and I sang a few show tunes that he knew. He was surprisingly good.

I had a captive audience. The *Standartenführer* made certain all his officers were in attendance, including Groener, though I was sure she would have been there anyway, and even Carson Evers sat in attendance. Without Ace the mule at the end of his arm, he looked sad and lonely. Well, drunk and sad and lonely.

During all of this, I made a show of drinking too much and getting a little sloshed. I didn't drink much. Trust me, the lovely plants around the dining room and the music room probably didn't survive the experience, and most of the drinks went down the toilet in the bathroom. Fischer was distracted by watching everyone watching me, and they weren't able to watch me as much as they'd wanted to out of fear of the *Standartenführer's* wrath.

Afterward, Fischer dismissed his guests and they retreated to their rooms. Elsa showed me to my room.

"I found some pants," she whispered to me at the door. "I left them behind the changing screen."

"Thank you," I said, and I squeezed her shoulder.

I walked to the electric lantern by the bed and switched it on. Elsa waved goodbye and Kilcher closed the door. The big guard locked the door behind him.

I wasted no time getting ready for Fischer. I knew he would visit tonight, and I knew he wouldn't be patient. He'd watched me too closely, and, when he'd caught his officers lightly flirting with me, he'd gotten angry and preened at the same time. Also, I deliberately hadn't been as deferential to him as he had wanted during the performance. He would want to show me who was master.

He would be coming soon, and I had to be ready.

I changed into the black dungarees I found behind the changing screen. Bless Elsa, she'd even thought to bring a pair of calf-high black boots that were only a little tight. I wondered how much she'd guessed why I wanted them, but I knew she couldn't guess what I was truly after. She probably thought I was going to try to escape.

After a couple of *Krav Maga* moves to make sure, I knew I could move well in the pants and the boots. From the earlier clothing choices, I selected a black turtleneck sweater. It might get a little hot, but, while wearing it, I'd be almost invisible in the night.

I prepped the bed by rolling the pillows in the bedclothes till it looked like someone was sleeping there. Then I switched off the lantern on the bedside table, hid behind the changing screen, and waited for my Luger-wearing, would-be Lothario to put in his appearance.

While I hid, I tried not to get too keyed up. Remaining calm even in the face of certain death was a must. I'd always struggled with that, and it didn't get easier. After all the missions I'd gone on, the list of things that could go wrong only grew longer. I thought about the flying wing and wished I knew more about the cockpit and the controls, but I trusted my abilities. I'd been trained by the best.

Not even ten minutes later, the bedroom door opened, and a rectangle of light fell into the room. Fischer hesitated at the door, then, drawn on by his lust, he followed the light into the room and closed the door after him.

With him inside the room, I started a mental clock. There was no turning back from this and playing the victim for him wasn't going to work for me. I'd rather die.

But I wouldn't accept failure.

Fischer walked to the bed and held his light up to inspect the bed. With his free hand, he drew back the covers and revealed the pillows I'd left there. He jerked upright and reached for the pistol on his hip.

By that time, I stood behind him and freed his lion-headed sabre with a quick hiss of razor-sharp steel. Before he closed his hand on the Luger or called out for assistance, which he was loathe to do, I reversed the sabre's blade, slit his throat from ear to ear, and shoved him face-down onto the bed in case he managed to squeak before he died.

Mercilessly, thinking of all the dead women and girls he'd buried somewhere out in the forest behind the castle, I climbed onto his shoulders and held him down. He fought and blood drenched the bedclothes, but I held him until his strength left him limp.

Breathing raggedly from my exertions and the emotions that banged around inside me, I remained as quiet as I could be and quickly relieved the *Standartenführer* of three extra magazines for the Luger and his keys. I slipped the magazines into my pockets, tucked the Luger into the waistband of the blood-covered dungarees, and hurried to the door.

Only dim light showed under the door. It was locked but finding the right key to open it only took seconds. Carefully, I eased the door open and peered out. No one was in the hallway outside the room, not even Kilcher. I supposed the *Standartenführer* hadn't wanted an audience, but men spoke in quiet voices somewhere below.

I'd already mapped out my exit strategy and headed for the window at the end of the hallway. I opened the window, no bars there, and looked down. The twenty-foot drop didn't bother me. I could stretch out, and I knew how to tuck and roll from parachuting.

A narrow spit of land stood out from the castle and disappeared into the moat. I didn't look forward to the swim, but there was no other way to get out without being seen.

I threw a leg over the ledge, hauled myself out, managed to swing the window shut, and lowered myself to hang by my fingertips. Then I dropped to the ground silently, went loose, and rolled. I got to my feet quickly and eased into the cold, dank water that surrounded the castle.

Breath tight in my lungs from the run across the broken terrain leading to the hangar, face smeared with mud from the moat to darken my features, I crept up to the building. The guards operated by moonlight and the occasional flashlight. The building was blacked out to prevent it from becoming a target to an Allied bomber that might have a couple of bombs left over from a run into Berlin.

I'd been lucky so far because the dog patrols were staggered and farther out, but I was also good in the dark. I wasn't so good while soaking wet, which I still was, but that had helped prevent the dogs from getting my scent. When I put my back up against the building, the wet clothing pressed against me, water drained down my back, and I shivered.

The clock in my head was ticking faster now. It wouldn't be long before someone checked on Fischer and found out he was dead and I was gone. I was quite sure his soldiers in the castle wouldn't believe I would go to the hangar.

That particular cat would be out of the bag soon enough, but for the moment I had a little more time.

Sentries on patrol of an area that didn't see much action lost their edge and got lazy. The same thing had happened to the guards tonight. Sure, when the *Standartenführer* was around, they were sharp as sharp could be. But how sharp did they have to be while hidden away and only watching over a few scared scientists with Fischer not around?

The guard at the door stepped away from the closed door to attend the call of nature. While he had his hands busy, I slipped behind him, relieved him of his knife without him knowing, and shoved it into the base of his skull. That type of attack killed a person instantly. He folded like an accordion, and I dragged his body into the deeper shadows at the corner of the building.

What I did might sound callous, but all those Nazis were killers. They served under Fischer, and he butchered women. Not to mention the family who had owned the castle. I wasn't going to give any one of them a chance.

I took the dead Nazi's Karabiner 98k rifle and slung it over my shoulder. I was familiar with the bolt-action weapon. It fired a 7.92x57mm Mauser round. I took the dead man's ammo kit and checked to make sure it held stripper clips that were loaded. I stopped counting at ten. Each clip held five rounds. If I needed more than fifty rounds, I was in trouble that the rifle wasn't going to help me escape.

I claimed his pistol too and shoved it in my waistband to join the one I'd taken from Fischer. I believed in having all the weapons I could get my hands on. This wasn't going to be a fade-into-the-woods escape.

Not if I got what I was after.

Armed, steady, and determined, I took his flashlight and slipped through the canvas tarp that covered the door and prevented the sallow light inside the hangar from escaping. I took a minute to allow my eyes to adjust, then I headed for the workroom that held the scientists. I easily avoided the two guards walking the hangar's interior.

As I slid through the gloom, I wondered if the scientists would be brave enough to follow me and seek their own freedom. I planned to present them with that chance because I didn't want to leave them behind if I could help them escape. If they didn't take that chance, they'd best stay out of my way.

Another guard stood in front of the workroom door. He snapped a match to life, leaned his head down to the flickering flame held captive in his cupped hands, and lit his cigarette. Once the tobacco was burning, he waved out the match, dropped it to the hangar floor, and sucked smoke into his lungs.

I thrust the borrowed knife into the hollow beneath his skull, caught him before he fell, and crushed out the cigarette on the ground under a boot. Holding the dead man in my arms, I backed into the workroom. His boot heels left scuff marks on the concrete.

As I pulled the corpse into the room, a few of the scientists, including Dr. Richter, woke and stared.

Before any of them could speak, I whispered, "Quiet!" and dropped the body on the floor. The dead man hitting the floor made a greater impact on them than my command. I brought the K98k around to a ready position, but I didn't threaten them. Not exactly.

Still, they knew the rifle was there and most of them shied away from me. They'd been in captivity for some time and had a lot of the resistance ground out of them.

"Dr. Richter," I said in German, "I'm an American agent. If you're willing, I can get you out of here." I looked at the other men. "You, and everyone else who wants to go."

"You can do that?" Richter asked. He looked doubtful.

I smiled at him grimly and looked as confident as I could. "I've killed three men tonight to get here. Including Fischer."

"You killed Fischer?" Richter gawked at me.

"I did," I said, "and I'll kill however many more it takes to get you men out of here."

Well, that actually depended on whether they followed me. I wasn't going to carry them.

"Where are the rest of your soldiers?" another man asked. Like Richter, he was skinny, almost emaciated, and wore thick glasses that gave him owl eyes. He peered past me and through the door as if expecting a platoon to be waiting out there.

"No other soldiers," I told him. "Just me."

His eyes got even bigger behind the thick lenses. "You've come here alone? Why…why that's insane!"

Richter whipped around to face him. "Bierstadt! Control yourself!"

"Did you expect to get out of here in a sane fashion?" I asked Bierstadt. "You need to get with the program, doc. You're not in a good place. Come with me and I can get you to one."

Bierstadt just stared at me through those thick glasses.

"Let's go," I told them. "You're wasting time. I'm leaving in the next couple of minutes, and you need to decide what you're going to do."

"What do we need to do?" Richter asked.

Some of the tension inside me unknotted.

"I need your research," I said. "All of it."

"We can't give it to you," Bierstadt said.

I made my voice harder. "Then I'll take it myself." I looked at Bierstadt. "If that's what I have to do."

Richter shook his head and held his hands up in a placating gesture. "That's not what Dr. Bierstadt means. When we are done working for the day, our Nazi captors lock up all our materials. We simply don't have them to give to you."

Okay, that was somewhat of a setback, but I was prepared to deal with it. I was not prepared to leave without trying to get that research. Not as long as I could keep my escape window open.

"Where do they keep those materials?" I asked.

Richter turned his hands palm-up and wore a hangdog expression. "We don't know. We aren't allowed to leave this room."

That was a *bad* setback, and I didn't have time for it. I had to work quickly.

"How are you going to get us out of here?" Bierstadt asked.

"In a plane," I said. I hadn't quite figured out the logistics, but the plan was in development.

Richter and his fellow scientists looked at each other.

"Oh brother," I groused. "Don't tell me you're afraid of flying."

"Some of us are not as experienced as others," a short man with scruffy eyebrows said.

"The problem," Richter said, "is that only one aircraft here can safely take all of us aboard. All the other planes are for patrols."

"Unless you are planning to abandon some of us," Bierstadt accused.

Because he was being such a pain, he was at the top of my list to jettison. I was pretty sure he knew that.

"I'm not abandoning anyone," I said, but the truth was that I would do whatever it took to get out of there with the research and, if I was lucky,

"Bierstadt! Control yourself!"

Richter. "Which aircraft?"

"The X-713," Richter whispered. "It is propelled by jet engines."

"I know," I said. "I got the ten-cent tour, remember?" I thought hurriedly and peeked outside the room at the big aircraft at the end of the hangar. It was an awfully long stretch of hangar away.

"Only a few of Fischer's pilots can fly that thing," Bierstadt said. "Jet engines are much different than propellers. A pilot needs training. Even if you can fly a propeller-driven aircraft, you can't—"

"I know. I've flown jets." I peeked back into the hangar. "Is the X-713 open?"

"They have a lock on the outside hatch."

That wasn't a problem that would take much of a solution. "Once I'm—we're—inside, will I be able to start the engines? Is there a key?"

"Yes, you can start them. There is no key."

Hey, that was a ray of light.

"Do you know if the fuel tanks are topped off?" I asked.

"They are," Richter said. "Fischer makes sure the X-713 stays ready. He is proud of it."

Well, that made things a little easier. I figured I could do with some easy.

"Okay, I'm going after the papers. You people stay ready. When I call, you need to come running."

"I'm coming with you," Richter said.

I couldn't see that happening. "Doc—"

"You will need someone to carry the research so you can keep your hands ready to fight in the event we're discovered," Richter insisted. "I can carry the research. I can't fight. I don't know guns." He adjusted his lab coat and stood a little straighter. "And I want to help you. That research is ours. It belongs to us. Not that megalomanic in Berlin."

He had me there. I nodded. "Keep up and stay quiet as you can." I looked at the others. "You men stay ready. When I call out to you, you have to get to the X-713 as quickly as you possibly can."

Bierstadt nodded. "Are you sure you can—"

"I'm sure, Doc," I said. "You can either be there or you can watch the rest of us fly out of here."

I left him with that and headed back into the hangar. I made sure Richter stayed a safe distance back from me. He moved more quietly than I expected. The only reason I let him come was because he was right about needing my hands free, and I'd gotten the impression I couldn't have stopped him if I'd tried.

I hoped the guards were as sparsely assigned as I believed. And I hoped no one from the castle raised the alarm any time soon.

Richter and I crept through the hangar. Five hundred feet farther on, about half the distance to the X-713, I spotted a guard sitting on the front tire of one of the three Messerschmitt Me 410 Hornisses sitting in the hangar. He was looking at a pin-up magazine by flashlight.

Quietly, I walked up behind him and slid the knife blade against his throat. He dropped the magazine and the flashlight between his feet. Neither made much noise.

"Say anything," I whispered in German, "and I'll slit your throat. Nod if you believe me."

Slowly, he nodded.

"Good." I watched the shadows around us. "Now you're going to slowly get up and take me to where the research materials are."

He stood slowly, and he was short enough that I had no problem maintaining my hold with the knife. I relieved him of his rifle and his pistol and left them sitting beside the fighter plane's tire. I was carrying everything I could.

"Stay to the shadows," I ordered.

He did as I commanded, and we walked a little farther on and turned to the left. Another room I hadn't seen on my tour was at the end of a short hallway.

He took out a ring of keys that clinked steadily because he was so frightened. A moment later, he had the door open, and we went inside.

The room was a small office that held radio equipment on a large wooden desk, notebooks, and models of various V2 rockets and the X-713.

A squat, ugly J. Baum Safe sat against the back wall of the room. It was just short of two feet tall, thirteen inches wide, and sixteen inches deep. I was familiar with the model. Many of them had been sold over the years and were in use in several of the places I'd visited.

Intending to kill the Nazi with a thrust to the base of the skull, I slid the knife from his throat. Instantly, he whirled and grappled me. He opened his mouth to yell and I shoved the point of the military knife into the underside of his jaw and up into his brain. He shivered. His eyes rounded and he stared at me in disbelief. Then he went limp, and I lowered him to the floor.

Behind me, Richter sicked up on the floor.

I focused on the safe. Even in the dark, I could crack it. I pressed an ear against the door, turned the dial, and listened to the numbers slowly click into place.

Only a moment later, I had the safe open and the contents—journals, sketchbooks, photographs, and ledgers—were revealed in the glow of my stolen flashlight. I took a canvas mailbag from one of the desk drawers and shoved all the books inside it. Surprisingly, all of them fit, but it was crammed tighter than Santa's pack on Christmas Eve. I pulled the drawstrings tight and handed it to Richter.

"Got it, Doc?" I asked.

Staring at the dead man, he tried to speak and settled for nodding.

"Don't look at him," I told Richter. "He's the past. We're looking toward the future now. Just think about what you're going to do after we escape."

I switched off the flashlight, stood by the door until my night vision returned, then I eased back out into the hangar. Richter followed me so closely he was almost stepping on my heels.

When one of the other Nazis swung into the hallway from around the corner ahead of us, we were forty feet from the juncture back to the main hangar.

"Edmund?" the guard asked.

I couldn't answer in my voice, and Richter wasn't quick thinking enough to respond.

"Edmund?" the guard demanded now. He stopped and raised his rifle.

I got mine up first, sighted on the center of his face from thirty yards away, and squeezed the trigger. The loud explosion of the gunshot rolled throughout the hangar. The guard's head snapped back and he sagged. Before he hit the ground, I worked the bolt action and seated a fresh cartridge under the firing pin.

Everything was in the wind now.

"C'mon," I told Richter. "The others will be coming."

I walked forward quickly with the rifle at the ready. The other scientists would be nervous too. My only hope was that the hangar was big enough that the other guards wouldn't immediately know where the gunshot had come from. I reached the corner, paused, and peered into the main hangar.

"How many other guards are there?" I asked.

"You have killed three men?" Richter asked.

"That was before the guard back there. The last one makes five." I slid into place at the corner at the end of the hallway.

"At night," the scientist said in a voice that trembled, "there are nine guards."

Four left, I told myself. "Always?"

"Yes. Always."

In the main hangar, one of the surviving guards aimed a flashlight in our direction and trotted toward us.

Before the bright yellow beam splashed over us, I took aim and squeezed the trigger. The bullet tore out his throat and spun him around. As he dropped, his rifle and flashlight clattered against the concrete. The light twisted crazily across the floor.

Three left. I worked the bolt action.

Richter tried to edge past me, probably because of freedom fever, or he knew the other guards would come at us.

I stepped in front of him and pushed him back with my shoulders. I kept the rifle ready.

"Wait," I hissed.

"The other guards will come," he whispered frantically.

"Wait," I hissed again.

Sixty yards away, two other guards came out of the darkness more slowly. Both only shined their flashlights every now and again and tried to remain hidden in the dark.

When I was sure I had their positions memorized and predicted, I squeezed the trigger, immediately worked the bolt action, and swung the iron sights to bracket the other man who was running to find cover.

I fired, but, when he ducked behind a Messerschmitt, I was sure I'd missed him. Sparks flew from the plane's left prop and the bullet whined into the darkness. I worked the bolt action and seated the last cartridge. On the other side of the plane, the guard crept toward the tail to use the plane as a barrier. I aimed at his legs below the fuselage and squeezed the trigger.

The rifle roared and I pulled it back because I was out of rounds. Behind the Messerschmitt, the guard fell and yowled in pain.

I opened the bolt action, pulled out a fresh stripper clip from the ammunition kit, and mashed five more rounds into the rifle with my thumb. The rounds caught for just a minute, then seated into the magazine. Automatically, I dropped the empty stripper clip into the kit and closed the bolt action so the rifle was ready.

The wounded man struggled to crawl away. I took aim, let out half a breath, and squeezed off a round that tore through his head and stretched him out flat.

A bullet slammed into the corner of the hallway a foot above my head. The ricochet screamed through my ears, and I ducked. I worked the bolt action and two more rounds cut the air only inches in front of me. Another bullet plucked at my wet shirt. I only realized then that the remaining guard had a fully automatic weapon. Probably a *Mashinenpistole 40*, judging from the sound of it. The MP 40 carried thirty-two rounds of 9mm in a box magazine.

I stepped out a little and ducked back. A flurry of gunshots ripped through the hangar. I had no way of knowing if the Nazi had expended all thirty-two rounds, but I couldn't—*we* couldn't—stay where we were.

I focused on the muzzle flashes, dropped to a half-crouch, and aimed in the center of where I thought the shooter was behind another Messerschmitt. I fired the remaining four rounds in the carbine and ducked back around the hallway corner.

As I shoved another stripper clip into the K98k's breech, the final guard rolled out from the fighter plane and lay still. I placed a bullet through his head to make sure, then I grabbed Richter's arm and hustled him forward.

I paused long enough to take out the flashlight, switch it on, and play it back over the other scientists. They had gathered around the doorway of their prison like children.

"Bierstadt!" I yelled. "Come on! It's now or never!"

The scientists poured out of the room hesitantly, then gained speed.

I sprinted past Richter and reached the ladder leading up to the X-713's access hatch. I paused only long enough to shoot the lock off the hatch, then I climbed inside and threw myself into the cockpit. The interior space would prove a tight fit for all the scientists, but I wasn't going to leave any of them behind.

The cockpit was familiar, and a quick glance at the controls with the flashlight reassured me I knew where everything was. I pressed the buttons to start the four engines and they immediately growled to life.

Boldness and confidence filled me.

"The doors," Richter said. "The hangar doors will have to be open."

Cursing in a most unladylike way because I shouldn't have forgotten something as important as that, I scrambled past the men and out of the aircraft. I carried the rifle and the two pistols thumped solidly against me.

The hangar doors were locked, but a round from the rifle dispensed with that problem in short order. I hauled on the hoist chains and easily lifted the massive doors out of the way. I stared out into the night and down the runway.

Then a snake of crawling lights roared out of the darkness to my left and shot across the valley. Fischer's body had been found, and maybe the rifle shots had been heard.

The jig was up.

Headlights from approaching trucks caught me briefly, but by then I was running for my life back to the X-713. Machine gun bullets chopped into the concrete and scattered sparks in all directions. I angled for the side of the hangar and tried to keep equipment and supplies between the machine gunners and myself. The large bullets knocked tools onto and across the floor, and they tore gaping holes in barrels and crates. Fluids sluiced out onto the floor.

I cut back toward the X-713 and ran for all I was worth. Unfortunately, I wasn't worth enough. When the truck engine roared up beside me, the truck's passenger door came out of nowhere and knocked me to the ground. The impact hurt and knocked the wind from my lungs, but I was able to control my fall and land facedown.

Two German soldiers hopped out of the truck bed with their rifles raised. I pushed up to my knees, pulled the Walther and the Luger I'd taken from one of the guards I'd killed and Fischer, respectively, whom I'd also killed—not so respectively.

I fired my pistols at about the same time they did. One of their bullets tore through my hair, it was that close, and the other burned across my arm but didn't hit flesh. My rounds punched them back and knocked them down.

I got one foot up and pushed off to stand. As the machine gunner tried to bring his weapon around, I shot him in the head twice. He crumpled and I killed the driver with my remaining rounds.

Weapons empty, I dove for one of the dead soldiers in front of me because other troops were arriving. Two trucks pulled in behind the first and I knew I wasn't getting out of this alive. I'd had a good run, and I was determined to take as many of them with me as I could.

I freed the dead man's pistol and tried to get it up. I barely glimpsed a figure before it smashed into me. Then *Hauptsturmführer* Groener knocked me to the ground.

As we struggled for the pistol I held, she called me a filthy name and spat in my face.

"Did you think I would kill you so fast?" she demanded. "No, I promised you a slow, excruciating death, and I will give that to you. You will beg me for your release."

"Don't make promises you can't keep, sister," I snarled. I tried to turn the gun on her.

Groener pinched a nerve in my arm and my fingers numbed. The Luger fell from my hand. Stubbornly, I managed to roll my hand into a fist and smashed it into her face. When she punched me in the throat, my moment of triumph flickered and died.

Gagging, trying to breathe, I stumbled back and concentrated on keeping my feet under me and clearing the spots from my vision. I raised my open hands in front of me. *Krav Maga* leaned into grappling as well as punching.

Groener had been trained too. In the murky darkness punctuated by the headlights of the trucks, her right leg came at me like a vicious blade. I barely blocked it with both my forearms, got severely bruised for my effort, and, when she delivered her follow-through, I caught another punch to my face that induced a moment of double vision.

I took another step back, managed to set myself, blocked another punch, and stepped into her to keep her off-balance. I drove a bunched fist into her left eye, got a piece of her nose, and knocked her back.

Rifles raised all around us. Bolt actions clacked. Behind one of the soldiers, Carson Evers grinned maniacally at me.

Groener threw a hand up to halt the soldiers. "I will kill the man who fires. She is mine."

Hesitantly, the rifles lowered.

Groener smiled at me and lipped blood that drained from her left nostril. We hammered each other with a flurry of kicks and punches. When she was far enough back, she tried the roundhouse kick again and counted on the murky lighting to hide it.

Instead, I ducked under the kick, dropped to my folded right leg in a baseball slide, and caught her supporting leg by the ankle with both hands. I twisted viciously, yanked, and heaved upward.

Groener upended and came down mostly headfirst as intended. Bone cracked, probably her skull and her neck, and she went limp. Still on my knees, I wiped blood from my mouth and stared down at her vacant eyes. Her head was turned farther on her neck than heads were supposed to turn.

"God in Heaven," one of the soldiers said, "she's killed her!"

"Quickly," another cried, "shoot her!"

I dove for the pistol Groener had forced me to drop, but I knew I'd never reach it in time. Gunshots echoed all around me, but I grabbed the pistol and still pushed myself up. I wasn't going to die lying down if I could help it.

All around me, the German soldiers, and Carson Evers lay unmoving and bloody. More gunfire cracked for a moment, but it was outside.

"Hey lady," a man called. He had a Brooklyn accent. "Don't shoot. You're among friends."

A match flared in the darkness and a rough-hewn face took shape in the darkness. His features were haggard and stubbled, but fierce. He could have been handsome. He wore a German coal scuttle, but I would have bet an American M1 helmet would have fit him better.

He touched the match flame to a cigarette in the corner of his mouth and blew the flame out in a fog of smoke.

"Sergeant, you're not supposed to be here," I said.

The man grinned. "Ma'am—"

"Don't *ma'am* me," I said automatically. "You *ma'am* your mother. I'm not your mother."

The man nodded and, in the soft glow of the cigarette's ember, grinned more broadly. Some of the men standing behind him laughed.

"Got yourself a firecracker, Sarge," a big man said.

"He *doesn't* have me," I countered.

"No," the sergeant said, "I don't. Maybe we ain't supposed to be here, dollface—"

I almost objected, but I packed that away. *Dollface* from him didn't sound so bad.

"—but you're not supposed to be here either," he said. "You're supposed to be gone." The sergeant looked around. "Since you started this little fracas, me and the boys were bored and figured we'd come on down and help out. We ain't ones to miss out on a fight." He pointed at the gun in my hand. "Maybe you could aim that somewhere else."

I lowered the pistol and smiled. "Sorry. I haven't been among friends lately. I've forgotten my manners." I squared my shoulders like I wasn't hurting from the fight with Groener. "As it is, neither one of us should be here. So, I'll be going." I looked at the men. "Thank you. Thank you all."

"You be safe," one of the men said. He touched his helmet.

I looked at the sergeant. "If we meet again, I owe you a beer."

"I do like beer," he said.

"I owe all of you a beer," I told Easy Company.

"We like beer," they said.

"You're not leaving?" I asked the sergeant.

He glanced around. "Figured we'd stay a bit while we're here, clean out this rat's nest a little."

"Go easy on the staff at the castle. They were hostages in this whole mess."

He nodded.

I took a moment and crossed over to Carson Evers's body. I took Tony Beeson's Zippo lighter from the dead man.

"What's that?" the sergeant asked.

"Something that jackass stole," I said. "I'm going to take it back to the good man he stole it from." Before I got back to the USO tour, I'd come up with a story about how I found the lighter.

I left Easy Company and returned to the X-713. Richter and Bierstadt had the other scientists organized and out of the way.

In the cockpit, I increased thrust to the jets and rolled forward. The X-713 was different from anything I'd flown, but I got her up in the air all right. There was only a little screaming from the peanut gallery in the back cargo area.

Before we were out of sight of the hangar, Bierstadt called out, "The hangar is on fire!"

I heeled over and came back around to observe the explosions that threw flaming debris high into the air. Easy Company's idea of cleaning out a rat's nest was thorough.

Leaving them to it, I flew west and settled in for a long flight. It wasn't going to be comfortable, but I hoped we'd be safe enough. When I got to my first rendezvous, I'd radio my contact and air command would establish a safe flight plan for us to return.

I looked forward to reuniting with Burt and finding out what our next mission would be.

And I wouldn't mind crossing paths with that sergeant again either. A girl can dream, right?

THE END

Tune In For Another High-Flying Adventure!

Ah, Radio Rita, I knew ye well!

Actually, I didn't, but I grew up on *Blackhawk* and World War II comic books. Johnny Cloud was the First American air pilot in those comics, and I seem to recall bombers featured in some of the magazines had drawings of beautiful women on them. At the time, I thought that was just comic books. I didn't know it was really a thing.

Later, when I majored in History and English at the local university, I discovered that those bombers actually had pinup girls (ahem, women) painted on them. The pin-up bombshell (literally) hasn't left our consciousness. That motif has been featured in several movie franchises and comics franchises. Dave Stevens's great *The Rocketeer* owes much to this legacy.

Much later, I (rediscovered) pinup artists like Gil Elvgren (mentioned in this story) and other artists when their work was collected and published in books. Mystery and suspense author Max Allan Collins has been responsible for the publication of several such books. Besides being a connoisseur of the artform, he's become something of a master of the history of those works.

When Cap'n Ron first posted pictures of Radio Rita, I fell in love with our favorite fly girl! I didn't know what her story was, but she was saucy, provocative, and just looked like a sassbasket! When the call was made to authors to come up with stories for Radio Rita, I couldn't resist throwing my hat into the ring.

Unfortunately, as life sometimes does, I was also dealt some hazards of my own along the way. A busy schedule, kids who needed me, and my own brush with a medical weirdness that I'm still not sure about. I got grounded for a while, but I stayed in the race until the finish line.

All of us were given instructions to produce a different Radio Rita. I kept overthinking the project (and I think my wildest idea was an incarnation of Radio Rita who lived in an old pocket-sized transistor radio from the 1960s—which still might be a fun idea at some time to play with, though in a different venue). Cap'n Ron stepped in and got me shipshape again, but there were still all those hurdles to clear.

After Cap'n Ron cleared the runways for a pin-up Rita, I dug in. I knew she had to be someone special, someone different. I hope Miss Rita Walker fits the bill. She's a pin-up girl, she works on radio (hence the "Radio" Rita, though we don't dig into that much here), and she tours with the USO with the likes of Bob Hope and Marlene Dietrich.

Since some males tend to overinvest in women as sexual creatures, I knew I wanted a German officer of the High Command (or something) to want Rita. The officer would arrange to have her kidnapped and brought to (I scrounged for other World War II motifs I wanted to use) a castle (because Captain America fought some of his best villains there—I'm looking at you Baron Zemo!).

Another standard of World War II sensationalized fiction is the SS she-wolf. I knew I had to have a female villain who could easily match up against Radio Rita. I think *Hauptsturmführer* Groener easily fits that fight card, and I enjoyed making her so bloodthirsty.

As a science fiction fan, and a Robert A. Heinlein fan in particular, I knew how important rocketry was to World War II (and didn't Bucky Barnes die while strapped to one of those?), so I wanted the V2 rockets in there as well.

My story was quickly stacking up with odds and ends that were pulling into what I thought would be a solid plot.

I plunked Radio Rita down alongside a USO tour just this side of the

Mercedes-Benz W31 type G4

German Flying Wing

front in France so she could get good and kidnapped. Of course, no matter what the evil German officer's designs on her were, our Radio Rita had her own plans as well.

The USO bits were interesting too. I knew something about them from movies and such, but I dug a little deeper with research and found out more. I think most moviegoers and fans took for granted what Bob Hope and his group did (and I only use him to spearhead the discussion, not that Bob Hope was the leader of the effort, but he was a hell of a spokesman). They were literally in the Fox Hole Brigade, right there in the thick of it trying to keep up the spirits of the American soldiers.

I had fun with Rita's relationship with Carson Evers and Ace the talking mule. I had fun dealing with the other people, and the soldiers, in those scenes. I think it was good theater and good history.

I also wrapped in FDR and Eleanor Roosevelt because, how could I not? Amelia Earhart and Howard Hughes had to be added to some degree because it was just too easy to do.

Some of my favorite heroes are kickass individuals. Black Widow and Mrs. Emma Peel come immediately to mind. I wanted this pin-up Radio Rita to be able to handle guns and hand-to-hand situations. So she learned how to shoot, and she learned *Krav Maga* from Imi Lichtenfeld himself. At this point, I feel she was stellar and well-rounded, with plenty of history of getting in and out of tough situations.

I also gave her Burt Kimble, whom I'd really like to write about again. I think he and Rita have had so many adventures that would be entertaining to write. Maybe they even have a post-war career that I haven't discovered yet!

I ended up creating a much bigger world for Radio Rita than I thought because it all came together so easily. I love this character and the adventures she has, and I love the possibility of continuing with her.

At the outset, I knew the story had to be told from a first-person perspective. No one could just coldly tell Rita's adventures. I wanted the words to come from her, and I wanted them to be the words she would choose, from the perspective she had. Hopefully, I've succeeded in that.

In the meantime, please enjoy "Operation Rocket Man" and I'll hope Radio Rita, as I have envisioned her, gets to fly again!

MEL ODOM - grew up in southeastern Oklahoma, where diehard country boys still eat possums and soft-shelled turtles, but now lives in Moore, Oklahoma, a wonderful town that unfortunately attracts Pecos Bill riding a twister on a regular basis. He's lived through hog-raising and F-5 tornados, surely two of the most dangerous things in the world.

Over the last twenty-plus years, he's written dozens of novels in many different genres, including some based on television shows like Buffy the Vampire Slayer and novelizations of Blade, Tomb Raider, and xXx. He's trekked through deadly forests and braved the Sword Coast in the Forgotten Realms, and written adventures of bioroid detectives in Fantasy Flight's Android game.

He teaches in the Professional Writing program at the University of Oklahoma and writes all the time. He can be reached at mel@melodom.net, www.melodom.blogspot.com, @melodom on Twitter, and on Facebook.

His current military science fiction trilogy, The Makaum War, has been hitting bestseller lists.

www.ingramcontent.com/pod-product-compliance
Lightning Source LLC
Chambersburg PA
CBHW051657260626
47170CB00004B/1548